# STORM CHASER

## SHEILA RANCE

Illustrated by Geoff Taylor

Orion
Children's Books

First published in Great Britain in 2014
by Orion Children's Books
This paperback edition first published in Great Britain in 2015
by Orion Children's Books
An imprint of Hachette Children's Group
Published by Hodder and Stoughton

Orion House
5 Upper St Martin's Lane
London WC2H 9EA
An Hachette UK Company

1 3 5 7 9 10 8 6 4 2

Text copyright © Sheila Rance 2014
Illustrations copyright © Geoff Taylor 2014

The paper and board used in this paperback are natural and
recyclable products made from wood grown in sustainable
forests. The manufacturing processes conform to the
environmental regulations of the country of origin.

A catalogue record for this book
is available from the British Library.

ISBN 978 1 4440 1102 9

Printed in Great Britain by Clays Ltd, St Ives plc

www.orionbooks.co.uk

# STORM CHASER

For Reg and Lily
where it all began

# Maia

*'Maia felt the song enter her bones.*
*She needed to run, to leap, to fly, to be free.*
*It was singing her name. "Sun Catcher."'*

**Maia the flame-haired.**
**Maia the outsider.**
**Maia, the stolen princess.**

Always an outsider, headstrong Maia longs for
life outside the watery world of the Cliff Dwellers.
Frightened of the sea, she dreams of training a hunting
eagle, but when she is named Sun Catcher she
discovers her destiny lies in a distant land.

# Kodo

*'Above him the silk hung waiting.*
*Kodo grasped a strip, tearing it from the thorns.*
*The silk was shrieking, commanding*
*him to free it . . .'*

Dreamer, friend, thief.
**Kodo the lizard boy,**
longs to leave the stilt village and his life
as an untouchable. His friendship with Maia
is forbidden. Valiant, loving and true of heart,
yet vulnerable to the silk's power he will lie,
steal and betray to possess it.

# Razek

*'She called me Storm Chaser.*
*Storm winds destroy the weed beds.*
*You are the storm I chased, Flame Head.*
*I can't go back without you now.'*

**Razek the Storm Chaser,**
the arrogant weed-master.
Driven by his love-hate relationship
with Maia, he first endangers her by
bringing the Wulf-Kin to their village,
then deserts his people to protect her.

# Tareth

*'A tall dark-haired figure swinging*
*on crutches, as if blown by storm-winds.*
*A man with eyes of fire and*
*an eagle feather in his hair.'*

**Tareth,** a crippled weaver
of the singing silk.
A warrior driven by his promise to protect Maia.
Maia calls him father, but is he?
His life is not his to give.
Long ago, the mysterious singing silk claimed him.

# Elin

*'A beautiful woman, with eyes like blue ice
and red hair that tumbled down her shoulders.
She held herself like a queen, but her robes
were worn, the fabric frayed.'*

## Magnificent. Dangerous.
## Death Bringer.

Elin is ruthless in her desire to destroy
her lost sister and claim the power of the sun-stone.
Imperious and corrupt, she believes she can catch
the power of the sun, only to find that some
things burn even brighter than her hatred.

# Caspia

*'Caspia glanced at her, grinned and took
hold of the sun-stone. Maia closed her eyes and
waited for the scream and the smell of burning.
Nothing happened. She heard the Wulf-Kin
exhale beside her, as if he too
had feared for the girl.'*

## Caspia, the thought thief.

Raised as a pawn in her parents' pursuit of
power, spoiled, damaged Caspia is no puppet.
As duplicitous and ambitious as her mother,
she dreams that one day she will seize power,
and bend Khandar to her cruel, childish will.

# ONE

Var lay hidden in the grass. His black rat scrabbled from the back-sack and gnawed at the leather cords binding the running blades to the bag. Var hissed at him. The rat thought better of the delicacy and nibbled at the shoots of new grass. He was quite safe. The vulture wheeling on the high updrafts was hunting for bones.

Var watched the large group travelling slowly across the plain. Horses, goats, eagles, people. A boy rode far out on the left flank of the untidy procession. He cast his eagle into the sky. Its huge, bronze wings beat powerfully, black tips almost touching the top of the tall grasses, as it skimmed the plain and suddenly dropped. The vulture swooped lower. No pickings there. The eagle had its prey trapped beneath its claw and its carcass would be too small to tempt a bone-smashing vulture to linger. It flew off towards the distant city. The tribe was going there too. So was he. But first he had to meet the red-haired witch.

He reached for his back-sack. Tiki, his rat, was gnawing the leather thongs of the running blades again.

'We must go too fast for you, little brother,' Var muttered, scooping the rat into his tunic. It curled up against his stomach, wedged against the ridge of his belt, as he tied on his running blades and set off across the plain towards the Sun City.

# Two

Caspia heard the Wulf Kin following her. Good. They were loyal to her, though they had never bonded with her mother, Elin, the queen. They had always been her father's creatures. Now they were hers and would help her to reach him in the Tower of Eagles, leaving the Queen to fight the imposter Sun Catcher, Maia. A weakling, who was afraid of her own power. Caspia had read her thoughts, had seen her doubts as the Wulf Kin had dragged her into the Sun Palace. She, Caspia, daughter of the Queen and Urteth, the Eagle Warrior, could have defeated her on her own. And what better way to prove that it was *her* destiny to become Sun Catcher? She would have enjoyed seeing Maia fall. She wondered whether Maia even had the courage to fight Elin, or whether she would meekly hand over the sun-stone.

Caspia remembered the moment when Maia had blocked

her thought-stealing. The jolt of losing contact had been painful. She frowned, tempted, for a moment, to return to the solar. Perhaps her mother had underestimated her younger sister. But her mother had dismissed her.

Caspia swept out of the palace. She could hear chanting in the city below. The palace boys almost fell over themselves in their hurry to bring her black mare to the foot of the steps where the two Wulf Kin ponies stood, lathered in sweat. The Wulf Kin waited for her to mount, their great beasts, more bear than wolf, crouched beside them. Vultek stepped forward, cupping his furred hand, and tossed her into the padded saddle.

The young Wulf Kin had ambitions to inherit the place of Zartev, her father's favourite. His thoughts were easy to read. Perhaps she would help him when Zartev became too weak to defend himself. But not yet. She pulled her foot free.

'We ride to the Tower of Eagles,' she said.

'You don't stay to see the sun-catch?' he asked.

She wanted that above all else, but frowned down at him. 'The Queen will catch the sun now she has the sun-stone,' she said. 'We go to Urteth.'

She rode away from the Sun Palace and the slender obelisk of the Catching stone, pointing like a finger to the sky, and into the square, sweeping past several riders. A dark-haired boy caught her gaze. He was wide-eyed, fizzing with excitement. Caspia felt the shock as their gazes locked and she looked straight into his thoughts. They tumbled pell-mell into her head, almost knocking her from the saddle with their colour and strength. Images of vast tracts of water, a boat, lizards, herself. No, not her. Someone who looked like her.

4

She turned in the saddle, prolonging the bond. In his thoughts she felt the thirst for a fight, the thrill of a mad pony ride and, hidden deep, caught in a net of lies, a secret. A silk secret. One of the Wulf Kin yelled and the contact between the boy and herself snapped.

Her back stiff, her gaze fixed on the flicking ears of her mare, she trotted along a maze of twisting lanes, through jumbled shacks, and emerged into the colour, smells and noise of a market.

Crowds scattered. A dyer's stall, festooned with hanks of brilliant yarn and banners of cloth, was knocked flying. A black-and-white mongrel wriggled from the wreckage, snapping at the ponies' hooves as they trampled the bright cloth. The merchant's shout died in his throat as he saw her. Vultek cursed as his pony stumbled. Caspia laughed and rode on through the chaos until they were through the vast city gates and onto the greening plain. She reined her horse in.

She thought of the boy. She was sure she had heard silk. But the whisper had been faint. She must have been mistaken. Only Elin still had silk. The rest had been lost, burned in a fire when all but one of her mother's sisters had died. The moth-garden had been torched and the moths had perished. The silk Weaver, Tareth, had vanished despite her father and mother's attempts to find him. Despite the Wulf Kin trackers with their wulfen.

Elin's anger and the tale of Tareth's treachery, his disappearance with the sun-stone and a child, had threaded the songs and stories of her childhood. She knew the tale well, knew how serious the loss of the silk had been. It had

5

signalled the end of everything they'd known. How could this stranger, a boy, be hiding thoughts of silk?

Vultek's pony bumped against hers. His wulfen howled. Caspia felt the hairs on the back of her neck stand on end. The Wulf Kin swung from his pony and knelt, pressing his ear to the ground.

'Something comes. Many footfalls. Horses.'

Caspia stood in her stirrups, shading her eyes, looking across the plains.

She saw nothing. Closing her eyes, she cast the catching net of her thoughts wide, probing the emptiness. Nothing. Whatever Vultek could hear was too far off. She squinted at the sky. Glimpsed the speck of a distant, soaring bird hunting above the plains.

'Traders?' She knew that, now the wolf-walk snow was melting, supplies would flow to and from the city as the frozen trade routes opened again. 'Herders? Bringing beasts for slaughter?'

Vultek rose to his feet. 'Slow-moving,' he said.

'Then we go to Urteth,' decided Caspia and, without waiting for him to mount, urged her horse into a canter.

A figure rose like a shadow from the grass. Caspia's horse shied, almost unseating her. By the time she had regained control, the Wulf Kin had flung themselves from their ponies and were attempting to wrestle the tall figure to the ground.

He eluded them and with a leap straddled Caspia's black mare, a knife held against her throat.

'Call off your beasts!' Var demanded. 'I came as summoned. I seek the red witch who calls herself Queen. Are you she?'

Caspia watched Vultek assess the threat. Choose not to attack the assassin. As the stranger's knife pressed into her neck she decided that she would make Vultek pay for that.

'I am Caspia, the Queen's daughter.' She was pleased that her voice was strong, contemptuous. 'Who dares call my mother the red witch?' She raised her hand to push the blade aside and gasped as it slit the skin of her fingers. Beads of blood oozed from the cut and dripped onto the horse's mane.

She tried to twist around, but he was swift, dragging her from her horse, clamping her wrist, keeping her at his side. From the corner of her eye, Caspia saw a large black rat scurry across her saddle and burrow into her mare's mane, reappearing between its ears. It planted its paws firmly and, leaning forward, nibbled the horse's forelock. Her horse snorted with fright and to Caspia's amazement slowly bowed its head and dropped to its knees.

'Who are you?' she demanded.

Satisfied that neither horse nor rider could flee, Var released his grip but continued to watch Vultek.

'Var,' he said. He pointed his knife at the Wulf Kin. 'He is angry. Does he do as you bid?'

'Of course.'

'Do you trust him?'

Caspia hesitated for a heartbeat. 'Of course,' she repeated.

Var sheathed his knife. 'Then tell him to wait where he cannot hear what he need not know. And quickly – unless you want this meeting known by those who cross the plains behind me.'

Caspia hitched up her skirt and strode away from her Wulf Kin escort. She spun round. The boy was right behind her, balancing delicately on strange wood and metal blades that made him taller than she was. He must move more quietly than the shadows, she thought. The black rat sat on his shoulder. Its beady eyes watched her closely, as did the bright, golden eyes of its master. Eyes like a bird of prey.

'Who are you?' she demanded again. 'What d'you want? Who is following you across the plain?'

'Not following. They make their own way. I passed them at sun-wake. Men and women with eagles. Children. Riders and herders.' He gestured towards the Sun City. 'I will enter the city with them and find the Queen.'

'Why?'

Var shrugged. 'To kill as the red witch wishes.'

'Who?'

When he remained silent Caspia's anger spilled over. 'I am the Queen's daughter. She has no secrets from me. Tell me. Who have you come to kill?'

Var was unmoved by her anger. 'If you, with your hair like fire, are daughter of the red witch, then you already know why I've come.' He reached to stroke the rat, picked him from his shoulder and tucked him into his tunic.

Caspia glared at him, but his golden eyes were a wall blocking the way to his thoughts. She clenched her fists. She would not fail. She would steal his thoughts. He smiled, blocking her probing. Caspia looked away. And suddenly knew that she didn't need to read his thoughts because she did indeed understand her mother.

'You have to kill the girl who claims to be the Sun Catcher. The queen wants her dead.'

Var did not betray even by a flicker that she had guessed the truth.

'Once she has the sun-stone, the Queen will not need the girl.' Caspia watched Var closely. 'Although she is her sister, she wants her dead. The last sister to die,' she said. She noticed his slight reaction. 'You are young for this work,' she challenged.

Var was amused. He couldn't remember when he had felt young. Perhaps it had been before the Finder had found him, a small child alone in the Hidden, separated from his pack in the barren land. The Finder had taught him everything. There had been no time to be young. He studied her. She was no older than he was.

'As are you,' he replied.

Caspia laughed. 'And when you have killed her, if you find that she has silk, bring it to me, not to the Queen. The Queen desires her death. I am tasked with looking for stolen silk and a story-coat. The girl may have brought it with her. Find the Tower of Eagles. Bring it. I will pay you well.' She held out her cut hand. 'My blood on it. Serve me and my father, Urteth.'

Var felt the rat nosing restlessly against his stomach. He didn't trust her. The girl's eyes were compelling. He felt her try to read his thoughts again and swallowed a snort of silent laughter as she failed. Despite himself he admired her audacity for trying even as his mind snapped shut like the secret catches on the Finder's box. The thought of the reward that she promised tempted him. The red witch queen had promised to pay well too. He pulled out his knife and let a drop of her blood drip onto the tip of the blade.

'A life. And silk,' he agreed.

'You will find her in the Sun Palace. Her name is Maia,' said Caspia.

# THREE

Maia sat sewing, aware but apart from the bustle around her. The old silk in her hands whispered. She tried not to listen to the voices but sometimes a picture drifted into her mind. Then she had to watch as one of her sisters walked unknowingly to her doom, hear her shriek as Elin locked her away forever. It was a relief when the whispers became smoke and the picture dissolved, even though she knew that the smoke was from the flames that had roared through the palace. A fire that had sent Tareth running, the baby, Maia, in his arms. Fleeing with the sun-stone and moon-moth cocoons. There were no cries in the smoke picture. No writhing figures. No night-wake waiting to visit her as she tried to sleep.

Maia tugged a fine thread through the silk, carefully stitching the last patch onto Elin's robe, and stabbed her finger with the fishbone needle. She sucked at the bead of blood. Each of the four patches torn from the story-coat had whispered the name of a sister, had started to murmur its own song. Xania whispered in the silk. She had come too late to save her sisters, but she had saved their song.

Maia had wanted to stuff her ears with beeswax so that she wouldn't hear. She had always done that when she had to visit the moth-garden hidden above her home in the Cliff Village. It was dangerous to spend too long listening to silk whispers.

Tareth had not wanted her to touch the silk patches. He hadn't wanted her to hear the death songs. But there was no one else to sew the silk to Elin's gown. No one who could bear the burden of the sisters' songs. Only Tareth, who had once woven the silk and now sat tethered to a strap loom, desperately weaving the last of the silk threads into eye-pieces for the sun-helmet. This silk was not old and tainted: it had come from threads the Warrior Women had unbound from the plaits attached to their bows, threads found by Kodo wrapped around the huge bronze wheels in the message tower, silk teased from the fraying hem of Xania's story-coat. He must finish before sun-wake when Maia would put on the helmet and the silk and catch the sun. If he didn't, she would have to face the sun's glare, her eyes unprotected. She would be blinded as the Watcher had predicted when she had named her Sun Catcher.

Maia glanced at Elin. She sat, stripped of her gown, wrapped in Tareth's salt-stained cloak, regal despite the travel-worn cloth and the circle of silent Warrior Women guarding her. Maia tied the final knot.

'Will it sing to her? Will she hear her sisters' torment?' Yanna asked, standing beside her, as if to help her with the burden of sewing the silk.

Maia cut the thread and slid the flint flake back into her belt pouch.

'I don't know.' She smoothed the patches, her fingers barely skimming the silk as she bid it farewell. It lay silent under her hand. Unless their song was woven among the other threads and stories in Xania's story-coat she would never hear their voices. She was glad she wouldn't have to listen again to their passing.

'Elin fears that it will,' she added. 'And because she does, she will hear the voices.'

Yanna nodded. She tossed the gown to Elin.

Elin pulled it on. Defiantly she glared at Maia and smoothed her hands across the patches. Her face contracted. She was not as immune as she would have everyone believe.

For a moment Maia regretted sentencing Elin to a life of whispering and bitter memories. But Elin had killed her sisters.

Yanna took the fishbone needle from Maia's hand and pinned it inside the pouch on her belt. 'It is well done, Sun Catcher.' She glanced at Elin. 'A fate better than death. She will remember and regret for all of her to-comes.'

Elin rose to her feet. The Warrior Women moved forward, tightening the ring around her, afraid she might spring free. 'What is there to regret, archer? I was betrayed by my sisters, by the Story Singer, by the weaver thief.' She pointed at Tareth. 'He stole the sun-stone. I was born to be Queen. I did what a queen must to rule this land. He is the one you

13

should judge and punish. He stole the sun-stone and left the sun unharnessed.'

'And kept the Sun Catcher safe from you and sent her back to us,' retorted Yanna.

'My daughter, Caspia, is the true Sun Catcher. The stone is hers. She will return to claim it and punish you for your treachery. The upstart will not save you.' She glared at Maia, her eyes like fire. 'Nor a lame weaver. And Urteth's Wulf Kin will rid Altara of your archers. He will burn the place to the ground. Your memory will be lost in the ashes.'

'Take her away,' said Yanna. 'I am weary of her. Let her sit alone in the darkness and listen to the silk.'

The noise of her departure woke Kodo, who had been dozing by the fire. He yawned and stretched. 'Is it time?'

'Not yet.'

'I'm hungry.' Kodo scratched his head until his hair stood on end like a dark raised lizard's crest.

Razek, lingering in the shadows beyond the fire, laughed. 'You are always hungry, lizard boy.'

'Trader,' Kodo corrected him.

'Lizard boy trader,' mocked Razek.

'Eat!' Zena flipped a flatbread from her blackened pan onto the pile she had made and set by the fire. 'We must go down to the Stone Court now. Otherwise there will be no place for us. Everyone will be there to see the Sun Catcher.'

Maia's stomach roiled. The smell of the warm baking bread suddenly making her feel sick.

Zena gave Kodo several flatbreads. 'To take. We will have to wait for the sun. You will be hungry again.' She watched as Razek left the shadows to help himself to food. He frightened her still, this strange, silent friend of her Sun Lady. She couldn't decide if Maia was pleased to see him. He had followed her across the Vast and haunted Altara until he had forced his way into the warrior's holdfast to find Maia and had been banished by Yanna. Maia had told him to return home. Razek had not listened. Didn't he understand that what the Sun Catcher commands must happen?

Razek glanced at Maia. 'We must wait in the Stone Court?' he asked.

Maia nodded. 'And don't look up when the sun comes,' she said. 'You must cover your eyes against the light.'

Kodo tucked flatbreads inside his tunic, reached for another and chewed it hungrily. He grinned at Maia. 'We'll find a good place and watch until we have to hide our eyes when the sun falls into your hands and you catch it like a honeycomb in the bee cave.'

Maia swallowed. 'And hope it won't sting like the Watcher's bees.'

Kodo's grin grew wider, although that shouldn't have been possible, thought Maia. He was trying to cheer her up, to give her courage.

'It will be a good sun-catch,' he encouraged her.

'A good sun-catch,' echoed Razek, and if he looked stern it was only because he had wanted to be the first to wish her well.

'Many, many people have come to see you, Sun Lady,' said Zena.

Kodo held out his hand. 'Come with us. You're too small to fight your way through the crowds.'

'You're not much bigger,' said Razek. He flicked his fingers in farewell to Maia. 'Come if you are coming,' he called over his shoulder as he strode from the hall. 'I will protect you from harm, little Lizard Keeper.'

Kodo rolled his eyes.

'If we don't go with him, he will get lost. Razek is not used to a city. He is from the weed beds. He lives in a cave. Whereas I have seen many places. I have sailed far on a trader ship. I could tell you many tales. Trader Bron, he is master of the ship . . . he saw me on my lizard swimming out to his boat and . . .'

With Zena trotting beside him Kodo skirted the fire and vanished into the darkness. Maia could hear him chattering still as he left the hall. The fire seemed a less comforting place with her friends gone.

Tareth, sensing her disquiet, looked up from the loom.

'It is not too late, Maia,' he said.

Maia heard Yanna's intake of breath. Felt her silent protest. Yanna had already told her what her destiny must be, as had her sister, Xania, while they crossed the Vast.

'You don't have to do this,' Tareth told her again. But his hands did not stop tossing the shuttle through the warp and beating the new line of thread tight against the rest of the precious silk in his frantic haste to weave the eye-pieces for the sun-helmet.

Maia thought of the Vast, of Xania dying from Wulf Kin poison, determined that Maia should reach the Warrior Women. She remembered the unquestioning loyalty of Yanna as she had taught her to be a warrior and taken her to the lake cave in the mountains to seek the hidden sun-stone.

She thought of Nefrar, Yanna's cheetah, who had pulled her from the water in the underground cave and become her shadow. Even now he stretched by her feet, the tip of his twitching tail almost in the ashes as he soaked up the heat. So many had helped her. The Eagle People had ridden to escort her into the Sun City. Tareth and Kodo and Razek had followed her. She thought about Elin. She thought about catching the sun to put an end to the long cold. She was afraid.

# Four

Razek shouldered his way through the shifting crowds. He bumped into a large man in an embroidered cloak, bounced off him and was aware of hawk-sharp eyes before they were swept apart and Zena was torn from Kodo's grip.

'Razek,' shouted Kodo.

Razek turned, saw Kodo's frantic wave and grabbed Zena as she was tumbled past.

'Careful, little lapran, or you'll be swallowed whole. Then who will guard Maia? And run with tales to Yanna?'

She hung onto his tunic, as he set her on her feet.

'And if you had not been banished you wouldn't have been in time to find the Sun Lady and see her catch the sun,' Zena said boldly. 'You would still be in Altara with your face always like a storm.'

Kodo laughed. 'Razek has to make the weed boys do as he says so he rages at them like a storm when they are slow and lazy. He's a Storm Chaser.'

'Much you know about it, lizard boy,' retorted Razek. 'And I didn't give you the right to use that name!'

Kodo whistled. 'The Watcher named you Storm Chaser?'

Zena gazed at Razek. He was frowning, his face as black as thunderclouds. He looked like a Storm Chaser. 'A good name.'

Razek shrugged. 'I didn't take the name. I am the Weed Master.'

'No weed here for you to master,' teased Kodo.

Zena looked from Razek to Kodo, only half-understanding the trouble between them. They were both Maia's friends but they didn't like each other.

Kodo punched Razek on the arm. 'But it was good to fight beside a fierce Storm Chaser in the palace garden.'

'It was a good fight,' Razek agreed. 'We fought well.'

'So did Maia,' said Kodo.

'She was always fighting with the weed boys,' said Razek. He followed Kodo's gaze to the Sun Palace. 'She was . . . is strong.'

Zena nodded enthusiastically. 'She will save us.'

'Save us?' A thin boy, his skin burned by countless desert winds, his leather tunic oiled and supple, was listening to them. A black rat nibbled the rag ends of his long hair which was carelessly caught at the base of his neck.

Zena held out her finger. The rat sniffed at it. Zena scratched between its ears. 'She will end the dark,' she said proudly. 'What's his name?'

19

'Tiki,' said the boy, lifting the rat from his shoulder and settling him on Zena's palm. 'And how will she do that?'

'She will wear the silk and catch the sun,' said Zena. She fumbled in her sleeve and drew out a flatbread, offering a corner to the rat. 'She came from a far place to find the lost sun-stone and bring it here.'

Kodo was looking as if he thought it a waste to feed flatbread to a rat. 'Come on, let's find a place at the front where we can see.' He could see men and women in faded cloaks of saffron cloth and carrying huge curling bronze horns make their way to the sides of the square. 'It will start soon.'

Zena handed the rat back to the boy. The rat, thinking his flatbread was being stolen, bit her. Zena squealed. The rat leapt from the boy's hand, picked up the bread and scuttled into the crowd.

'You've lost him,' said Razek.

The boy hitched his back-sack more securely over his shoulder. 'He'll find me again when he's eaten.'

Razek, intrigued by the sight of two strange curved sticks hanging from the sack, watched him go. And lost sight of him instantly. He blinked. The boy had slithered away like an eel's shadow slipping among seaweed fronds. It was as if he'd never been there.

'Did you see that?' he asked Kodo.

'Does it hurt?' Kodo was asking Zena as she sucked the small puncture marks on her hand. 'Why did it bite you?' He shuddered. 'Never trust rats. The lizards hate 'em. They burrow into the hatching pen. And when we bring the eggs back from the lizard scrape they eat the eggs . . . and even the hatchlings.'

'Did you see how he slid away?' demanded Razek. 'Did you see his sticks? Were they hunting sticks? Throwing sticks?' He gazed across the crowd. He could see no sign of the boy but, like Kodo, noticed the horn bearers. They stood facing the Sun Palace. They were wearing tall hats with eyeless masks painted with swirls of gold, red and white.

The rising sun warmed Razek's shoulders. The light changed. The gloom of the square brightened, became tinged with pink. Beside him, Zena twisted to watch the light.

'Wait. Watch Maia. Don't look at the sun,' said Razek. 'The Catcher comes!'

'She greets the sun,' called another. And pitched full length on the ground, hiding his face in his arms.

It was as if this was a signal. Everyone was falling, tumbling like the giant kelp cut from its holdfast. Razek saw the tiny figure of Maia in the glinting, golden helmet high above him. Saw stars gleam about her as the light touched the crystals sewn across the story-coat.

Her hands were moving.

Razek buried his face in his arms. But even through flesh and cloth Razek saw the blaze as the sun fell on his back and the bronze horns roared their greeting. The wave of sound and light bounced around the square, pinning the crowds to the ground. Razek felt as if he was dissolving in light. Warmth washed over him. He tried to look up to see Maia somewhere at the brilliant epicentre of heat and golden sound but he couldn't move.

Then it was over. The horns fell silent. The crowd drew breath, stirred, dared to believe. Then a murmur began and swelled to a roar. A roar which the horns picked up and tossed joyfully around the Stone Court in a bright waterfall of sound.

'Sun Catcher! Sun Catcher! Sun Catcher!'

The crowd rose to their feet, pointing at the shining stone. At the giant, stone-locked crystals throwing light across the Sun Palace and out across the hillside.

'Sun Catcher!'

# FIVE

Maia padded barefoot through the great hall. The fires had collapsed into heaps of white ash studded with glowing embers. A boy was feeding sticks into one of the mounds. He blew into the slumbering fire, sending puffs of ash in the air as the new flames crackled round the kindling. Grabbing an animal-skin bag, he used the bellows to fan the flames.

Maia wondered if he would be in trouble for letting the new Solstice fire die. Was the fire that had taken so much effort to catch so unimportant that it could be left untended? She had had to carry the Solstice flame into the hall to set the new fires alight. A fire born by her catching the sun.

She rubbed her eyes and the boy and the fire wavered in the grey light as if she was underwater. Her eyes hurt. But she wasn't blind. The Watcher's words were not true, then.

Catching the sun had not darkened her sight. Her eyes were clouded as they had been after the first time she had caught and used fire to kill the wulfen and save Kodo. The Watcher had used eyebright. There might be gardens in the palace or the city where it grew. Kodo had promised that he would hunt for a cure for sun-blindness. Perhaps that was where he was even now.

'Eyebright,' she croaked. Her voice seemed to have been crisped by the sun. 'Where can I find eyebright?'

Aware for the first time that he was not alone in the cold hall, the boy almost fell into the fire. 'Lady,' he stuttered. He scurried backwards on all fours and disappeared.

Maia stared after him. Had he heard what she had asked? She rubbed her eyes again. Maybe he had gone to find eyebright, she thought hopefully. There was no one else to ask. The palace seemed deserted. The night-wake which had sent her tumbling panic-stricken from her sleep platform had obviously not visited anyone else. She hadn't woken Zena, who had insisted on sleeping beside her. Now she wished she had. Zena would have brought her chay and flatbreads and chatter to chase away the night terrors.

As she continued across the hall, Maia heard furtive sounds behind her. The palace boy was creeping back to tend the fire. He froze as she turned to look at him as if they were playing the childhood game of stalking a sleeping wolf. She moved on and heard him creep forward.

Not everyone was asleep. Elin was sitting in the dead moth-garden. Her fingers were tugging at the silk patches on her gown, then stroking the twigs of the thorn bushes.

'Dead,' she muttered. 'All dead.' She saw Maia hesitating

at the edge of the garden. 'Except you, sister.'

Maia flinched from her venom.

'And you'll soon join them,' threatened Elin. 'You won't see another sun-catch. Caspia will be Sun Catcher.'

Caspia was welcome to the dizziness, the headache and the risk of blindness, thought Maia. 'I never desired to be Sun Catcher,' she protested. 'I had no choice.'

'I have summoned your death,' hissed Elin. 'As I summoned theirs!' She moaned and wound her arms about herself as the voices in her head screamed. 'I desired it,' she whispered to her unseen sisters. 'The fire took you. But I wished it. I wished you dead.'

Maia fled. She didn't belong in the Sun City, but nor had she belonged in the weed beds. Not like Razek, who must already be planning to return to the cliff-tops. He might even go with Kodo when the trader ship set sail. She would be alone. Alone except for Tareth, the raving Elin and terrified palace boys.

She would find Tareth. Perhaps he would send Elin away. And agree to her plan to find an eagle. An eagle would help her to see. Its far sight would become hers. If the sun-dazzle lasted, it would not matter so much. And she would belong in this Land of Eagles if she had an eagle.

Tareth was propped in a fur-lined chair, drinking chay. He looked weary. As Maia entered he was stroking the eagle feather hanging in his hair. She knew that he still missed Magnus, his sea-eagle. There was a stranger with him, bearded and as plump as a breeding seal, his blubber not diminished by his huge height or hidden by his decorated tunic. His boots were embellished with stitching and appliquéd designs, circle and crosses and a strange winged bird. Even with her hazy vision she could see that they were beautiful. He was a man who thought highly of himself.

Maia took an instinctive dislike to him.

'Sun's greetings, Maia. This is Azbarak. Keeper of the palace stores. He has been telling me that the city granaries are nearly empty.'

Azbarak flicked his fingers in a greeting and lowered his head so that his eyes did not meet hers. Before his gaze slid away Maia saw his expression and the quick crossing and uncrossing of his fingers. This man was almost as wary of her as the palace boy had been.

She nodded. 'What must we do?'

'We will take the new crops that will grow now that the Sun Catcher has warmed the land and replenish the granaries.'

'Take?' frowned Tareth at him. 'The Sun City always had its own fields and grew enough to feed the city. They traded for more if needed.'

'And does still,' replied Azbarak smoothly. 'But the long dark and snows of wolf-walk have brought poor harvest and kept the traders away.'

'The traders will come once the river ice melts and the landing beach below the rapids can be used,' said Tareth. 'Kodo tells me that Trader Bron will come soon.'

And take Kodo away with him, thought Maia sadly.

Azbarak nodded. 'That will be good. It's been a hungry time.'

Maia looked at Azbarak's girth. He didn't look as if he had gone hungry. Her distrust increased.

'We must send hunting parties into the mountains once the passes are clear,' continued the Keeper. 'If the Sun Catcher permits?'

Maia wondered what the decision had to do with her. She glanced at Tareth.

'The Sun Catcher will do whatever is best, as always.' Tareth smiled at her. 'The Eagle People will want to go back to the mountains. They rarely visit the city. They stay only to see the Sun Catcher. The hunters will leave with them.'

More loss.

Maia decided that she would go with them. She would find her eagle in the mountains. And so would Tareth.

Meanwhile she would make Tareth tell her more of her past, her family and what it meant to be Sun Catcher. She sighed. She wasn't Elin. She couldn't rule as Queen. She had never imagined such a destiny. Not like Caspia, who must always have thought that she would be a queen.

Caspia had powerful gifts. Maia shivered, remembering how she had had to block Caspia when she had tried to steal her thoughts. She'd read Maia's mind before she'd realised the danger. Caspia was like the silk. It listened to thoughts too.

'I would be happy to take the Sun Catcher to the granary so that she may see for herself our need for food,' suggested Azbarak.

'Later,' said Maia. 'I wish to speak with my father.'

Azbarak shot her a look. Maia decided she didn't care if the overfed Palace Keeper had guessed that she didn't like him. He had obeyed Urteth and Elin. He had kept himself and them well fed while the land had grown hungry.

As Azbarak flicked his fingers and departed, Tareth poured chay into a bronze beaker and handed it to Maia. 'Take care, Maia. Sun Catcher power is strong. The people look up to you.'

'They are afraid of me,' she said.

'A Sun Catcher is to be feared,' said Tareth.

'Is that why you hid me away? Why you kept the secret of my family from me? Why you fled?'

'I hid you from Elin. She would never have let you live. As a baby you were helpless. When Xania saw the danger she wanted to keep you safe until you came of age and grew into your gift. She gave me you and the sun-stone to hide.'

Maia sipped the hot chay. The steam got into her eyes, making them water. 'Why didn't you tell me?'

It would have been easier if she had known why she was different from the weed children. Instead she had lived among them, an outsider. She rubbed the moisture away with the palm of her hand.

Tareth hesitated. 'When your silk was lost, drowned in the storm, and yet we were saved, I thought it a sign. Your to-come changed.'

'But, the silk wasn't lost,' objected Maia. 'You made a moth-garden. The moon-moths made more silk. You started to weave the silk in secret.'

Tareth was silent for so long that Maia thought he had fallen asleep. Finally he stirred. 'Yes. I started to weave again. Like you, I discovered that I had no choice. No more choice than moon-moths have. They must lay and spin cocoons and I must make silk.'

'Must?'

28

Tareth sighed. 'I was the Queen's Weaver. I learned how to tend the moth-garden. I made the silk for Xania's story-coat.'

'And became more than they knew,' Maia repeated the challenge Tareth had thrown at Elin.

'Became more than they knew,' agreed Tareth. 'More than I wished. Elin, for all her desire for power never understood Xania and the story-coat. They were the true strength of the land.'

'Yet now Xania lies on the Cloud Plains and there is no silk for stories because the moth-garden here is dead,' said Maia slowly.

Tareth nodded. 'But now the Sun Catcher has come,' he said, 'she will find new silk and I will weave it. She will rule well. She has the story-coat.'

'But she is too young to rule as Queen instead of Elin.' Maia stared down at her bare toes. 'Nor does she want to.' And she didn't want the story-coat. She looked at Tareth. It was difficult to face him. 'There must be another way.'

She saw Tareth shake his head.

'There is always another way,' she said fiercely. 'I want to have an eagle. I want to fly an eagle.'

'A Sun Catcher has never flown an eagle. They are birds of the mountains, of cold skies. Sun Catcher fire would burn them.'

'Magnus flew with me,' protested Maia.

Tareth looked uncertain. Then he shook his head. 'Before you caught the sun.'

'I can be different. I have always been different,' Maia tried not to sound bitter. 'I want to tame an eagle. An eagle has far sight. An eagle can help a Sun Catcher see when the sun burns her eyes.'

Maia knew she was sounding like a fractious child.

'If I must be a Sun Catcher, I will. If you show me how, I will learn to listen to the silk.' She pulled a face. 'I will even speak softly to Azbarak, the fat Keeper.'

Tareth grinned.

Emboldened by this glimpse of the old Tareth who had guided her through the stormy days of growing up among the weed people, Maia pressed on.

'I will search for new silk so that you can weave. I will learn to be Queen if I must. But not yet. First I need to find an eagle. The Eagle Hunters gave me Fionn. They will give me an eagle . . . if I ask.'

Tareth shook his head. 'It's not a gift they can give. An eagle chooses where it will fly. It's true that the hunters catch young eagles and hope to hunt them. But many remain wild and are set free. Your place is here. You are the Sun Catcher.'

# Six

Maia tugged the hood of the cloak over her head, hiding her hair. No one would recognise her. She wasn't going to be kept a prisoner in the palace like Elin. Azbarak was an old woman. He claimed the city was not safe. Had told her to stay in the palace. That she should only go into the city if the archers went with her. Tareth had agreed with him.

'Come on,' she urged. 'Before someone comes.'

'Is it safe?' asked Zena.

'Of course. Razek and Kodo will protect you. And I'll protect them.' She grinned at their indignant faces. 'Come on. I want to see if the traders have hoods for eagles.'

Razek watched the crowds milling around the market. It was worse than a Gather back at home. Chaos, noise, smells. He longed for space, the emptiness and rhythms of the weed beds, the sounds of families in the caves above the beach, the chatter of the weed boys, the rise and fall of the sun-deeps, the jewel-bright seaweed swaying beneath the water. He needed to go back. But how?

He frowned at Kodo. The lizard boy was trying to persuade Zena to barter for a golden fox-fur hat. Who needed fur? The sun was hot, beating on his shoulders, bouncing off the stone.

The timber buildings oozed resin. The sun was making the crowds livelier, the traders' cries were worse than the endless screeching of nesting gulls. He shrugged irritably. His tunic stuck to his back. Maia had pushed back her hood. Kodo's face shone with sweat.

Razek remembered Kodo had said that Trader Bron would arrive in the city soon and then Kodo would join him. He wondered if the trader ship would pass close to the cliff-tops. Would he need more crew? Kodo had talked his way on to the boat with Tareth. If a lizard boy could find work on a trader ship, so could he.

It would be good to leave even if it did mean a voyage across the unknown far-deeps.

As if in tune with his thoughts, the crowds surged like ripples running across the surface as a pack of hunter fish chased a shoal of silver flicker-fish into the shallows. Movement caused by a boy being chased by a burly, bearded man, brandishing a stick and yelling. Darting and dodging, the child narrowly missed crashing into a pile of hazel wand cages. His pursuer did not.

The stack swayed, toppled. The cages fell, several splitting open as they hit the ground. Chickens spilled out. The crowd swirled, hands reaching, plucking birds from the ground. Several disappeared beneath tunics as the whirling shoal of spectators sucked them up.

A city of thieves, thought Razek contemptuously. How could Maia think of staying here? The weed beds were her home.

'I'm going to ask Kodo's trader if he will take me on his boat,' he announced.

Maia was silent.

'Kodo thinks he'll come to the city soon,' added Razek.

'I'll be sorry when you leave. You will be glad to return.'

'I must be glad,' said Razek. 'I don't belong here.' He glanced at her. 'Nor do you.'

Maia bit her lip. 'I was born here. I will learn to belong.'

'Come back to the weed beds, Maia.'

'I can't.'

'You said they are afraid of you. The Cliff Dwellers don't fear you. Come back with me.'

'The Cliff Dwellers don't like me.'

It was Razek's turn to fall silent. 'Selora treated you as a daughter,' he said finally.

'She would rather have Laya,' retorted Maia swiftly. The Salt Holder's daughter was rich. 'Selora only liked me because she thought Tareth would be a good cave mate.'

She saw that she had startled him. 'Too late now. Tareth will never return to the weed beds . . . this is his home and mine!'

She could see Zena and Kodo returning, their hands full

of flatbreads. Kodo, blueberry juice trickling down his chin, cheeks bulging, was juggling his flatbreads as they burned his hands.

'Trader is sure to need extra crew. You can leave with Kodo.'

'No! Maia!' yelled Razek and shoved her hard.

Maia tottered backwards and fell as Razek hurled himself at her. They crashed to the ground. As her head banged the stone and breath exploded from her chest, she struck out at Razek. They struggled as he tried to keep her pinned beneath him and caught her fists to stop her hitting him.

'Razek. Get off!'

Then suddenly he was gone.

'Razek! What are you doing?' yelled Kodo as he dragged Razek off her, dumping him at Zena's feet.

Razek sat up, dabbing at the blood welling from his split lip. 'I saw something.'

He examined a slit in his sleeve and the thin red scratch marking his skin. He rolled onto his knees, searching the ground.

'There!' He picked up a small throwing knife.

'A knife!' said Kodo. 'Someone has just thrown a knife at you.'

'Not at me. At Maia.'

They closed in a tight ring around her as she got to her feet. She examined the scratch on Razek's arm.

'We should go!' said Razek. 'It's not safe.'

The whole city was a midden of danger sheltering thieves, cutpurses and who knew what else, flotsam washed in to see the sun-catch. The sooner he left the Sun City the better he would feel. He stepped closer to Maia.

She saw the black-handled knife in his hand. 'You saved my life,' she said.

'Go!' commanded Razek. He tugged Maia's hood over her red hair. 'All of you. Quickly.'

Moving as one, with Maia penned in the middle, they hustled her forwards, warily watching the crowds.

A black rat scuttled into the light, grabbed the flatbread Kodo had dropped and scurried past the tumble of chicken cages to vanish into the shadows.

# SEVEN

The knife was black, the hilt polished wood. Maia turned it over in her hands. It gleamed darkly in the sunlight. She could see lines scratched onto it. She frowned, turning the knife to try to decipher the pattern. It looked like a long-legged figure with raised feathered arms. A wading bird? A man with wings?

Kodo peered over her shoulder. 'A throwing knife.'

'An assassin's knife,' said Razek.

'Assassin?' protested Maia.

'It was thrown at you. Someone tried to kill you,' said Razek.

Maia swallowed. 'Not a very good assassin,' she said.

Zena moaned softly. 'Lady not safe here.'

Maia smiled at her. It was a shaky smile. 'I won't stay in the city. I'm going into the mountains. To hunt eagles. I need an eagle. Tareth needs an eagle.' She glanced at Razek. 'Will you come with me, before you leave?'

'To find an eagle for Tareth?' asked Razek. He could redeem himself. Help her find an eagle.

'You can't replace Tareth's eagle,' said Kodo. 'Sea-eagles don't hunt here.

He watched Razek's changing expression. The Weed Master was as easy to read as the currents across the sun-deeps. He didn't like the way Razek was looking at Maia. Kodo felt his stomach twist and this time it wasn't hunger that growled like an angry lizard.

'Tareth will not want another eagle . . . just as Ootey, my grandfather, would never replace his lizard. He didn't take another lizard when Oon was killed with my father. He didn't take another son when my father drowned.' He stared hard-eyed at Razek. 'You cannot replace the dead.'

Maia sighed. 'The Eagle People fly golden eagles. Tareth would have flown an eagle when he was a boy, just as Huan does.'

'Magnus was a sea-eagle. You wanted a sea-eagle. You asked me to look for a nest,' said Kodo.

Maia nodded. 'But there are no sea-eagles here. Huan can take us to where the eagles nest. I can find an eagle. A female fledgling. She can become my far sight when . . . when the sun-catching burns my eyes,' she added quickly.

Kodo felt the breath leave his chest as if the cold blade in her hand had slit him open. He'd promised to search for an eye cure before the sun-catching. He had told her he would travel with Bron as he traded along the coast seeking remedies to help, as the Watcher's eyebright had helped when Maia had brought down fire to destroy the wulfen. If Maia wanted an eagle to help her see, she must think he would fail in that quest.

Maia was looking at Razek now. 'Before Bron comes, will you come into the mountains to hunt eagles?'

'Bron?' The cold, stone knife in Kodo's lungs was burning now. Did Maia think Razek could have a place on the trading ship, *his* ship? Kodo glared at Maia.

Maia looked at him and misread the fire in his eyes. 'No, Kodo. There's no news. But Keeper Azbarak told Tareth that he expects traders to arrive soon. Once he can come up the river, Bron will be here. Then you will be gone. Come to the mountains with me first.'

'I don't like high places.'

'It will be like honey hunting,' Maia said, realising that she had somehow offended him. 'You liked that. Come to the mountains before Bron arrives.'

Kodo felt his sulks disappearing. 'A beast attacked me when I went honey hunting.'

'I saved you.'

'I got stung!'

'Eagles don't sting.' Maia grinned at him. 'And the honey was sweet. Even Grandfather Ootey was pleased.'

'They don't sting . . . just tear your eyes out,' muttered Razek. 'Don't come if you're afraid, lizard boy.'

Kodo ignored him. 'Maybe we'll find another honey cave.'

Maia nodded. 'We'll ask the Eagle People. You'll come?'

Kodo glanced at Razek. He so did not want a lizard boy to go with them.

'Bron will wait for me. I'll leave a message.' He crossed

his thumbs behind his back. 'He won't leave without me. I'll come and see where eagles nest.'

'And I,' said Zena. 'To make flatbread. Not catch eagles.'

Razek glanced at the knife in Maia's hands. 'And Tareth? Will he think it safe to go to the mountains when you tell him what happened?'

Maia slipped the knife through her belt. She would hide it later beneath her sleeping furs. 'Nothing happened. There is nothing to tell,' she said.

Tareth had asked the boy to set a bench beside the fire. Now he sat, his feet almost in the circle of white ash. The palace boy placed another huge log and, as Maia stepped into the firelight, backed away and disappeared.

Maia leaned against the bench. She pulled off her boots and stretched her toes towards the flames. Rather than look at the fire, which seemed too bright for her sun-dazzled eyes, she watched the shadows the flames threw onto the walls.

'He's afraid of me, just as he was afraid of Elin.'

'She can do no harm,' said Tareth.

No, thought Maia. But if she could, she would harm me. She frowned at the fire.

She felt Tareth's gaze. 'Has anything happened? '

Maia shrugged. 'Something happened in the market,' she admitted.

'The market? You went to the market despite Azbarak's

warning? Did Yanna and the warriors go with you?'

'No.'

'Maia!'

'Azbarak worries like a dog with fleas. I was with Razek . . . and Kodo. Zena too.'

Tareth sighed. 'What happened, Maia?'

'There were thieves . . . stolen chickens. Gossip. Traders. But no Bron.'

Maia crossed her thumbs. Would he guess that she wasn't telling him everything?

'I asked, but no ships have reached the leaping water. Kodo wants to be gone. Razek too. They don't like it here.' She clasped her arms around her knees. 'Neither do I,' she confessed.

'Many came to watch the sun-catching and will leave soon. They cannot stay long. They will leave to plant early and hope for a good harvest.'

'Which Azbarak will claim for the Sun Palace and then they will hate me more,' muttered Maia.

'Azbarak must fill the granaries so that if another harvest fails the Sun City will not starve.'

'So catching the sun was not enough?'

She twisted to look up at him. She could not bear the bleakness on his face and turned away to stare at the fire.

Tareth laid his hand on her head. 'It was enough. More than enough.' He touched the eagle feather in her hair. 'Yet, even with the sun, harvests can fail. If there is not enough rain . . . a plague of flying beetles, that devours the crops. Azbarak is wise to plan for disasters.'

Maia groaned. 'Shall I become a Storm Chaser, a Rain

Bringer and a Bug Slayer too? Nefrar might develop a taste for beetles.'

As she had hoped, Tareth laughed.

'Must I go to the mountains to find stones and make them into runes and rattle them in a bag as I walk, like the Watcher? And blacken my teeth and throw ash in my hair so that everyone knows that I am old and wise?' She flapped her hands and the shadows danced like a scatter of black crows wheeling above the Watcher's cairn.

'Easier to bring the Watcher to the city,' said Tareth.

'She wouldn't come,' said Maia, her own laughter dying. 'She belongs in the open spaces where her crows can touch the sky.'

She remembered her last glimpse of the Watcher, lying injured beside the stone cairn. She and Xania had left her for dead as they'd fled from the Wulf Kin. She blinked.

'She wouldn't come. She wouldn't like it here.'

'As you do not,' sighed Tareth.

Maia shrugged. 'I will learn to like it . . . as I learned to like the Cliff Village. As you did,' she added, remembering that Tareth had been a stranger to both the Sun City and the Cliff Village too. 'Does it take long?'

Her question was met with silence. Questions always were. Surely now she had become a Sun Catcher he could tell her the truth. He began to speak, his voice soft with the song of the has-been.

'I didn't love the city, or the Sun Palace. I loved the mountains. I wanted nothing more than to fly an eagle.

'Urteth dreamed of becoming a warrior, but eagle hunting was enough for me. Our father hunted with his eagle, as his father had before him and his father before that. We were Eagle Hunters. And would be still if Xania hadn't reached our valley and I heard silk sing. Xania and the silk claimed me and I came to the city, learned how to care for the moon-moths and became a weaver.'

'A Warrior Weaver,' murmured Maia, remembering what Sabra, the Watcher had called him on her Naming Day.

Tareth rested his fist on his crippled leg. 'A poor excuse of a warrior. And as for being the Queen's Weaver . . . for that I must have silk.' He fell silent, remembering.

Maia couldn't bear the bleakness in his voice. 'And an Eagle Hunter,' she added.

Tareth sighed. 'That, too. Once I found Magnus,' he agreed.

Maia turned and knelt, resting her forearms on Tareth's knees, staring into his face.

'That's what I wish for. I want to go into the mountains and find an eagle.'

'You're the Sun Catcher. You cannot be an Eagle Hunter.'

'You're a Warrior Weaver and an Eagle Hunter.'

'No longer.'

'You could be again. Come to the mountains with me and find another eagle. Then we can go to the cliffs. To the moth-garden. Collect more silk.'

Tareth's eyes were as dark as the knife she had hidden in her sleeping furs, his face as cold as the stone blade.

'I'm no longer an Eagle Hunter. And you must learn the secrets of the silk now that Xania is no more. Secrets that even I can't teach you. Someone must sing the silk songs.'

'I'm not the Story Singer. The coat isn't mine.'

'Xania left it with you. Who else will wear it now?'

'There's Caspia.'

'Caspia? Elin's daughter will *never* wear the Story Coat.'

'Why not?'

'How can you ask that after all that Elin has done?'

'Elin. Not Caspia. Is Caspia to be blamed for what her mother did?'

Tareth shook his head. 'Caspia is not the Story Singer.'

'She is like the silk. She . . . she sees thoughts I felt her reach into me, seeking to know me,' said Maia 'She whispered in my head just as the story-coat does.'

'Elin's daughter is not the Story Singer,' said Tareth.'

'Nor am I.'

'Then we must find one. Khandar needs its stories. And new silk. '

'I need an eagle . . . not stories '

'You will never be able to tame an eagle, Maia.'

'Why not?' demanded Maia fiercely, desperate now. 'I learned to fly Magnus. I learned to live in the weed beds. I learned to fight like the warrior women. Why can't I learn to fly an eagle.'

She was never going to change his mind. He might look weary but he was as fixed and unchanging as the tall rocks guarding the cliff village against storms. Yet even rocks were worn away by wind and waves. She would be like the waves and the rain and the wind. She would show him that he was wrong. She would fly an eagle.

'I know I can learn to fly an eagle. I learned to catch the sun.'

She rose to her feet. 'I told Kodo and Razek that I'd take

them into the mountains before they leave. I will catch an eagle. And then . . . then I will find new silk and a Story Singer.'

Tareth hesitated. Maia held her breath. Finally he nodded.

'Go to the mountains, if you must. Take the story-coat. Keep it with you. Learn its stories.'

He lifted his finger to forestall her protest.

'You may find it easier to hear its stories away from here.' He glanced up at the huge banners hanging from the roof. 'Away from Elin's great hall, and her evil. Guard it well. And remember that Kodo has listened to the silk. He is brave and strong, but the silk is stronger. Do not trust him near the coat.'

'I would trust Kodo with my life.'

44

# EIGHT

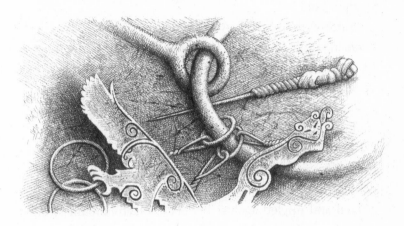

Kodo liked the eagle boy. Huan had let him hold his bird. It sat on his fist and took the gobbet of raw meat he held out, trapping it beneath its talon as it tore at the bloody flesh. Even in the dim light of the stable Kodo could see the brightness of its fierce eye, sense the power of the folded wings. No wonder Maia wanted to fly such a bird. Behind him other eagles, hooded and restless, shifted on their perches as the Eagle Hunters moved among the horses, throwing on the felt saddles, fitting the bridles with their dangling gold ornaments. A tiny golden stag, a leaping cat and a swooping eagle hung from Huan's bridle.

'My father made them,' said Huan, seeing Kodo's interest. 'And gave them to me when my eagle made his first kill. This one,' he touched the gold eagle, 'was my mother's birth gift. I must carve my own . . . or trade furs to have more for my horse.' He patted his horse. 'He is swift and beautiful and deserves to wear much mountain gold. When the snow melts I will try to find the burrows of the ant-bears and dig for their gold.'

Kodo's eyes widened. 'Ants? Gold?'

Huan saddled his horse and slipped the leather hood over his eagle's head. 'He has eaten enough. Too much and he won't hunt.'

The eagle stepped onto his gloved fist, swaying to balance as Huan mounted.

Kodo's arm felt suddenly weightless now the eagle was gone. The other Eagle Hunters were leading their horses from the stable. Shaking his bridle so that the gold animals swayed and jingled against his neck, Huan's mount strode after them. Kodo, his hand on Huan's ankle, scurried alongside.

'Ants?' he queried.

Huan grinned down at him. 'Ant-bears living between the mountains and the river.' He tapped his nose. 'Gold digging ant-bears.'

'Is it true?'

He had promised his mother gold earrings to match her gold stab pin. Trader had never found gold, despite his many voyages. Kodo had begun to think that he would return empty-handed to the stilt village when the ship reached the horse marshes below the Marsh Lord's holdfast. If Huan's story was true! If he could persuade the eagle boy to show him the ant-bears! Kodo felt a lurch of excitement.

'It was only a story told around the fire until one day my father was thrown from his horse. He was angry. He dug

46

into the burrow to find the creature that had felled him. He found golden dust instead.'

Huan touched the golden stag. 'Enough to cover this with gold. Since then, many look but few find. Even the Story Singer when she heard the tale did not believe it. My father is a good teller of tales. But, I will find such a burrow and make a mountain lion for my horse with the gold I find.'

'Take me with you,' said Kodo. 'I would like to find an ant-bear.'

Huan gathered up his reins. 'I've promised to take the Sun Catcher into the mountains to find an eagle.'

'After the eagle hunt,' Kodo called after him as the horses filed through the palace gates.

He thought that Huan hadn't heard him. The gates swung closed behind the Eagle Hunters.

'After the hunt,' called Huan. 'You'll need a horse.'

'I need a horse.' Kodo upended his leather pouch and poured tokens onto the floor. Zena retrieved the ones rolling past her. Kodo spread out the tokens. 'Will these be enough?'

Zena looked doubtful. 'Good horse much,' she said.

Kodo counted the tokens. He was afraid that Zena was right. If only Bron had arrived. He would be up for an adventure. The lure of gold would be strong. He would be sure to delay the departure of his ship and follow the story-trail to the ant-bears. And if he didn't go himself Kodo was sure Bron could be persuaded to give him the goods to barter for a horse.

Maia arrived. She looked and felt hot and cross.

Azbarak, the Keeper, had insisted that she be taken through every room in the palace to inspect her new domain, from the huge bronze wheels in the tower where once silk stretched over the wheels to sing their messages, to the treasure room where the sun-helmet lay, and then into the vast, nearly empty, granary.

Everywhere she went she had felt or heard the retreat of the palace boys. And it wasn't because Nefrar, the cheetah, padded at her heels. How could she live in a place that seeped terror whenever she was near? And then Azbarak had suggested that he show her the city. She had turned aside the suggestion and escaped, telling him she had to spend time alone in the moth-garden. She would make sure she was long gone into the mountains before the fat Keeper came to find her again.

She looked down at the tokens scattered across the floor. Kodo started shovelling them back into his leather pouch.

Kodo dropped the last token in his pouch, pulled the thongs tight with more force than was necessary, and shoved the bag out of sight in his tunic. He glared at Zena, wishing he had never told her about Huan's offer and the story of the ant-bears, willing her to keep silent. He wanted to surprise Maia with a gift of ant-bear gold. Some for Jakarta, his mother. Some for Maia, so that she too could hang a gold ornament on her horse's bridle.

'I need a horse to go eagle hunting.'

'Razak's gone into the city to find us horses.'

Kodo didn't feel the relief he should have done now that his problem was solved. What did a Weed Master know about horses?

'So go and help him choose, horse dealer,' laughed Maia, when he told her what he thought.

The old man was filthy. Fleas crawled over his sweating face. His tangled hair was alive with lice. He smelled of old age and rotten meat. Var shivered and tried to roll further away from the heap of rags that were all the old man wore. He rolled into another bundle of filth, snoring in the dark doorway. As he touched the bundle a cloud of flies rose from the body. Var felt a wave of nausea. He swallowed a mouthful of vomit. He was sick. Everyone in this alley was sick. He had to get away. The city had made him sick.

He pushed himself to his knees, trembling, his bones aching as if he was an old man too, and crawled towards the sunlight at the end of the alley. Tiki fell out of his tunic, his fur damp with Var's sweat, and scurried in front of him. At least the rat had not caught the fever. Did rats catch fevers, wondered Var, as his delirium played havoc with his thoughts.

He fought off the swirl of pictures that tried to pull him back into the night-wake where he burned under the desert sun and desert spiders stabbed him with their poison and rolled him in their sticky webs so he could not move. He was parched. Tiki brought him scraps of food. Waste food, food he could barely eat. Food often as grubby as the alleyway in which he had slept since the fever had struck. But he had made himself eat. He had to throw off the fever. He had a task. He had failed once.

At least the red-head's companions had not torn aside the shadows that concealed him and dragged him into the marketplace. He had managed to slip away and had woken next to the filthy old man. He didn't know how long he had lain there. He had to find water. Find light. Find air.

He pulled himself to his feet, gripping the edge of the wall to stop himself falling. He was still near the marketplace. The sun was sinking below the roof tops. He could hear water. Someone walked by leading a horse. The horse lowered its head, drinking great, gusty gulps of water from a shallow stone trough. Var swayed forward, drawn irresistibly towards the water.

He lurched as another figure joined the first, also leading a horse to water.

'They could be worse,' called a voice, 'but not much.'

'I'd like to see you doing better,' came the reply.

Var wiped the sweat from his face and shrank further into the shade. Even through the haze of sickness he recognised the voices. He had heard them before. He stood swaying, remembering.

Tiki ran out of the alley and dashed across towards the water, slipping under the drinking horse's nose, swimming across the trough, over the far edge and away.

The horse reared. The boy holding her jerked up in the air. As he landed he bent, grabbed a stone and hurled it after the disappearing rat. He missed. He turned to his companion.

'Did you see that? Rats. Everywhere. The sooner we leave this place, the better.'

Var discovered that he had been fingering the handle of his knife. At least he hadn't been robbed while he lay senseless. The feel of the wooden handle beneath his fingers seemed to lift the fever. If the man had hit Tiki, he would have felt a knife between his ribs.

As if he had felt the wave of venom, the figure holding the horse turned towards the alley. It was the tall boy who had knocked the flame-head from the path of the knife. Where he was, she would be. He could follow and find the girl who looked like Caspia, the blue-eyed daughter of the red witch queen.

The horse was being led away. Var pushed himself off the wall. He took a step. Darkness roared in his head. His knees gave way.

# NINE

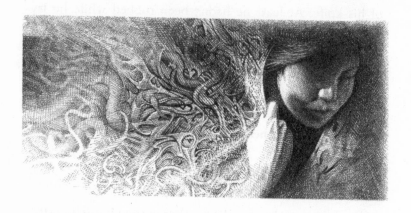

Tareth hadn't changed his mind. She could go to the mountains, but she had to take the story-coat. She didn't want to. She'd argued with him. He wouldn't listen. She had never loved the silk. It wasn't hers to claim as the sun-stone had been.

Reluctantly, Maia collected the back-sack from Azbarak's storeroom. There must be another way to learn the story of the has-been. Somewhere in the echoing vastness of the Sun Palace there must be someone, something, that would help her to understand.

Perhaps the pictures hidden beneath the fire stains in the moth-garden would tell her more of her sisters. Azbarak had promised that he would set the palace boys to work restoring the moth-garden.

Azbarak had lied. The walls of the moth-garden were still

smoke-blackened. Maia sighed and polished a small piece of the wall, revealing part of a flowering tree. A head appeared. A red-haired girl like her. She was feeding the tree.

Maia spat on her sleeve and wiped it across the tree. They were not flowers, but painted moths. And the girl was feeding them. A moth hovered on her hand drinking from a dish on her palm. Maia could see its long tongue curling into the dish. The moth was so lifelike that Maia almost expected it to clap its wings and fly off.

Interested now, she scrubbed at the wall, smearing soot across the image of another girl who was picking the cocoons from the tree and dropping them into a basket at her feet.

Maia abandoned that painting and crossed the dead moth-garden. Using her filthy sleeve she exposed another figure. Maia rubbed some more. It was Xania, or someone like her, standing, arms raised, light streaming from her shoulders, swirling like waves around her. It was the story-coat.

Maia shivered and wiped her grimy hands on her tunic. She wished that she had buried the coat with Xania. It belonged to her. But perhaps she had had to keep the coat safe for Caspia. Maia studied the picture again. She had been wrong about many things.

Tareth was right about her need to know the stories of Khandar. He could tell her some, but he'd been gone for many star-shifts and didn't know the stories Xania and the coat had learned while he was away. The coat could tell her if she dared to listen. It held the stories of her family, secrets that Tareth could never know.

Maia nibbled her thumbnail, frowning at her wayward thoughts. She did not used to be so indecisive.

Tired with her own shilly-shallying she tugged the story-coat from its bag.

Sighing at its release, the silk tumbled over her hands, cool and soft as the sand in the lizard scrape in the chill before sun-wake. It seemed welcoming. Maia ran her finger across it. It rippled beneath her touch like Nefrar's fur when she stroked him. Maia closed her eyes and remembered wearing the coat with Xania as they'd escaped from the Gather and again on the Vast as Nefrar watched over her.

Swiftly, before she could change her mind, she twirled the coat over her shoulders and plunged her arms into the long, loose sleeves.

The coat screamed. Voices howled. Hands reached, tugging at her, pulling her into a red cauldron of writhing, fighting figures. Flames roared. Hissing, smoking serpents with gaping red mouths and flickering purple forked tongues coiled round her body, squeezing and smothering her. She couldn't breathe. She opened her mouth. A child wailed.

She was ripped from the serpent and plunged into darkness, suffocating against cloth and jolted through the seething mass of struggling bodies. Beneath her cheek a heart thudded, its erratic beat becoming hers.

Threading through the smoke she was aware of a tantalising smell, at once strange yet comforting. She fought to remember what it meant, struggled to free herself from the swaddling cloth.

A shout; a howl; the clash of blades; shock waves from the blow running through her. Fire and blood. And the dreadful howl of a mortally wounded beast. She burst free of the dark into firelight as the armoured man fell.

Maia yelled, ripped the coat from her shoulders and threw it to the ground. The silk wound around her feet. She could still hear the voices, the screams. She kicked the silk away, wiping her hand across her mouth. Her hand smelled of smoke and fire. Why had the coat shown her that? She drew in a deep sobbing breath. She hated the silk. It wasn't to be trusted.

'Did it frighten you?'

Maia's heart missed a beat. Elin was standing behind her.

'You should take care when and where you wear the coat.'

'It was here,' whispered Maia. 'Fire. Fighting.'

'Here,' echoed Elin. She looked round.

'I was carried. A man died.' Maia shuddered.

It had been real. The flames, the fight, the death. Real, not just a story locked in the coat. 'I was saved from the fire.'

'Tareth stole you.'

'I would have died.'

Elin stroked the worn panel of silk on the front of her gown and gripped it in her fists, screwing the fabric tight, crushing it as her face twisted with the effort to shut out the voices of the sister silk she had been condemned to wear.

'No loss,' she hissed. 'Caspia was to take your place. You should never have been born. A child of our mother's old age. She should have perished carrying you, but you both survived.'

Elin shuddered. 'I did not start the fire. I did not burn the silk.' Her voice rose. 'It punishes me, but I didn't destroy the moths. Tareth did. Did the coat tell you that? Tareth brought ruin and death to the land when he killed the moths and stole you and the stone. Did the coat tell you that? The stone and the silk are mine, for me and those of my blood!'

Maia bent and gathered the coat. There were no voices. She felt its listening silence. She shook the silk. It flared and touched Elin.

'Is it yours? Ask it. Can you wear the coat?'

As the silk touched her, Elin flinched.

'Are you afraid, sister?' demanded Maia. 'Afraid to listen to its stories?'

Elin backed away. 'They are not for me,' she gasped as the voices in the silk overcame her strength to resist. 'Nor you,' she cried and rushed from the room, pursued by voices only she could hear.

The coat lay silent in Maia's hands. Hardly daring to breathe, Maia shoved it deep into the back-sack. She couldn't take the coat into the mountains. It must stay in the palace, hidden until the next sun-catch. Hugging the bag, she fled through the palace to the small room Azbarak, the Keeper, called the treasure store, tucked the sack beside the sun-helmet and escaped.

# TEN

Wings half-closed, tail tilted, the golden eagle glided in the wind. Purple cloud shadows chased across the hills. The sun was high, the sky a brilliant blue streaked with high white cloud. Fionn picked her way, sure-footed, across the tumbled rocks littering the valley. It was good to be with her friends. Listening to their chatter, Maia realised that she was happy. Happy to share the eagle hunt. Happy to be free of the Sun City.

Zena was happy too, singing to herself as she clung to her pony's mane. Kodo was as at home on his horse as he was riding his lizard. He was talking to Huan. It looked like a serious conversation. Only Razek seemed ill at ease, sitting awkwardly on a sturdy pony, his long legs dangling almost to the ground. Nefrar wasn't helping either. The spotted cat leapt into the stream, sending water spraying over Razek's pony so that it shied, almost unseating him.

Maia felt a bit guilty about Nefrar. The cheetah had appeared after they had left the Sun City. She hoped Yanna would understand. As always, Nefrar chose his own path; she hadn't lured him on the eagle hunt. She looked at Huan's eagle now spiralling lazily on the updrafts. If Huan hunted him maybe there would be a fur to take back for Yanna to make up for Nefrar's absence. The Warrior Woman would need warm furs for wolf-walk in Altara.

Huan deserted Kodo and caught up with his father Egon who had promised to show them the eyrie he had seen when he had taken his own eagle hunting after the sun-catch.

Maia rode alongside Kodo. 'Well, did Razek find you a good horse?' she teased.

Kodo glanced back at Razek and grinned. 'Better than his. He would have taken this one but fell off twice in the stable.' He patted his horse. 'It's as well he doesn't have to ride a lizard.'

Seeing Razek wincing in the saddle, Maia felt a twinge of sympathy. Her first ride had been with Xania. The Story Singer had held her on, otherwise she would have been in as much trouble as Razek was now.

'We'll make camp soon,' she called.

Razek waved to show he had heard and fell off.

Kodo smothered a laugh as Razek climbed to his feet, found a rock to stand on and hauled himself back on his horse.

'Have you and Razek quarrelled?' asked Maia.

Kodo shrugged. 'He never forgets he is the Weed Master, even with Huan.'

'I'm glad you like Huan. He and Egon gave me Fionn.' Her horse, hearing her name, tossed her head. Her bridle ornaments jingled as her long mane fell over Maia's hands. Tareth might have doubts about an eagle bonding with her now that she had captured the sun's fire, but Fionn showed no fear of her. Maia patted her. She would have her horse, her eagle and, when Nefrar mated, her own hunting cat too.

'What secrets were you and Huan sharing?' she asked.

'No secrets,' said Kodo. 'We were talking about the hills and looking for sight balm and . . . and the animals that live here, snow leopards and foxes . . . and wolves.'

'Here?'

Kodo gestured towards the distant peaks. 'Higher. His father is going to ride on and hunt while we catch our eagles.'

Maia nodded. She knew that Huan wanted to be the one to take them to the eagle's nest. 'Sight balm?' she asked.

'Huan says that there's a plant that his people use to ward off mountain blindness. Maybe it's like the Watcher's eyebright. We'll search for it.'

He wanted to tell her Huan's story about the ant-bears and the gold to be found in their burrows. But he wanted to surprise her with gold even more. And if he did tell her she might tell Razek. He frowned. He didn't want his secrets shared with Razek.

Maia didn't understand his frown. 'It would be good if Huan can find an eagle and a plant that works like eyebright, wouldn't it?' she said.

'Of course,' said Kodo. 'And when I sail with Trader, I'll keep looking for other cures too. I won't forget.'

Maia woke before the first rays of sun probed the valley where they had camped. She could smell the scent of warm chay, hear the crackle of a fire. Someone was awake and up before her. Her stomach clenched with excitement. Soon she would be clambering down the rock face to capture a young eagle.

She wriggled out of her sleeping fur and pulled on her boots. Nefrar grumbled in protest as she dislodged him and slid into the warm hollow she had left, burying his nose in her back-sack. The back-sack shouldn't be so empty. It wouldn't have been if she had not brushed aside Tareth's instructions and left the story-coat hidden in the Sun Palace.

Huan was saddling the horses. Razek, crouching over the fire, stirred the pot of steaming chay. He didn't look as if he had slept. As he stood up to fetch the beakers he winced.

'It will be easier when you ride again,' said Huan. 'Unless you want to rest here while we find the eagle? Kodo can take your place.'

Egon had told them that their party was too large to approach the nest. Three would be enough, he said. One must be Maia since the eagle was to be hers. Huan was to go too. The others had drawn the dried stalks from his hand. Razek had drawn the longest straw. Kodo's indrawn hiss of breath had signalled his disappointment. He had scowled at Razek,but Zena had been delighted that she too had a short straw.

Razek stretched until his joints cracked. 'I'll hunt,' he said and hobbled to his horse.

'It's more like a climb than a hunt,' said Maia, wondering if Razek would feel safe on the steep slopes. She'd never seen him scale the cliffs to steal gulls' eggs with the weed boys. Perhaps that task was below the dignity of a Weed Master. She knew Kodo could climb almost as nimbly as she could.

Egon crawled from the shelter. He flicked his fingers.

'Sun Catcher,' he greeted her, then scanned the lightening sky. 'The parents will hunt early. You need to reach the nest while they are away.' He sipped his chay, leaving a band of froth along his lip. 'Unless you wish to battle with eagles protecting the nest and increase your legend, Sun Catcher?'

The twinkle in his eye suggested he was not serious. He glanced at Razek and Huan.

'You will have two fine hunters to protect you if the eagles return.'

'Then we'll leave now,' said Maia.

The stack of untidy sticks was wedged in a crevasse just below her feet. If she leaned out from the surface of the rock she was clinging to, she could just see the downy heads of two birds. Above her, Huan's face peered over the edge.

'Take care,' he called.

Maia hooked her fingertips into a crack and lowered herself down, dislodging the side of the nest.

A yellow beak hammered at her ankle. She stepped carefully onto the ledge, one foot in, one foot out of the nest, trying not to step on the fledglings. One bird was bigger than the other. The female. That was the one she should take. Leaning against the rock face she slipped off her back-sack and pulled out the cloth Egon had given her. The young eagles were baiting, backing away from her. The female tried to strike her again. She picked it up, folding its wings close into its body, careful not to damage the feathers, and wrapped the cloth around it. The eagle's yellow claws broke free; its talons gouged her hand. It hurt. Maia caught at them and tucked them into the cloth, wrapping them tightly. It was a fierce bird. Once tamed it would make as good a hunter as Tareth's sea-eagle, Magnus.

'Gently, fierce one,' she crooned.

It was important for the eagle to hear her voice. Once used to it she would be easier to tame. At the sound the eagle writhed in her hands. Maia almost dropped the bundle. Pressing it against her chest she absorbed the eagle's struggles but lost her balance on the precarious edge.

She heard Huan's anxious cry and Razek's shout and slammed herself back against the rock wall, almost stepping on the squawking male chick left in the nest. Waiting for the dizzying swirl of mountains and sky to subside, she tried to calm the wriggling eagle.

The eagle stabbed at her as she edged up the rock face, nearly sending them both tumbling to their deaths. Huan hadn't said that catching wild eagles was this difficult.

Her hands scrabbling for purchase, toes seeking the smallest hold, Maia crawled to safety. Razek, flat on his belly, leaned out and grabbed her shoulders, hauling her over the top, cursing as the eagle's stabbing beak hit his wrist and drew blood.

Huan pulled her to her feet. 'A fierce one. A queen of eagles. Fit for a Sun Catcher,' he said.

The eagle screamed.

Huan scanned the sky. 'We should leave before the small one's calls bring the mother.' He slipped a leather hood over the eagle's head. 'Peace, little one.' Instantly the bird quietened.

Razek was sucking his bloody wrist. 'You only brought one. There were two in the nest.'

'This was bigger,' said Maia.

'A female,' nodded Huan. 'They make better hunters.'

'I hoped to take an eagle for Tareth,' said Razek. 'I'll climb down and get the other.'

Huan shook his head. 'We leave one,' he said. 'We can find another eyrie' – he looked at Maia – 'if the Sun Catcher wishes to have two eagles.' He sounded unsure of the wisdom of his suggestion.

Maia shook her head. She hadn't known what Razek planned.

'No,' she pulled a face. 'This one will be more than enough. Tareth will find his own eagle,' she told him. 'He hasn't forgotten Magnus yet.'

Razek flushed. Maia realised she had been cruel. Razek was only trying to make amends. He didn't know that that was impossible.

'It's the way of the Eagle People,' she said gently.

# Eleven

Kodo glowered at the distance. He was a good climber. Razek was a webbed-toed paddler from the weed beds. What did he know about heights and steep dangerous climbs? Maia should have taken him, not Razek

He scuffed his feet in the dust and was in such a bad mood that he didn't grin when his pony blew nosily down his back then nosed at his tunic looking for food. He wiped away pony dribble and watched Zena edging crab-like round a rock.

'Come,' she called.

Kodo hobbled his pony and scrambled across the rocks to where Zena had been. She had vanished. He stood, gazing around, feeling silly and cross. He wasn't in the mood for games.

'Here!' Zena's voice was somewhere under his feet. He slid

down the rock. It was steeper than he realised. He landed awkwardly in a dusty gully.

'Where are you?'

A fall of earth splattered across his feet. He heard a grunt. Zena's dirty face appeared and then the rest of her wriggled from a shallow hole in the earth. She was holding a wriggling, dark-furred creature.

'Ant-bear,' she called.

Kodo squatted beside her, avoiding the scrabbling curved claws of the creature. It had been burrowing. Dirt was smeared across its snout. Its tiny, round, black eyes blinked in the sunlight. Flecks of yellow gleamed in its fur. Gold.

Holding it firmly by the scruff of its neck, Zena placed the creature on the earth. 'It feed,' she said. 'I catch. Let go and it run to burrow. We follow quick.'

Kodo nodded. Zena lifted her hand. The creature seemed to puff up to twice its size and then, nose to the ground, it scurried off. Darting from rock to bush along the gully, the ant-bear raced for safety. A helter-skelter chase followed round rocks, through a stream. Zena tripped, screamed and fell. Kodo ripped his tunic as he wriggled under an overhanging slab of rock. He tugged himself free to the sound of more ripping. The ant-bear's rump vanished into a scrubby bush. Kodo hurled himself forward and fell down a hole.

'Find,' Zena crowed. 'You find burrow.'

And had been lucky not to break a leg, Kodo thought, as he hauled himself out of the hole. The ant-bear was nowhere to be seen.

Squatting at the edge of the burrow, Zena was digging

through the loose earth. She held up a handful of dust and let it trickle through her fingers. As it fell, flecks of gold glinted in the sun.

Kodo lay in the dirt, his fists holding gold-flecked earth to the sky, staring at the sun blazing overhead and laughed until he had no breath left.

'Find. Find.' Zena, already in the hole, was tossing up handfuls of dirt.

'I'll dig,' he said. 'You can sort through the dirt and pick out the flakes.' He hauled Zena from the burrow.

Zena sat and spread her skirt to dry. Filling her cooking pan with dust, she carefully tossed the dirt into the air. Dust blew in the wind. Kodo downwind of her, ducked. After several flips and dust clouds she examined the pan, stirring the remaining earth with her finger. She grunted, unwrapped the scarf Maia had given her and picking tiny flakes from the dirt laid them on the fabric where they stuck to the damp cloth.

'Keep safe,' she said. She glanced at the sun. It was much lower in the sky than when they had left Egon. 'Go back to others?' She broke a twig from the uprooted bush. 'Make fire. Stay?'

Kodo uncovered a tiny nugget. It was smaller than his fingernail. But it would make a gold ear stud for Jakarta. He put the nugget in his belt pouch. His stomach rumbled.

Egon had insisted that they carry food in their saddlebags.

'Stay,' he decided. 'We'll dig first and eat later.'

They could water the horses in the stream. It was fortunate that Zena never went anywhere without her small cooking pan, no matter how much Razek had teased her about tying it to her sash. He could find more gold while Zena made flatbreads, and return to Egon's camp before dark.

Slipping his knife from its sheath, Kodo lowered himself into the ant-bear burrow.

# Twelve

Caspia saw the two figures in the valley below. She reined in her horse. The wulfen crowded her, making her horse jitter across the track. She hissed at them and they slunk away.

She was unaware of them as she dismounted and peered over the edge of the path. She watched the curly-haired boy bent double in the half-dark, stab his knife again and again into the earth. Saw him fill a pan with earth and pass it above his head to a grubby girl. His face was streaked with dirt, his dark eyes gleamed, his mouth gaped with effort as he started hacking at the earth again. His thoughts were strong. The mind-picture a strange swirl of huge swimming lizards, a snuffling baby, earth-falls and gold ear studs. She felt dizzy with thought-stolen excitement. The scattered mind-pictures were confusing. They demanded her attention.

She had seen him before, yelling with excitement. He was the boy who had ridden into the Sun Palace as she had left the city. A boy who dreamed of endless sun-deeps and lizards and a flame-headed girl. A follower of the Sun Catcher. A follower the silk had chosen. And he was here.

Why? What was he doing? And was the Sun Catcher with him? Caspia cast her thought-stealing net wide, trying to read more of his thoughts. Nothing now but effort, sweat and thirst. Hunger so sharp it made her own stomach clench. Then the thought of flatbreads warm from the bake-stone and a glimpse of the boy sniffing like a hunting hound and straightening to stand in the light.

'What is it, lady?'

The smell of the Wulf Kin, sweat, fur, leather, as Vartek nudged his pony alongside overpowered the sense of hunger, blotted out the smell of flatbread and again the image dissolved. The Wulf Kin's narrow face with its swirling blue tattoo and pointed teeth replaced the curly-haired boy.

'What d'you see, lady? Is it Urteth?'

Caspia drew back from the edge of the track. She hid her irritation at the loss of her mind-pictures.

'My father is in the Tower of Eagles,' she retorted. 'Why would I see him here?'

Urteth might be injured, dying as the usurper Sun Catcher had claimed, but he was still the Wulf Kin's master. So long as they thought he lived and was strong they would follow his daughter.

'Do we ride through sun-sleep?' Vultek's eyes with the black slit pupils could see almost as well in the dark as the light. She could not. And her horse spooked in the darkness.

Vultek knew that. He was trying to intimidate her. To take control of their journey. She would not allow it.

'No! We'll rest here. I have dreams to watch. Something is happening.'

Vultek nodded and gnawed at a flea in the fur covering his hand. Caspia relaxed. He was still a little in awe of her ability to thought-steal. He would obey and serve her while he believed she had that power, and not just because she was Urteth's daughter. She stored away the knowledge.

'You will be safe while you dream-seek, lady. We will watch over you.'

'Send Jadhev to catch lizards.'

Vultek stared at her. 'Lizards?'

'A handful. Alive. Unharmed. I will need lizards after sun-wake. Search while the rocks are still warm and they sleep in the sun. Then make a fire.'

She heard him think that spit-roast lizard would make a good change from the dried strips of yak they had eaten since leaving the Sun City. She didn't tell him that the lizards had a different fate. They were bait. Unless he hunted, Vultek would have to content himself with another jaw-aching meal.

Despite Elin's command, she had lingered in the mountains instead of riding to Urteth. She had felt the sun-catch. Felt the land start to warm. Her mother must have taken the sun-stone. She thought about returning to the Sun City, but Elin would be furious if she disobeyed. And she did want to see Urteth. She had much to tell him.

Caspia settled herself on a sun-hot boulder and wound her skirts around her long booted legs. Then, resting her chin on her knees, she stared into the distance and began to thought-weave the events which had sent her and the two Wulf Kin fleeing from the Sun City into the mountains. Thoughts of a usurper who had arrived to challenge her mother, Elin. A flame-haired girl who looked like her and claimed to be the Sun Catcher, a role her mother had raised her to believe would be hers when the sun-stone was discovered. The girl had found the stone. But Caspia knew her mother had summoned an assassin.

She tried to recapture the image of the bird-eyed boy who had waylaid her on the plain. She frowned when his face refused to form. If he should fail to rid them of the Sun Catcher it wouldn't matter much. When she reached the Tower of Eagles, she would tell Urteth to send Zartev, the old one, to find and kill her. The ancient Wulf Kin hadn't failed her father yet.

A whisper drifted through the smoke of her thoughts. Her mother's voice. It sounded strange. Caspia turned her gaze away from the fierce thought-face of Zartev and listened. Where was Elin?

Elin stumbled. The silk coat was heavy. It shouldn't be this heavy, but at least it was silent. She carried it on her back, silent and safe in its bag. She had wrapped the sun-helmet in the billows of silk before she had stuffed both in the back-sack and left the palace. She dared not stop. If Tareth discovered her gone, he'd send the Warrior Women and their hunting cats after her.

The patches sewn to her clothes rustled and whispered as she moved. Only if she stood still did they fall silent. But she couldn't pause long. She must cross the mountains and reach Urteth and Caspia in the stone stronghold. Then, dressed in the coat and wearing the sun-helmet, Caspia could claim her birthright to be the new Sun Catcher.

# Thirteen

Something was wrong.

Maia knew that an eagle swaddled in cloth, hooded so that it was in the dark and couldn't see, should be quiet.

This eagle was frantic. Maia's back-sack pitched and heaved as she rode. She could see Huan glancing anxiously across at her. He was probably worried that the eagle would damage its newly forming flight feathers.

She took a breath and sang the song she had heard Tareth sing to Magnus as they sat on the ledge outside their cave and watched the sun sink into the sun-deeps. She thought the eagle listened, stopped struggling. Encouraged, she sang again and the eagle fought frantically to escape.

'What am I doing wrong?' she called to Huan.

The eagle boy shrugged. 'Perhaps she is hungry. We should stop and see if she'll feed.' He had strips of meat to feed his own eagle in the pouch on his belt. He wondered if there would be enough to satisfy the fledgling too.

Maia nodded. Huan had caught a lapran on the journey to the nest. It dangled from his saddle. Fresh meat might calm the captive bird.

'The lapran?' she asked. Huan might have caught it to vary the diet of flatbread, nuts and wizened fruit Egon had insisted they carry. Not good eagle food. She wished she had thought to bring prepared meat on the hunt, but she had intended taking the eagle back to their camp before she fed it. She had wanted Egon to be there when she freed the eagle. She trusted Huan, but his father must have trained many eagles.

The eagle wriggled. Maia felt its hooked beak hit her shoulder. If only Tareth was here. But he didn't want her to have an eagle. He didn't think a Sun Catcher could fly an eagle.

The bird's beak thudded into her shoulder again, but less hard now. Perhaps it was exhausting itself. Maia bit her lip.

'Can she eat the lapran?' she asked.

Huan nodded. He glanced again at Maia's back-sack. Even hooding the captured eagle had not reassured it. This fledgling was not scared, she was furious. She didn't need blood to fuel her anger and make her even more intractable. It would be better if Maia's bird was calmer, thought Huan wryly, and wondered if they should press on and return to the others so that Egon could help with pacifying the young eagle. He opened his mouth to suggest it, but Maia was already dismounting and slipping the back-sack from her shoulders so he said nothing.

Sighing with relief, Razek slid from his horse and watched as Huan pulled off his leather gauntlet, deftly skinned the lapran and cut off thin strips of flesh, then pulled a wooden dish from his saddlebag and filled it with water. He took off his own eagle's hood, letting her drink before he returned her to her perch on the short wooden crutch he had lashed to his saddle before they had set out. Then he dropped the strips of meat into it, prodding it with his finger, washing away the blood.

Maia opened the neck of the back-sack wide and gently eased the bundled eagle from the bag. Placing it on the ground she knelt beside it and, with Razek's help, fastened jesses to the eagle's legs just as Huan had told her. The eagle flexed its talons but lay still, the breeze ruffling its dark feathers. Quickly pulling on the thick leather mitten, Maia set the hooded eagle on her arm, tucking the trailing jesses under her thumb so that the bird could not fly off.

The eagle's head swivelled, trying to see through the close-fitting hood. Its strong talons gripped her gauntlet. Maia rocked her arm, as Huan had showed her. It was partly to check the eagle's balance, partly to start its training. If the eagle could not balance well it might not make a good hunter. Maia held her breath. Wings folded, the young eagle adjusted its grip, swaying easily on her arm. Perfect. Maia's breath escaped in a relieved sigh. The eagle's head turned, seeking the sound.

'Ay! Ay!' whispered Maia softly, mimicking the cry Huan used to call his bird.

The next move was to remove the hood. Her hand brushed the eagle as she reached for the hood.

Instantly the eagle's wings rose as she hurled herself from Maia's arm, pitched forward, fell and swung head-down from the jesses, her beating wing tips almost brushing the ground.

Huan shouted a warning. Maia struggled to hold the eagle clear of the ground. It twisted and spun from the short length of the jesses. One wing tip slammed against the ground as the eagle beat its wings, trying to escape.

'Gently! Gently!' she sang. The sound of her voice seemed to enrage the eagle. Her wing beating became more frantic. On tiptoe, her arm stretched high, struggling with the dead weight of the eagle, Maia tried desperately to stop its wings hitting the ground.

Then Huan was there, ducking the beating wings, grasping them and folding them against the eagle's body out of harm's way, gentling the panicking eagle against his coat. The eagle's hooded head batted against his shoulder, the movements slowing as Huan stroked her plumage. He opened his hand. Shaken, Maia slid the jesses under his thumb and Huan took the eagle from her, wincing as the talons gripped.

Razek grabbed Huan's thick leather gauntlet and tugged it over his hand. Huan smiled his relief and thanks as he transferred the eagle to his gloved fist. Calm now, the bird balanced there, turning her head as Huan continued to stroke her feathers.

'Ay! Ay!' he crooned. 'Sky Warrior.'

The eagle bobbed her head at the sound of his voice.

'Ay! Peace, little one,' chanted Huan softly. 'Ay. Ay. She's beautiful,' he whispered 'Strong. And brave. She'll make a fine hunter. Sky hunter, wind rider,' he sang to the eagle. He glanced at Maia. 'She will fall like a sword from the sky on her prey.'

Maia stripped off her gauntlet. 'But not for me,' she said. 'She will not ride the wind and rule the sky for me.'

She turned away so that neither Huan nor Razek would see the sudden rush of hot tears. Tareth had been right. There was to be no eagle far-sight for her. Her sun-fire had hurt and frightened the eagle. She would never fly her own eagle.

# FOURTEEN

Kodo ripped off the end of Zena's long scarf. Flecks of gold, which reminded him of lizard scales, had caught in the stitching. Zena watched wide-eyed as he placed the three tiny nuggets he had scratched from the burrow into the torn scrap of cloth. He rolled and tied it carefully before tucking it inside his tunic.

'I'll trade for a new one,' he promised. 'In the market.'

He glanced at the sky. Fingers of pink and gold brought by sun-wake were stretching up beyond the dark hills. He was starving. And cold. The sun hadn't yet warmed the flat rock they had slept on. He had been glad to huddle over the fire as he tended it during the dark.

Zena wrapped the torn scarf around her shoulders and pulled a fold over her bald head. She shivered, holding her hands to the flames, and then touched the streak of sunlight licking the surface of the rock.

'Warm soon,' she said.

Kodo stood, stamping his cold feet, flexing his aching shoulders. Nefrar would have kept Maia warm, stretching alongside her as she slept. Zena would have slept curled against the cat too. He looked at Zena's pinched face, her dirty clothes, her torn scarf and felt guilty. He should have returned to camp, not dug until he couldn't see and forced them to spend the sun-sleep in the open.

'Warm soon,' he echoed. 'I'll look again in the burrow now it's light. And then we'll ride to find the others.'

With a lingering glance at the sun, Zena scrambled from the rock and retraced the ant-bear tracks to the tiny stream.

'Stay close,' called Kodo.

She didn't look back. Kodo wondered if he should go after her. He turned to follow. A winged shape high in the sky distracted him. An eagle. He wondered if Razek had managed to catch an eagle and pushed aside a stab of jealousy that the weed boy had gone on the eagle hunt. He touched the small bulge under his tunic. He had done better than Razek. He had found gold. And there might be more.

The burrow was empty. The entrance destroyed. An earth slip had filled the tiny tunnel he'd dug out. The ant-bear would have to dig another home, thought Kodo. Even though the sunlight spilled into the earth, there was no glint of golden dust. To find more he would have to burrow deeper. Zena had vanished. Kodo hesitated then began to dig.

The sun blazed onto his back. His tunic was sticking to his back. His only reward for digging had been the discovery of a chip of rock with a smear of gold no bigger than the tip of an arrow gleaming on its surface. He wiped his sweating forehead with the back of his hand. There was no more gold here. To find more he would have to excavate deeper. Perhaps even find another ant-bear burrow. He glanced up and was dazzled by the sun high above. He hadn't been aware of its climb. He should take Zena back to the others.

He scrambled out of the pit. There was no sign of her. Only the hobbled horses, their muzzle dripping water. Zena must have gone back to the stream and returned with water for them. He could see her long green scarf stretched out, the corners pinned under stones, on the flat sleeping rock. She had washed it.

Kodo, aware of the dirt in his clothes, tucked the tiny rock in his tunic, sheathed his knife and attempted to beat the dirt out of his tunic. He had emptied his boots of grit and earth and was pulling them on when Maia, her hair the colour of flames in the bright sun, appeared near the horses. She crossed to the rock and bent to examine the fire that Zena had let go out.

'Maia,' called Kodo surprised. 'Is Zena with you?'

The figure slowly stood and turned. 'The small one? No, she is sitting by the cool of the water.'

Kodo stared. The girl smiled. She was Maia, yet not Maia. Maia with eyes the clear blue of the shallows near the lizard scrape.

Kodo stared at her and it seemed to him that he was slipping beneath deep water. Water that washed away the dirt caking his hair, his clothes and the grime on his face. He shook his head to clear it and saw the small lizard perched on the girl's shoulder, its face peering through her long red hair. Another clung to the front of her tunic, a long scarlet strand trailing from its neck. One end was fastened to her hand where another grass-green lizard sat panting in the sun. It too was attached to a cord.

The girl smiled and sat, putting the two lizards on the boulder beside her. She ran her finger across them. Kodo saw them change colour, growing paler and then golden as they merged with the sandy rock. The girl scooped the third lizard from her shoulder and placed it on her palm. She wrapped its slender cord around her thumb and held her hand out to Kodo.

'Come and see my lizards,' she invited.

The small lizard on her hand stood on tiptoe, its throat throbbing, its blue tongue flickering from its open mouth.

Kodo stared, fascinated. The lizard was like a tiny, jewelled Doon. All it needed was a red crest. As Kodo watched he thought he saw a red crest open and close behind the lizard's head. He blinked and stared at the girl again.

'Who are you?'

'My name is Caspia,' she said. 'And I like lizards too.'

Zena knew that she ought to return to Kodo but the stream led her on. She followed it, scrambling over the tumbles of rock that blocked her path until the sun made her thirsty. She knelt, cupped her hands and drank. The water tasted like the bronze beakers in the Sun Palace. Sitting back on her heels, she could see the trail winding across the foot of the valley. She shaded her eyes. There were mounds of earth, dark as piles of dried berries heaped in the flat woven baskets in the market. Perhaps they were the dirt spoils thrown from more ant-bear burrows. She would go that far and look, then go back to tell Kodo what she had found.

She had almost reached them when she saw a clump of yellow flowers with huge fleshy leaves like shiny green horns on the far side of the stream. Was that the sight balm leaf Huan had told them to look for? Where the water curled under the shade of an overhang and vanished, there were more flowers.

Zena splashed across the stream and bent to examine them. The flowers were the shape of horns too. Bronze-coloured horns, like the ones that had roared and greeted Maia's sun-catch. Deep inside its throat, red speckles the shape of an eye patterned each flower. Long stamens with purple pollen sprouting from the centre of each looked like the pupil of an eye. This could be eye-balm. She wondered if the balm came from the flower or the leaf.

Zena peered more closely. A fly settled on the edge of the flower and crawled into the centre. The flower snapped shut. Zena could see the silhouette of the fly through the thin petals. The long stamens twitched and curled round the fly. A puff of pollen dust hid the insect. When it cleared there was no sign of the fly. Zena took a step back. A fly-eating flower?

She reached to touch another blossom. The flower snapped

shut but not before tiny specks of pollen shot from the mouth of the horn and covered her hand. Her skin started to itch. Zena plunged her hand into the stream. The dust washed away, but her skin prickled. Zena scratched. This could not be eye-balm.

Disappointed, she snapped off a leaf. If she took it back to Huan perhaps he could tell her what plant this was. The stem was sticky with sap. It oozed onto her hand. Zena wrinkled her nose at the stench. No one would rub this around their eyes. It smelled just like the churned-up ground of a sheepfold at the end of wolf-walk. But where the sap had touched her skin, the itch was gone. Zena rubbed the cut end of the stem across the back of her hand. There was no itch. It was balm.

Pleased at her discovery, Zena folded the leaf and tucked it in her belt pouch. Paddling along the winding stream she stopped at each plant, gathering the fattest leaf, and saw a lake. A figure crouched at the water's edge.

# Fifteen

Elin shivered. All her family feared water.

She stared at the water lapping at her toes. She could feel the silk shivering. It muttered fretfully as she shrugged off the back-sack and dropped it on the shore. Her breath ragged, her heart pounding, she stepped into the lake. The water covered her ankles, her trailing robe. She watched the stain creep up from the hem. She felt the recoil of her own silk as the water reached it. Felt the faintness, a curious weakness in her limbs as if all the blood was draining away as the edge of the silk was submerged.

She lurched out of the water. Instantly, the sisters' voices began to accuse her again, their voices rising, mingling until they sounded as one. But beneath the chorus she could hear doubt and anxiety. Now she knew how to free herself. Swiftly, before she was overwhelmed again by her sisters' screams,

Elin bent and ripped at the old silk band running down her skirt. Her frayed silk sighed as she pulled the band from the dress. It was hard. Her hands shook. The silk complained. She tried to soothe it, to tell it that she meant it no harm but it twisted from her fingers, streaming free, attached only to the bodice of her gown. Dazed by the incessant voices of the sister silk patches, she almost forgot why she was freeing her own silk. Swiftly, before confusion overwhelmed her, she reeled in the band of silk, wrapping it around her neck and tucking the torn end inside her gown.

She waded into the lake until the water reached her knees and sat. The freezing water lapped about her waist. The cold kidnapped her breath. She couldn't feel her submerged limbs. As her skirt floated she pushed the cloth beneath the water, drowning the silk patches. Tiny trails of bubbles rose from the silk and drifted away in the water. The bubbles changed colour, blue merging to lilac and pink, fading to rose and becoming transparent. The voices in her head murmured, fell silent. She touched the necklace of bubbles. Several popped and her second-youngest sister whispered a complaint before her voice dissolved. Elin's own silk hissed a warning as water splashed onto it. Fighting her desire to beat at the surface, to destroy all the drifting skeins of bubbles, Elin started to laugh. She was winning. Her sisters' songs were drowning in the lake.

Zena stood transfixed. How could Elin be here, her voice echoing against the rocks so it seemed as if the lake was full of Elins?

Zena backed away. Elin mustn't see her. She must return to Kodo. They had to warn Maia that Elin had escaped from the Sun Palace. As she turned to run she saw the bag Elin had tossed onto the pebbles. It was the one from Altara, the bag that she had carried across the plains to Maia. It held the story-coat.

Without thinking, her feet sent her running towards it. Running towards Elin. Scurrying like a hunted lapran, Zena ran to seize the story-coat. She twisted her ankle, swallowed a gasp of pain, staggered the last few strides and reached the bag.

As she grabbed it and turned to flee, a blood-curdling scream froze her in her tracks.

Elin had seen her. She surged from the lake, a rock in her hand. Zena saw Elin's arm raised, heard her scream a challenge. She ran but was too slow. The stone glanced off her shoulder. She lurched, almost dropping the bag. Elin leapt after her, pausing only to grab another rock and hurl it. It thudded between Zena's shoulder blades.

She pitched forward, and fell. Elin pounced.

Her fingers clawed at the silk. It was soft. It slipped through her fingers like water: she couldn't hold on to it. She clutched at it again. A whisper fizzed up her hand. She cried out. Clenching her fist, she tugged and pulled a fold of silk clear.

Elin screeched. Grabbing a stone, she hammered it down on Zena's hand. Zena's fingers jerked, the silk slipped free. Lifting the rock again, Elin slammed it against Zena's head.

# Sixteen

Caspia trailed her finger across the back of the small lizard. It shivered and changed colour. Its legs turned blue, its head red, its body became a bilious green.

Kodo stared, fascinated.

'Isn't it pretty?' said Caspia. She picked it up and dropped it in Kodo's lap. Instantly the lizard became the colour of Kodo's grimy tunic.

'It likes you,' said Caspia. 'See how it becomes one with you.' She eased the cord from its neck. The lizard remained on Kodo's lap. 'And stays with you too when it could run away.'

She picked up another lizard and dropped it onto her skirt. Unseen by Kodo, she shortened the knotted cord attaching it to her hand so that it could not escape. The lizard turned a dusky blue and merged with her skirt.

Kodo gently scratched the head of the tiny lizard clinging to his tunic. Ootey's giant lizards had never changed colour like this. True, their crests flared red when they were angry, but these small ones were like bright jewels.

'Do all creatures answer to you like my lizards do?' asked Caspia, her voice friendly.

Kodo glanced at her and was dazzled by her smile. He shook his head.

Caspia laughed. 'Or do all creatures answer to the Sun Catcher? Where is she?'

'Searching for an eagle,' Kodo blurted out as her probing fell like spindrift over his thoughts. He felt its warmth and friendship. The red-headed girl was his friend.

'With Razek,' he muttered. And felt again the warmth of Caspia's understanding. She wouldn't have abandoned her friends as Maia had done.

'And left you here?' Caspia's eyes widened with surprise.

Kodo shrugged.

Caspia placed another lizard in his lap. 'If I was hunting for an eagle I would have asked you to accompany me.'

Kodo risked staring at her. She was very like Maia. The same hair. The same smile. They could be sisters, but for the eyes. Maia's were often stormy, often bright like fire, the colour of chunks of amber which sometimes washed up near the lizard scrape. Caspia's eyes were wide and clear as the endless blue sky. Kodo felt as if he was falling into sunlit water.

'You want an eagle too?' he asked.

'No.' Caspia gestured to the distant peaks, still glistening under their caps of snow. 'My father is an Eagle Hunter and has been far, like you,' she said. 'He goes to many places beyond the mountains to the sun-deeps. As I wish to.' She touched the grey lizard in her lap and it turned pink, then blue. 'He flies an eagle, Azara. She is old, but powerful. He would let me fly her if I wished. But I'd rather keep my lizards and let my father hunt eagles over the mountains.'

'You don't need an eagle to cross the sun-deeps,' agreed Kodo.

He knew Maia would never cross the sun-deeps. She feared them. This girl was braver. The stories of his adventures skipped through his thoughts. Such tales he could tell her. Since his arrival in the Sun City, Maia had been too busy being friends with Razek to listen to him. Only Zena had listened, wide-eyed and admiring. She had even shared his excitement at the discovery of the ant-bear. He felt a pang of unease. Where had Zena got to?

'You must have seen many things,' continued Caspia, thought-stealing.

'Many,' said Kodo, forgetting Zena. 'And I'll see many more when I sail again. More than Razek will ever see,' he boasted.

'As wonderful as this?' asked Caspia. She slipped a woven band from her wrist and dropped it into Kodo's hand.

Without thinking, Kodo's fingers closed round the silk band. Whispers tingled up his arm. Dreams prickled, needle-sharp, longings curled about him. Bright images dazzled, were gone. Caspia prised his fingers open and took the silk. As his vision cleared Kodo saw her slipping it onto her wrist. He rubbed his forehead, trying to recall the dreams the silk had shown him.

'What was that?' he stammered.

'The to-come,' said Caspia.

'The to-come?' Kodo sounded and felt befuddled.

'If you dare to find it.'

'Find it?' repeated Kodo. He wanted to hear the silk again. He held out his hand.

Caspia smiled and tossed him the blue-grey lizard. It hit Kodo's outstretched palm, tumbled to the ground and scurried off, trailing its coloured leash.

In a daze Kodo watched it go. He should chase it, catch it and free it. It was Caspia's lizard. Why wasn't she following it, to reclaim it or release it from the cord which could snag and tangle and trap it? A Lizard Keeper would never be so careless. Ootey would have bellowed his disapproval, but perhaps these tiny jewel lizards were different from Doon and Toon.

Caspia was turning the woven braid on her wrist. Kodo's eyes were drawn to the coloured silk. He wanted to hold it again. It brought good thoughts. He remembered the old silk he had taken from the moth-garden. That silk had held promises too and shown him the to-come when he would be a trader. He had even seen Bron on his ship in the silk-dream.

'You have already found it. You stole it. And lost it,' Caspia reminded him.

Somewhere deep inside him, tucked away from her thought-stealing tentacles, Kodo felt a faint quiver of alarm. How could Caspia know that he had once stolen silk? He had hidden that. Maia knew. So did Ootey, although his grandfather hadn't believed him. He had told Tareth. No one else. He would never confess to anyone else. It had brought trouble and the Marsh Lords to the stilt village. It was his fault, the silk's fault, that he had had to flee his home.

Caspia smiled, reading him. 'You know where there is enough silk for us all.'

Her voice was like a song. 'The silk belongs to everyone who can hear it sing. To you. To my family. To me. My mother's sister, Xania, wore the story-coat. She would have taught me the silk stories had she lived. And soon I will need silk, for the stories I find. You should have silk, too. Silk that will sing to you alone. Silk that will learn your story. A story the Lizard Keepers will want to hear when you return.'

'Yes,' said Kodo. Jakarta his mother would want his stories as much as the gold earrings he would bring her.

'You must look for silk.'

'Yes,' said Kodo.

'It will sing to you when you find it.'

'It already has,' admitted Kodo.

Caspia smiled. 'And when you find it, you could bring it to me and I will teach you its secrets.'

A tiny part of Kodo still struggled. 'Maia . . .' he began.

'The Sun Catcher!' Caspia's voice was sharp.

Kodo flinched at her anger.

'She won't tell you her secrets! She . . .' She paused, her head lifting as if she heard something. Her attention slipping from Kodo, her eyes searched the cliffs.

'Maia,' muttered Kodo. He was not sure if her name was a protest or a plea. Before he could marshal his thoughts, Caspia turned back to him and her voice, honey-sweet, was weaving its spell again. She smiled at him, watching him, her eyes as blue and bright as the sky.

'Maia is the Sun Catcher. The sun-stone is hers. Razek will find her an eagle. You can give her silk too when you find it.'

Kodo nodded. He knew where to find silk. In a moth-garden. The moth-garden he had . . .

Caspia was too eager. Kodo felt her thought stab like his fishing spear. It hurt. Instinctively he protected himself: his mind shut with the snap of a lizard's jaw crunching a scavenged carcass dragged from the sun-deeps.

Thwarted, Caspia spun away, gathering the lizards.

'When you have the silk, we'll meet again,' she said. 'My silk will sing with yours so you can learn its secrets.' She turned back to him. 'We'll learn together. The silk song will be strong in you, Kodo, Lizard Keeper. You have come from far to help find silk to renew the old coat.'

She smiled at him, her anger hidden and forgotten, determined to lull him into trusting her. 'May the sun rise and rise on your quest.'

Kodo rose to his feet. 'And on yours,' he responded.

'It will,' laughed Caspia. 'Until we meet again, Silk Finder.'

When she had gone, it was as if the sun had shifted lower in the sky.

Kodo shivered. The ant-bear burrow was in shadow. The horses stood close together, nose to tail, ears pricked. There was no sign of Zena. One end of her sun-dried scarf had worked free of the rock weights and was flapping in the wind.

Then the screaming began.

# Seventeen

Zena lay sprawled at the edge of the lake. Slipping and sliding across the rocks, Kodo raced to her. He fell to his knees beside her. Blood seeped from her head.

'Zena!' He touched her hand. Beneath his searching fingers he felt the smallest, slowest flutter of a pulse. Not dead.

He looked around. Just rocks and the trickle of a stream feeding a lake, its water dark under the clouds streaming from the peaks. He saw a dark arrowhead drifting high in the sky. An eagle. Was it Huan's? Perhaps the eagle-hunting party was close. He thought he saw a flash of blue among the rocks.

He turned back to Zena. How had she fallen? Scattered along the beach were wilting green leaves. She had been looking for sight balm.

His fingers lost the flutter in her wrist. 'Zena! Zena!'

Anxiously, he felt for the beat of life below her ear. Blood oozed onto his fingers. The wind off the lake ruffled her skirt. For a wild second he thought she had moved.

'I'm here. I'll get help.'

Kodo was in an agony of indecision. Should he leave her and ride for help, or move her? He glanced round wildly. He didn't dare leave her alone, unprotected. Huan had warned that foxes, wolves even, occasionally a snow leopard, prowled in the mountains. Then there were birds of prey looking for carrion. And Zena was so still she seemed dead. If only Caspia was still here.

He cupped his hand to his mouth. 'Lady,' he called.

The echo bounced back to him. Kodo drew in a deep breath. He tore a strip from the edge of Zena's skirt. It was cleaner than his tunic. Folding it into a pad he bound it to her head with another strip of skirt.

'Lady!' He threw back his head and called again and endured the mocking answer from the mountain.

*'Lady, lady, lady.'*

'Caspia!' he howled

*'Caspia, Caspia,'* mimicked the mountains.

Carefully, Zena's head lolling against his shoulder, he carried her across the beach and under the overhang. He had to leave her on the earth by the burrow as he unhobbled the horses and threw on the saddles. Struggling to mount with Zena limp in his arms, Kodo gentled his horse into a walk, trying to sway with its gait, and cradle Zena against the motion. The pad and binding was stained red. He dared ride no faster when every step seemed to jolt Zena's head against his shoulder.

The horses splashed across the narrow stream. He could see the hoof prints still deep in the mud at the edge of the water. Zena's riderless pony dropped its head, drank noisily and then rushed after them, nudging Kodo's mount. Desperately Kodo tried to knee it away. The pony leaned closer, trapping Kodo's leg between the two horses, pushing with its shoulder against its companion, almost unseating him.

Kodo yelled. The pony shied. Filling his lungs, Kodo bellowed at it. Star-shifts of calling the lizards in from the sun-deeps had strengthened and deepened his voice. Again Kodo roared and the horse took fright, stampeding ahead and disappearing along the track.

'Go back, find the others,' Kodo shouted after it, as if it could understand. Let Maia and the others be at the camp, he thought. Let the pony remember that there's fodder and company at the camp and find her way back.

Caspia found her mother crouching in a hollow, clutching a bag, rocking herself backwards and forwards. She looked up as Caspia slid down to join her.

'They thought they could punish me. Thought they could keep me prisoner, keep me from Urteth. How little they know!' She stared at Caspia, the wildness in her eyes dying. 'What are you doing here, daughter? I sent you to Urteth. Where are the Wulf Kin?'

'Waiting,' Caspia looked at the bag her mother was holding. 'I heard you call.'

'I had to hit her. She tried to stop me.' Elin shrugged. 'She will die in the mountains. The beasts will find her and rip her to shreds.'

'Maia? You have killed the Sun Catcher?'

Elin looked at her blankly.

'I hit the girl. She tried to steal from me.' She moaned, rocking over the bag in her lap. 'Be still. Be silent,' she grunted. 'Weaker, weaker, but still they torment me.' She glared at Caspia. 'Water weakens them,' she hissed. 'But still they whisper.' She lifted her fist and howled at the sky. 'Be silent. I will tell the tale. I will sing your stories if you will be silent!' She twisted her hair back from her face, pulling it tight, using the pain to quiet the voices in the silk patches. 'I must think. I must reach the Tower of Eagles.' She became aware again of Caspia's presence. 'Why are you here? I sent you to Urteth.' She held out her arm. 'Help me up. We must find Urteth.'

'Lady!' The call drifted across the mountain. 'Lady!'

Elin's fingers dug into Caspia's arm. 'Already! They have followed already.'

Caspia shook her head. 'A boy only. No danger.'

Elin saw the lizards, clinging to Caspia's clothes. She shuddered with distaste. 'What are you doing here?' she asked again. 'With those?'

Caspia ripped the cords from her wrist, plucked the lizards from her arm and tossed them away.

'Caspia!' The cry was desperate.

Caspia looked over the lip of the hollow and saw Kodo

staggering along the lake edge, a bundle in his arms. She dropped out of sight as she saw his head turn to scan the mountainside.

Elin had slipped the bag onto her back

'Come, daughter. Find the Wulf Kin. They will take us swiftly to the Tower of Eagles. I have much to tell Urteth.'

Caspia watched her mother climb towards the narrow animal track which snaked along the slope. She cast her thought-stealing net after her but caught nothing. She frowned. She had never been able to steal Elin's thoughts. She didn't know what her mother, with her ripped robe and wild hair, was doing in the mountains.

She peeped back over the edge of the hollow. Kodo had disappeared. For a moment she considered scrambling after him. That way, she could find Maia, the ursurper Sun Catcher, and lead the Wulf Kin to her. Two Wulf Kin and their wulfen could easily overpower Maia and her companions.

An eagle screeched as it drifted across the valley. She heard a distant Eagle Hunter's cry as he called his bird.

'Ay! Ay!'

The eagle screamed a response.

'Come, daughter,' called Elin.

Caspia shrugged. Who knew how many hunters were with the Sun Catcher, or how many eagles. Eagles would not hesitate to attack the wulfen. Kicking aside a lizard whose cord had become tangled with a rock, Caspia hitched up her skirt and climbed after her mother.

Maia watched Egon's serious face as he fanned out the young eagle's flight feathers and felt along the wing bone. His hand beneath the wing, he supported its weight as Huan carefully smoothed the feathers back into place. Maia stepped forward to help him. The eagle saw her, and lunged. The jesses, held under Egon's thumb, prevented her launching herself, talons raised to strike. Her injured wing slipped from Egon's hand and hung awkwardly.

Shaken, Maia moved out of the eagle's line of sight. Nefrar nudged his head under her hand. She scratched his fur, comforted a little. The eagle stopped baiting and her wings dropped over Egon's hand, mantling as if she were defending her prey. The injury to her wing was obvious even to Maia.

'We cannot release her,' said Egon. 'She will never fly.'

Huan looked at his father. Maia read the swift exchange.

'You can't kill her,' she protested.

'She'll never hunt. She cannot survive,' said Egon. His hand brushed across the spikes of juvenile feathers sprouting from the eagle's head. It was a gesture of farewell.

'No!' said Maia.

Huan looked at his feet. Egon started to turn away. The young eagle pecked at his padded coat, as if looking for food.

Maia fought back hot tears. This was her doing. Her fault. She was not destined to have an eagle. She had refused to listen to Tareth when he'd warned her. She was a Sun Catcher. They didn't fly eagles. It didn't matter that she had always dreamed of flying her own eagle like Tareth. Did not matter that she had never wanted to be Sun Catcher.

'No!' She drew herself up, becoming a Sun Catcher,

powerful, dangerous. The eagle would not die because of her.

'The bird lives. It can be healed. I will find silk to pad and bind the wing. The bird shall not die.'

She would give it the silk she still wore. Silk made by the moon-moths and woven in secret by Tareth. It had protected her on the long journey across the Vast. Had kept her safe in the crystal cave where she had found the sun-stone. Her strange silk that had never sung. She knew that silk was not just for stories. It protected too. It was important to her family, to Khandar. Her task had been to restore Khandar with the sun-stone. But sun-catching was not enough. Silk was needed too. Tareth had told her that she must find silk. Had told her to learn and listen to the story-coat. She had disobeyed him and an eagle was hurt.

She had to find more silk. She would leave, go to the moth-garden above the weed beds and bring the silk-moths to Khandar. She would help Tareth renew the burned moth-garden in the Sun Palace as she had promised. What better reason could there be to bring the moths back to Khandar than to heal the eagle she had harmed because she wouldn't listen?

'We'll take the eagle to Tareth,' she said.

Egon nodded. 'We should return quickly so that the bone can be set.'

Maia felt the fire drain from her. The eagle would be safe now. 'Kodo and Zena,'she began.

'I'll wait for them,' Huan offered.

Egon glanced at the mountains and frowned. 'Keep the fire burning throughout sun-sleep and your eagle unhooded and close. I will leave Garha with you too.' He was easing the hood from his eagle as he spoke.

Maia looked at him in surprise.

He met her gaze. 'Something tells me that all is not well,' he said.

'Then I'll wait with Huan too,' said Maia. She lifted her hand to silence his protest. 'The eagle needs Tareth and I can't take her,' she said. 'You've seen how she becomes crazed when I'm close. She would harm herself trying to escape. You'll have to take her, Egon.' To cover the hurt this admission cost her, she grinned at Huan. 'And I will remain and save Huan from the dangers of the mountains.'

Egon hid his laughter in a snort as his son's wind-burned face flushed red. 'So be it, Catcher. He will surely be safe with you and two eagles.'

'Since my father cannot, I will protect you, Sun Lady,' said Huan frostily, glaring at his father.

'And I,' said Razek. 'I'll chase away the storms that come. It'll be safer than riding through the dark with Egon. I won't be able to see where to fall off.'

Maia laughed. The laughter died in her throat as Zena's riderless pony trotted into camp and ambled across to stand nose to nose with Fionn.

Huan knelt and laid his ear to the ground. 'Another comes,' he announced, getting to his feet. 'Slowly.' He slipped the hood from his own eagle. 'Nothing follows,' he said.

Maia, tugging the black-handled knife Tareth had given her from its shoulder sheath, ran from the camp. Nefrar loped after her, pursued by Razek.

'Wait, Maia,' he shouted. 'Wait.'

She heard Egon scramble onto the rocks at the edge of the camp. He would be there, bow in hand, his eagle ready to strike. Huan followed her, his eagle powering ahead of him, climbing to gain height, ready to plummet and fall like an arrow.

Then both eagles were circling above a horse and rider. A rider huddled in the saddle, his head bowed as he allowed his horse to pick her way along the track.

'Kodo!'

Was he hurt? Maia saw his head lift and that he had been bending over a bundle he held in his arm. A bundle that wore Zena's skirt.

Fear lent her feet wings.

'Zena!'

Zena didn't stir. Maia touched the hand which flopped against Kodo's knee. It was ice-cold.

Razek arrived in a rush. He grabbed the reins and led the horse towards camp. Maia trotted alongside, her hand holding Zena's limp one, trying to pour warmth into the freezing flesh.

Egon met them. Kodo allowed him to take Zena from him and slid off the horse. He was filthy, his tunic ripped and blood-stained.

'Are you hurt?' asked Maia, shaking out her sleeping fur so that Egon could lay Zena on it.

'No,' Kodo collapsed to his knees.

Razek placed a hand on his shoulder to steady him. Kodo shrugged him off, his gaze never leaving Zena as he watched Egon feeling for the beat of life in her neck. He saw Huan bring water and start to wipe the blood from her face. Maia crouched beside Zena, holding her hand as Egon carefully eased aside the band Kodo had wrapped around Zena's head. He clicked his teeth at what he saw and crossed to his saddlebag, returning with a handful of lichen and strips of cloth.

'What happened?' demanded Maia.

'I don't know. She must have fallen. I heard screaming. There was blood on the stones,' sobbed Kodo. He managed to drag his gaze away from Egon's hands as he lifted the dark-stained pad from Zena's head and cleaned the wound before covering the seeping gash with woven bands.

'She was looking for sight balm. She wandered off while I was in the ant-bear burrow.' He heard Huan's intake of breath. 'We found one,' he told the eagle boy. 'Then a girl came. I thought it was you. She looked like you. She said she was Caspia.'

'Caspia,' said Maia. 'She was there?'

'She expected to find you. We talked. She had lizards.'

'Caspia? Lizards?' Maia could hardly make sense of what he was saying. 'She's here?'

'She left,' babbled Kodo. 'Then I heard screaming and I ran and found Zena.'

'Caspia did this?'

'No. No.' Kodo rubbed his filthy hand over his hair, trying to recall exactly what had happened by the burrow. 'Zena fell. She was climbing near the lake looking for sight balm. I ran. I found her. Caspia had gone. I shouted but she didn't hear, didn't come to help. I carried Zena to the horses.'

He found he couldn't look into Maia's stormy eyes so he looked at Egon instead.

'Zena wouldn't wake. Her horse ran away. Will she live?'

'The mosses will stop the bleeding,' said Egon. He had pulled Maia's sleeping fur around Zena. 'This will keep her warm.' He smiled at Kodo. 'You did well to bind her head and to carry her here. Now, she needs a healer.'

Razek got to his feet. 'I'll bring one.'

Egon gazed at the sky. His lips moved as if he were debating with himself. 'The young eagle needs a healer too. I will take the child.' He glanced at Razek, changed his mind and said, 'Huan will take the eagle. She'll be calm with him. We'll ride together. Garha will take a message.'

Huan, anticipating his father's decision, brought him a thin cord. Egon twisted and knotted the cord, setting some knots separately, binding others together, looping several others in a circle. He called and Razek had to duck to avoid the eagle's yellow talons as Garha swooped over his head to land beside Egon. He attached the knotted cord, smoothed his hand down her feathers, whispered to her and cast her off.

They watched as Garha circled the camp then, wings beating strongly, she set off along the mountain pass.

'Come,' said Egon. 'We must hurry.'

# EIGHTEEN

Tareth, Azbarak and a healer were waiting for them at the Sun Palace gates. Grim-faced, Tareth greeted Egon, ignoring Maia and Huan with his bundled eagle. As the palace boys led the horses to the stables he followed the weary party into the solar, sending the grey-haired healer and Azbarak after Egon as he carried Zena to Maia's room.

Only then did Tareth turn to Maia, his face closed, his eyes dark with anger.

'Well?' he demanded.

'She fell,' said Maia.

She knew she should have watched over Zena, should have kept her with her.

Nefrar nudged the back of Maia's knees and settled across the doorway, his unblinking golden eyes watching. Azbarak stumbled over the cheetah's long twitching tail as he bustled off to summon Yanna, the Warrior Woman.

Maia didn't dare think what Yanna would say about Zena's accident.

'Was she alone?'

'It was my fault.' Kodo sprang to Maia's defence. 'Zena was with me.'

'But in my care,' said Maia. 'I'm to blame. I should never have taken her eagle hunting. Should never have tried to find an eagle.'

'Yet you return with a young injured eagle.'

Huan, holding the eagle, almost wilted under Tareth's fierce eyes. He managed not to turn tail and run.

'I harmed her,' confessed Maia. 'We couldn't release her. She's hurt. I thought you could heal her,' she whispered.

'Heal her?'

The eagle's head swivelled at the sound of Tareth's voice. Her bright eyes watched him over the top of the bundle.

'My father thought it best to kill her, since she will never fly well.' Huan managed to find his voice.

'She mustn't die,' Maia pleaded. 'You can mend her wing.'

'Mend it so you can have an eagle?' demanded Tareth.

'No.' Maia faced his anger. 'I can't fly an eagle. They are birds of a cold sky.' She blinked and turned her back on her dream. 'I am the Sun Catcher.' She spread her hands. 'These catch sun and fire. The eagle knew the wrongness of what I was attempting. She tried to escape and was injured. But you can heal her.' Her hands curled into fists and she thrust them out of sight. 'Please, Father.'

He was not her father, but he had saved her from the flames as a baby, had taken her to safety in the Cliff Village and brought her up. Tareth was the only father she had ever had or ever needed. She needed him now to forgive her, to mend the eagle's damaged wing. Yet he was looking at her so coldly, that he seemed a stranger. And he looked weary, old. She was frightened.

'Please. I was wrong. It will be my fault if she never flies. She needs your help.'

She nodded at Huan. The eagle boy unbound the bird. Freed, it half-flew, half-fell. Instinctively Tareth reached out and it landed on his wrist. Maia saw the sudden brightness in his eyes and heard his indrawn breath.

The young eagle stood on Tareth's fist, her damaged wing trailing. She leaned forward. Her curved beak touched his cheek. Tareth's eyes glowed.

His finger smoothed her plumage. The eagle bobbed with pleasure.

Maia felt dizzy with relief. This at least was going to be all right. She had feared he would reject the eagle.

'Her name is KiKya, Sky Hunter,' said Tareth softly. He looked at Maia, his expression stern. 'And if she is to fly we will need silk to heal her, Maia.'

'She sleeps still,' Maia answered Kodo's unspoken question as she joined him.

The palace was in darkness. Yanna, Nefrar and the healer kept vigil in Maia's room, watching over Zena. Tareth brooded in the charred moth-garden, a dozing KiKya on his arm. Her injured wing was bound in strips of silk. Despite Tareth's protests, Maia had torn them from her own silk.

The frayed edges felt strange against her skin. The silk woven for her at the edge of sea-deeps had never sung. Perhaps it was only silk woven in Khandar that could whisper and dream. Maia touched it. It had brought her comfort as she crossed the Vast. She hoped it would bring her comfort now. Hoped her friends would go with her.

Razek gazed at the moon and stars painted on the high ceiling. They gleamed in the flickering firelight. Maia sat beside him and tried to see the constellations in the scatter of silver stars. She didn't recognise any. These were the star patterns of Khandar, not those shining above the weed beds.

She picked up a stick and poked at the embers.

'Healer has told Yanna to talk to Zena, hoping that she will hear and wake. When Yanna sleeps, I'll take her place.'

'I'll help too,' said Kodo.

'And I,' said Razek. 'If hearing me doesn't frighten her. She thinks I carry storms with me.'

'You might scare her awake then,' muttered Kodo.

Razek ignored him. 'How long must we watch?'

Maia shrugged. 'For as long as she sleeps. Yanna won't return to Altara until she can take Zena with her. Some of the Warrior Women will stay, so there will always be a voice Zena knows to call her from the darkness.'

Kodo was silent for a moment. 'When Bron arrives, I must leave.'

Maia nodded. 'Keeper Azbarak expects traders to arrive with the horned moon.'

'Bron will be the first,' said Kodo confidently.

'Good, because I must return to the cliff-tops,' said Maia.

'Yes! I knew you would. And I will go with you.' Razek slapped his fist into his palm. 'We can be there before the Gather. There is always much work to be done in the weed beds then. Elder will be glad that the Weed Master has returned.'

Kodo stared at her. 'Go back?'

He wanted to remind Maia why they had left, pursued not just by Wulf Kin but also the Marsh Lord. The Wulf Kin might have followed Maia to Khandar, but Helmek, the Marsh Lord, was still in his holdfast at the edge of the sun-deeps and he wouldn't have forgotten the flame-headed girl, nor his desire for silk.

'But you're the Sun Catcher,' he protested. 'Your place is here.'

'She belongs with the Cliff Dwellers,' said Razek.

'I must return. Will you help me cross the far-deeps?'

Kodo stared at her. Maia didn't like water. She couldn't swim. She was always sick, even when she had sailed with Tareth to his home in the stilt village. She would never choose to cross the far-deeps.

Razek's voice broke the silence. 'I will go with you. The far-deeps hold no terror for a Weed Master.'

Kodo looked at him with scorn. What did a weed boy living by the shallows know of the far-deeps? Razek's world of weed was small, bordered by sun-deeps and cliffs. Maia, the Sun Catcher, would never stay there.

Suddenly he knew what she was going to do. Maia was not returning home to the Cliff Dwellers, to the weed beds and Razek as the Weed Master dreamed. She was returning to the hidden moth-garden and the moon-moths. She was returning to the silk as Caspia had said she would.

'I'll come,' he said.

# Nineteen

Tiki, the black rat, peered into the room. Ash falling from a burned log and soft breathing were the only sounds he heard. He scurried away as a hand appeared beside him on the stone ledge and scampered down the wall, across the darkened room towards the glimmer of a fire.

Var slithered through the oriel and dropped silently to the floor. Part of the shadows, he waited and listened and, like the rat, heard the sound of breathing as his eyes adjusted to the gloom. Not for the first time he wished for the dark sight of his rat. The palace boy hadn't told him that anyone slept in the large hall. From the boy's description he knew the room and the sleeper he sought. At least this one slept and he would make sure that they didn't wake and raise the alarm.

Following the rat, he crossed to the dying fire. Two forms

lay on either side of the hearth. One curled like an unborn child in its mother's belly, the other straight and stiff as a body awaiting burial. It would be easy enough to slit their throats.

Var slipped a knife from his belt. One sleeper stirred as the black rat's tail trailed across his hand. The glow of the fire lit his face. Var recognised him. It was the tall boy from the Stone Court and the market. The one who had pushed the flame-head aside so that his hastily-thrown knife had missed its target. If it had not been for him, Tiki and he could have completed their task and left this stinking, fever-ridden city. The sleeper had taken the black knife. It had been a favourite throwing knife, his best. Another reason to end a life.

Var felt along the boy's belt. No black knife, merely a broad curving blade with a thick handle. Tools for the fields, not a warrior's weapon. Var drew the clumsy knife from the belt and placed it in the ashes.

He crossed to the second sleeper. And again recognised him. It was the curly-haired boy he had seen watching the sun-catch. He had no quarrel with him. But the boy slept lightly, his breathing shallow, his eyelids twitching as if he was caught in the skeins of a night-wake. He might wake. Var knew he couldn't let him live to raise the alarm. He leaned forward, knife drawn. Tiki was sitting on his hind legs by the boy's ear, his tail draped across the neck of the boy's tunic like a slender torc. He would have to move him to make the swift, killing slash or cut off the rat's tail.

The rat's eyes gleamed dark as an ebony knife handle. He licked his paws and groomed his whiskers. Var hesitated.

The rat watched him, then his tail quivered and he was off, running across the solar towards a door at the far end.

It was a sign. Var sheathed his knife. He pressed his fingers beneath the ear of the boy. The boy sighed deeply, his breathing slowed and he fell into a deeper sleep. The second sleeper didn't stir as Var laid heavy sleep on him too. He would be long gone, his task completed, far from the crowded city and running towards the dry, hot emptiness of the Hidden before they woke. He went to find the girl.

She was not alone. The murmur of voices came from the room the palace boy had described. Var stood in the darkness and listened. Not voices – one voice, he decided. And it was a voice that droned as if the speaker hung on the cusp of sleep. Var risked a look.

The room was lit. A floating wick in the small dish of oil resting in a niche burned brightly. The light flickered across the sleeping platform. The girl lay there. A woman sat beside her, holding the girl's hand. It was her voice that he'd heard. A large spotted cat snoozed at her feet. As he watched, the woman's head drooped and she jerked herself awake.

'You should sleep, Yanna,' said a woman, stepping into view. 'I will keep watch.'

'She needs to hear me. To know I'm here.'

'I will speak to her. If she can hear us, she'll know she's not alone. Go and rest.'

Yanna rose to her feet, stretching. 'Speak to her about Altara, so that she knows we are here. I'll return before sun-wake. If she wakes, send Nefrar for me.'

The sleeping cat's tail twitched. He opened one eye. His claws unsheathed, his paw lashed out. Var heard a squeak.

Tiki! The black rat, ever inquisitive, had scuttled into the room. Now he lay pinioned beneath the cat's paw.

'Rats!' hissed the woman, reaching for the flat bronze dish which lay on the floor. She raised it above her head.

Tiki squealed. He writhed under the cat's paw, twisted and bit hard. The cat's paw lifted and the rat squirmed free and ran under the sleeping platform. The bronze bowl clanged against the wall as he scampered up the wall and squeezed through the wooden shutters.

Var melted into the shadows but not before the cat's tawny eyes turned towards the doorway. He paced towards the opening.

Var sprang across the passage. Fingers scrabbling for a hold in the uneven surface, he shimmied up the wall, swung out onto a beam. Lying flat, he pressed himself against the resinous wood, held his breath and closed his eyes so that no tell-tale glint of light in his blackened face would be seen from below.

He heard the women come to the doorway.

'What is it, Nefrar?'

The cat's soft growl rumbled. Var could imagine its tail swishing, its gaze searching the dark passage, testing the air for scents.

'Rats! Is your cheetah forced to eat rats now, Yanna? You must take him hunting.'

Var waited until they had turned away, until he heard the cheetah follow and grunt as it lay down. The girl he sought was not the one who lay in the deep sleep. The palace boy had lied to him.

He waited longer. The droning voice of the woman

continued. Someone left the room and walked away yawning. The black rat ran along his leg up his back and down inside his tunic. Var felt him curl up against his belt. Eventually he heard the gentle snore of the cat. Var stretched and lifted the rat from his tunic.

'Seek,' he breathed. Then swung down from the beam and soundlessly began to search the palace.

Tareth stoked KiKya's plumage. His fingers skimmed across the silk which bound her damaged wing. Strips Maia had torn from the last silk he had woven for her above the sundeeps. He must weave more. He was the Weaver. He would grow weak if he didn't have silk. He had been without it for too long. He could feel his strength draining from him. Maia had promised she would bring him silk.

His fingers stroked KiKya again. What a gift she had given him.

He frowned at the burned moth-garden and saw the bushes move. Dead trees didn't move. A shadow shifted. Tareth's fingers tightened round his crutch. He felt KiKya shift on his arm. Then the eagle half-fell, half-flew. There was a squeal. And the eagle was mantling over something she had caught. Tareth was just in time to raise his crutch and strike as a shadow rushed at him. He heard the crunch as it struck bone and whirled away to strike again, using it as a fighting stick.

He felt the blow land and grabbed the knife arm slashing towards him. He was jerked forward. Frantically he jabbed his crutch into the ground, trying to keep his balance. His twisted leg gave way and he fell, pulling his assailant with him.

Tareth shouted. A rat ran across his face. KiKya screeched. The intruder yelled as the eagle's talons ripped into his shoulders. Dislodging the eagle, he tore himself free.

And ran straight into the bulk of Azbarak.

The Keeper tottered, bellowed, hit out with the lamp he carried and, more by luck than judgement, struck the intruder's head.

'I have him,' he gasped as Yanna, bow in hand, her unbound hair tumbling to her waist, rushed to his aid with two of her Warrior Women.

They made short work of the stranger's struggles and following Azbarak's breathless instructions dragged him away to lock him in a secure room.

Azbarak bent to pull Tareth to his feet.

Tareth reached for his crutch and with the Keeper's help levered himself up. 'The eagle?' he asked. 'Is she hurt?'

Kodo and Razek arrived, sleep-dazed. Razek stooped and offered his arm. The eagle stepped onto it. Razek bit his lip as her talons gripped. He didn't feel the rat with a broken tail run across his foot.

'What happened?' asked Kodo.

Azbarak retrieved his lamp and threw dirt to quench the small flames in the spill of oil. He picked up a black-handled knife.

'Assassin,' he said.

Tareth took KiKya from Razek. 'Assassin? Who was he intending to kill?'

Razek recognised the knife.

'Maia,' he said.

# TWENTY

Var lay where the Warrior Women had flung him. His forehead stung. The black band tied around his head smelled of oil from the fat man's lamp. He'd been lucky that it hadn't caught fire when the oil splattered his face and head. It had been ill fortune that a man with a fierce bird had been hiding in the dark.

Var sat up. He'd fallen among bundles and sacks. The room was small. In the gloom he could just make out the shape of a shutter set high in the wall. He explored in the dark, his fingers feeling the cold stone surface, searching for finger and footholds so that he could climb to the opening and force open the shutter. He found the door. A cool draught blew under it. He knelt, and the breeze sighed past his hand, brushing across the floor. There must be another hole.

He crawled across the floor, following the stream of air

until it dissipated beneath a tumble of grain sacks. He felt beneath them, his fingers finding spilled seed, rough wood and a gap that the breeze slipped into. Perhaps he would not have to climb after all.

He was pulling the sacks to one side when Tiki squeezed under the door. Var scooped up a pinch of the fallen grain and offered it to his battered rat. Poor Tiki, caught first by a huge spotted cat and then pinned beneath an eagle's talons. He was a true survivor. The rat sat up, his whiskers twitching, and looked towards the door. Var just had time to shove the sacks into an untidy heap and collapse against them before the door opened.

The fat man stood there and by his side a tall, dark-haired man leaning on wooden sticks. There was no one beyond them and the open door, just a dimly-lit passage. Var assessed the distance and wondered briefly if he could escape. The dark-haired man's head moved as if he too was calculating the risk, and Var saw the eagle feather brush the man's shoulder.

The fat man was talking. Var tore his attention from the stranger with the sticks and eagle feather. The voice tickled a memory.

'Who are you?' the fat man demanded. 'Why are you here?'

Var stared dumbly at him.

'Where are you from?' It was the voice of a bully. A voice from the has-been.

Var decided to say nothing. His hand closed about Tiki. He could hurl the rat at the fat man's face, brush aside the man with sticks and run.

The dark man read his thoughts, shifting his weight so that one crutch was free and poised as a weapon.

Var hesitated and the man smiled.

'Perhaps he doesn't understand you,' he said. 'Or perhaps since he came in secret he intends to keep his secrets.'

'He will tell me,' said the fat man. 'He will be glad to.' He seemed to swell in size as he drew a breath and stepped forward.

'No, Keeper.' The man's voice was sharp. 'Urteth and Elin no longer reign here.'

Var's eyes swivelled to the fat man.

'So, you do understand.' The man with the dark eyes was talking to him now. 'I will not harm you. But I cannot let you go free.'

'I am Tareth,' said the man. 'The guardian father of the new Sun Catcher, Maia. I am tasked with protecting her . . . with my life.'

Var was conscious of the man's searching gaze.

'We need the Sun Catcher,' the man continued. 'She has ended the dark and cold of wolf-walk. She will help us to make the land green. We are happy that she's returned to us. Yet you came in the dark with a knife.'

Azbarak opened his hand and displayed the knife he held. The slender blade glittered in the lamplight. 'This knife,' he said. 'An assassin's knife.'

Var didn't look at the knife. He stared, unblinking, at Tareth.

'Did you come to kill my daughter?' asked Tareth.

Var remained silent. He could hear his own heart marking the distance the silence made between them. The man's eyes never left his face as the silence stretched further and further.

'Did Elin, the queen, summon you to kill my daughter?' Tareth asked.

'You'll get nothing out of him,' boomed Azbarak. 'The rat has eaten his tongue.'

Tareth ignored him.

Var's glance flickered to the fat man and back to Tareth. He was the leader here despite the fat man's noise.

'You went to her sleeping place,' said Tareth. 'Yanna says you were there. She didn't see you, but she knows you were there looking for my daughter. Her cat heard you. He caught your rat.'

Var scooped up his rat and tucked him in his tunic. He felt Tiki wriggle against his chest as if he was listening too. The rat's claws scrabbled against his skin. He cupped his hand over the bulge and the rat lay still.

'Whoever sent you couldn't have known that my daughter was not there. Who told you where she slept? Who sent you to kill my daughter?' asked Tareth softly, dangerously.

Var felt a slight shiver run up his spine.

'He'll never speak. His sort are taught never to speak,' said Azbarak harshly. 'We should leave him locked here. Forget him. We'll learn nothing from him.'

The tall man hesitated. 'Until we find who sent you, you'll stay here. I will send food.' His eyes searched Var's face. 'And the healer with a salve to soothe that burn. She is a warrior. Do not hope to escape when she comes. She protects the Sun Catcher with her life. As we all do.' He turned to leave.

'Tell the healer that the sick one moved. When the pot she threw at the rat hit the wall and the noise was like a singing sword in battle, the girl moved,' said Var quickly, surprising himself.

Tareth spun round so swiftly he almost toppled. Azbarak

put out a hand to steady him. Tareth ignored him.

'Zena! The sick one moved?'

Var nodded.

'I must find Maia.' Tareth's crutches pounded against the floor as he propelled himself along the passage. 'My thanks,' he called as he disappeared.

Azbarak looked down at Var. 'So the rat doesn't own your tongue.'

He held his lamp higher and studied the shutter high above Var's head.

'He will send the healer. And when she's gone you will be alone. No one comes here. Only I seal and unseal the door. Only I collect the grain.'

His gaze dropped to the pile of sacks that Var slouched against.

'I saved the Sun City from starvation when the harvests failed because the Sun Catcher was lost.'

He watched Var from beneath lowered brows. 'Don't let your rat gnaw the sacks. When I lower the sacks through the trap in the floor to the traders waiting beneath, I don't want to find that the seed has spoiled.'

He glanced again at the floor.

'Things have changed in the Sun Palace. Elin is no longer queen. We do not obey her. We have a new Sun Catcher. We will follow her, not the queen some call the red witch.'

He turned away. 'Choose well. The city is no place for one used to the silences of the Hidden.'

Var heard the bar drop into place. He was locked in, but the fat Keeper had shown him how to escape.

# Twenty-One

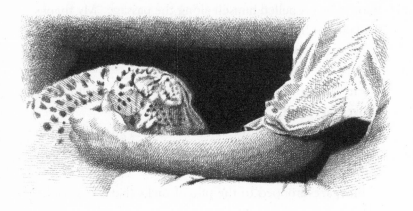

Maia could feel Tareth and Yanna crowding her as she knelt at Zena's side.

'Zena. Can you wake?'

Nefrar padded to the side of the bed. His breath fluttered the sleeve of Zena's tunic. He started licking her hand.

Maia could hear the rasp of his tongue then the cheetah reared to place his forepaws either side of Zena's shoulders and breathed on her face.

Maia saw the twitch as Zena's nose wrinkled at the smell of warm cheetah breath.

'Zena. Wake up. You're safe at the Sun Palace. Kodo found you.' She held Zena's hand.

There was no response. Maia glanced at Yanna.

Yanna understood. 'Wake, idle one,' she said. 'How dare you sleep when the fire is hot and there are flatbreads to be made? Fetch your pan. You have lain here for long enough. Wake before the Catcher finds another to serve her and I send you back to Altara.'

They all saw the struggle on Zena's face. Her fingers twitched in Maia's grip. She opened her eyes. Her lips moved.

'She take.'

'Rest, child,' soothed the healer.

'She have,' Zena whispered. She stared straight through Maia at something that no one but she could see. 'Kodo.'

'He's here,' said Maia swiftly and heard Yanna leave to find him. 'He's coming.'

'She take,' gasped Zena, her fingernails dug into Maia's skin.

'Take what? What is it, Zena?'

'Take ... story,' sighed Zena.

'When will she wake again?' demanded Maia.

Yanna, warming her hands round a beaker of steaming chay, shrugged wearily. 'Zena is strong. She has woken once and will wake again. The healer won't leave her.'

'But I must?' asked Maia.

Tareth nodded. 'You must go before sun-wake so that no one sees you leave.' He handed Maia a knife. It was twin to the one Razek had saved her from in the market. 'The city isn't safe. Until I find who sent the boy it will be better if no one knows where you are. They must think you are here with me.'

'I will send Nefrar with you,' Yanna said.

'But . . .' began Maia.

Yanna leaned forward, her long loose hair concealing her face as she fondled her cheetah's ears. 'He would follow you anyway, Catcher. Didn't he follow you into the mountains?'

'But—' Maia seemed incapable of finding another word.

Tareth nodded. 'A small group will not attract attention. Razek will go. Kodo too. No Warrior Women.'

A large spotted cheetah was likely to attract a lot of interest, thought Maia, but didn't say so.

'She is nowhere,' announced Razek as he and Kodo joined them by the fire.

'She hasn't been seen since we left on the eagle hunt,' added Kodo. He squatted beside Maia. 'Zena?' he asked softly.

'Sleeping still,' answered Maia. She glanced at Tareth. 'Who is missing?'

'Elin,' said Tareth grimly. 'She must have managed to control the sister silk. I thought it wouldn't allow her to leave the palace, since this is where she killed her sisters.'

Maia saw again the flames and heard the screams that happened when she had tried to wear the story-coat. She frowned. Elin must have great power if she had managed to silence the patches of silk sewn onto her clothes.

'Where will she go?' she asked.

'The mountains. To find Urteth. To the Tower of Eagles.'

'And will pass close to Altara. I'll send a message. They will watch for her.' Yanna frowned, her fingers twisting the braid on her wrist.

'The Eagle Hunters will find her when she crosses the mountains,' said Tareth.

Caspia had been in the mountains, thought Maia. She had met Kodo and Zena. No, not Zena, remembered Maia. Zena had been looking for sight balm. Had Caspia found Zena? Was that what Zena was trying to say? If so what did she have? What had she taken? She looked at Kodo, wondering suddenly if Zena's fall had been an accident.

Kodo shifted under her gaze. He knew what she was thinking.

'No,' he hissed, a red flush staining his cheeks as if he had moved too close to the blazing logs. 'Not Caspia. She was with me. I heard Zena scream as she left.'

Tareth noticed Kodo's flash of anger. 'You searched everywhere?' he asked.

Kodo nodded. 'Keeper Azbarak searched too. The sun-helmet is also missing. Azbarak thinks Elin has taken it.'

'The helmet? Why would Elin take that?' asked Maia, still smarting from Kodo's sharp response. Caspia was a thought-stealer. Who knew what she was capable of doing? There was no need for Kodo to spring to her defence so swiftly.

Tareth frowned. 'If Elin wants Caspia to pose as the Sun Catcher then she will need the symbols of the Catcher's power: gold, silk, stone. In the sun-helmet she will look like the Catcher, like you.' He smiled at Maia. 'If Caspia had Xania's story-coat it would add to the illusion,' he added, 'but you have that safe. And Elin cannot take the sun-stone. The stone cannot be touched until it dulls in the long dark of wolf-walk. Elin will wait. We will guard the palace and the stone.'

Maia felt as if a storm wave had sucked her into the sun-deeps and slammed her onto the stone levees of the weed beds. She had left the story-coat with the sun-helmet because she had been too afraid to take it.

'Maia?' asked Tareth.

She tried to breathe. Tried to recall what Zena had said. She had been trying to tell her something important.

If the 'she' was not Caspia because Caspia had been with Kodo, could Zena's 'she' be Elin? And the 'have story' of Zena's whisper be the story-coat?

Maia got to her feet so suddenly that blackness swam around her and she almost staggered. Tripping over Razek's long legs, stretched out by the fire, Maia ran.

'Maia?' said Razek, rolling to his feet and following. 'What is it?'

'Maia!' Tareth's voice halted her in the doorway. His face was gold in the firelight, his eyes dark. She was glad she was in the shadows where he couldn't see her face. She dreaded what he was going to say.

'I left the story-coat behind when I went into the mountains,' she said. 'I left it with the sun-helmet.'

# Twenty-Two

Maia hugged the cheetah, burying her face in his fur. It was stiff with salt. Yanna had been kind. Had told her that her archers would easily track Elin. She had even sent Nefrar with her, which made leaving Tareth easier. She would be glad to have the cat at her side when she climbed to the abandoned moth-garden to gather the silk cocoons. She must find them and return swiftly to the palace so that Tareth could make a new garden and weave silk again. He had looked so weary, so old. Even Kikya had not banished all of the shadows on his face. She pushed away her fear. The silk she would bring would help to make him strong and well again.

A wave broke over the bow, tossing spray into the air. It splashed them both, soaking them, and ran in snaking sea-serpents along the planking, drying almost instantly in the sun. The sky was as blue as Bron's eyes.

She could sense the Trader sitting propped against the mast, his hands busy baiting hooks on a long cord, his attention on her rather than the task in hand. She knew Kodo was braced against the sweep oar, steering the boat through the troughs and waves. She wondered if he deliberately put the bow into the largest waves so that she was regularly soaked. She looked back at him and his grin confirmed her suspicions. Or was Razek, who was hanging over the side as he hauled in a line, his real target? Razek had quickly found a place among the crew. Razek who watched the clouds and the waves. Razek who seemed to be a Storm Chaser, keeping them safe from storm winds until even Kodo had started to believe.

Another deluge hit her. Perhaps she should move, but she was out of the way here, and it was better sitting on the wet deck than below, among the cargo. Maia blanked the thought of the depths of water beneath her, the creatures that must live there and the distance still to be covered.

Maia's arms tightened round Nefrar. She would not, must not, fail again. KiKya needed silk to bind her injured wing. Tareth needed silk to weave. He must have it to wind round the bronze discs so that messages could sing again in the towers. If they were to defend Altara, the warriors would need all their courage and skill to replace the strands they had given her so that Tareth could weave eye-pieces for the sun-helmet.

She had torn strips from her own silk before she had left the city. She hoped it would protect them just as it had protected her when she had crossed the Vast. Hoped they could unravel the strands and plait them in their wrist and bow braids and that they would hear the silk threads sing on their bows. Yanna had promised that the story-coat would be found and placed in Tareth's safe keeping. Maia believed her.

Yanna wouldn't falter as she had. Maia knew she should have kept the coat with her. She had wanted to join Yanna, to search for Elin. But she had to return to the moth-garden. Only she knew its secrets. Only she could collect the cocoons for Tareth. He had wanted to go with her. But this was her seek. A task easier to do alone. Neither Kodo nor Razek could go with her into the moth-garden. Only Nefrar. There was no need to fear that the silk would whisper to him. She rubbed the stiff fur behind his ears and heard him grumble with pleasure. When she had the silk, she must return swiftly for the next sun catch. She looked at the sky. She needed storm winds to send the boat swiftly to the cliff village and the moth-garden.

Razek pulled in the line he was holding, deftly unhooked the wriggling fish, dropping them into the leather bucket at Maia's feet.

'Fish for later,' he said.

Maia's stomach heaved at the thought. She fixed her gaze on the dipping horizon and swallowed. Bron had told her the sickness would pass. It was better, but she would never love the sea-deeps as Kodo did. He was at home here. So was Razek.

Razek grinned at her as he dropped the line over the side and pointed to a bank of cloud building ahead of them. 'More wind,' he said cheerfully and climbed onto his favourite perch on the cross pole high above the decks.

Another storm, thought Maia and shivered. Razek seemed to like battling through the squalls that swept across the deeps. The Watcher had named him well when she had called him Storm Chaser. Nefrar grumbled deep in his chest and turned his back on the approaching waves. Maia scratched the salt-stiffened fur behind his head. She wasn't alone: Nefrar didn't like the far-deeps either.

Razek glanced at Maia from his perch on the cross pole. She looked pale and thin. But her courage hadn't wavered. Unless there was a storm too severe to be chased away or avoided, she sat like a figurehead in the bow with Nefrar staring at the way ahead, searching the horizon for her first sight of the cliffs. She was glad to be going home. So was he.

He looked across the deeps, looking for the sail he had seen at sun-wake as they had passed a group of rocky islands. Bron had warned them to keep a look out for the Sea Thieves. Seth, the oar master, had delved below deck and carried up armfuls of flint-tipped spears, a collection of bows and even several bronze swords, and stacked them round the mast.

Maia had sat, fletching arrows and showing Seth the fighting thrusts she had been taught by the Warrior Women in Altara. Kodo had watched her sparring with Seth with interest and Razek had seen him later examining the swords and when he thought no one was looking swinging the blade as if attacking an enemy. Any Sea Thief daring enough to waylay Trader's vessel would have a fight on their hands.

But as the islands fell away below the horizon the tension eased and the sail disappeared. Razek slid down the mast too quickly, skinning his hands and knees. He just avoided landing among the stack of spears.

He saw Kodo grin at his unsteady progress. He was still not as sure-footed around the boat as the lizard boy. 'Still no sail,' he told Bron. 'But, there are clouds growing over the islands.' He pointed. 'Wind before sun-sleep.'

Bron squinted. 'A storm?' he asked.

Razek glanced at Kodo, making sure that he had heard the Trader's question. Once Bron had discovered Razek's strange affinity with the wind he had often listened to him, interpreting the to-come from Razek's description of what he saw. As a result he'd been able to avoid one storm by seeking shelter and had chosen to ride out another by sailing further from land. Kodo was not the only one who was useful on board!

'Yes,' said Razek.

He was right. There was no chance to outrun it. The storm howled down on them at sunset and drove them across the deeps. The ship's timbers groaned, the sail was ripped to shreds before Bron could secure it, the mast broken. Huge waves washed over the stern, foaming white in the darkness. Bron had lashed himself to the sweep oar so that he was not swept overboard, but even he couldn't keep his feet. Seth was hurled along the deck and saved when Kodo fell on him as he was tumbled past and managed to hang onto the shattered stump of the mast until they could both struggle to their feet.

The cargo was flung about below decks and Maia and Nefrar, sent there by Bron when the storm hit, were in danger of being crushed. When Maia wedged herself among the cargo, bracing herself against the side of the hull, she discovered that the caulking stuffed between the planks was leaking. Water spurted through the gaps and sloshed among the cargo. One of the huge amphorae smashed and the pottery stored inside spilled out. Nefrar scrambled onto a half-submerged stack of copper ingots. As the boat pitched the stack shifted and he was flung into the bilge water. Knocked off her feet, Maia floundered. She surfaced panicking, choking and spitting water.

The storm pursued them from sun-wake to sun-sleep until it was hard to remember that there had ever been a time when the wind didn't scream, the waves didn't curl above them and the boat didn't seem to lie lower and lower in the water.

Kodo's face appeared above her. Then Razek was half-lifting, half-pushing her on deck. Kodo threw a rope round her waist and lashed it to the remains of the mast before securing the line around Razek.

'Hold on,' he shouted as a wave broke over the side of the boat and he disappeared beneath the deluge.

As the bow rose above the waves Maia could see that the boat was being driven along the coast. Above the noise of the storm she could hear the thunder of distant surf as the waves hit the cliffs.

This sun-wake brought no relief. Black clouds filled the sky so that it seemed as if the sun had not risen. The distant cliffs were closer. The crashing waves louder. The trader ship settled ever lower in the water and rolled through the churning deeps. Razek, hugging the broken mast, his gaze fixed on the coastline, suddenly shouted. As the boat climbed a wave Maia saw the line of the cliffs. There was a light gleaming high up.

Bron had seen it too. He roared his challenge at the waves then he, Seth and Kodo were pushing with all their might trying to turn towards the shore. Maia was aware that some of the oarsmen had risked injury and had run their oars out and were attempting to pull the boat around too.

'The weed beds,' shrieked Razek.

Running with the waves as they surged towards the shore, the boat seemed to hurl itself forwards. The white line of surf drew closer.

'We'll sink,' screamed Razek.

Kodo yelled and pointed. 'Doon!'

Head held high, red crest a splash of colour in the monochrome world of dark water and spray, the huge lizard was swimming towards them. Then it was gone, diving beneath the deeps.

'We're sinking,' yelled Razek again.

Maia saw Nefrar in the water. The current was tugging the cat away. She pulled her knife from her shoulder sheath and frantically sawed at the rope tying her to the mast. As the next wave broke across the boat, the rope parted and she was washed over the side.

'Maia!' Kodo sprang after her as Razek tried desperately to cut himself free.

Water roared in Maia's ears as she sank. She kicked furiously and bobbed to the surface only to sink again as a wave broke over her head. Something nudged her hard in the small of her back. Flipped her like a juggler's ball at the Gather. Once again she surfaced. Her clawing hand found something solid. She tried to grab it but there was nothing to hold on to. Someone seized her am. The water swirled beneath her, trying to suck her back as she was dragged out of the water and onto the scaly neck of the lizard.

'Hold on,' bellowed Kodo. He hauled her upright, holding her as she swung her leg over the lizard's neck and guiding her hands onto the wide leather yoke the lizard wore.

'Nefrar!' she shrieked. A broken timber and a tangle of ropes floated past.

She could see the boat disappearing through the flying spray. She glimpsed Bron as the boat crested another wave.

The lizard turned towards the shore, swimming strongly towards the line of breakers. Maia saw what looked like a piece of oar. She couldn't see Nefrar in the heaving water.

'Nefrar!'

Kodo pointed. She could see dark smudges of caves in the cliffs, and a line of figures on the shore. The Cliff Dwellers. Some of them were wading out, braving the waves which broke over the stone levees enclosing the weed beds. Something flew through the air and struck the lizard on its shoulder. A stone hit her thigh. She heard Kodo shout and recoil as he was hit too. One of the figures was brandishing a long stick. The people on the shore were running, picking up rocks, standing on the edge of the deeps and hurling the stones at the lizard. A splatter of spray spat around them as the stones hit the water. A skimming flat stone bounced against the lizard's chest. Maia saw a small weed boy leaping and waving his arms. She ducked as another stone whistled past her head.

'Stop!' she screamed, waving.

Kodo turned the lizard away from the shore.

'Cliff Dwellers!'

The lizard swam through the debris washed from the trader ship. Nefrar was not clinging to any of it. The sun-deeps must have swallowed him.

# TWENTY-THREE

A flurry of tattered black crows wheeled round Doon. Kodo ducked as one of the birds' wings brushed his head. He lifted his fist but the bird was already dipping over the lizard's crest and flying towards the shore. The others arrowed after it.

'Look!' Maia pointed to a figure like a huge black bird with billowing wings which was scrambling down the cliff. The crows flew to the figure, swooped back towards the swimming lizard and then performed the same erratic flight again. 'They want us to follow,' she yelled.

The cliff-climber gained the beach and stood at the edge of the water, waving.

Maia wiped the salt spray from her eyes. It couldn't be! Sabra, the Watcher, had died in the attack on the cliffs when the Wulf Kin had entered the caves. She and Xania had found her on the cliff path when they were escaping. She had told Razek to hide her body safely in the cairn so that the wulfen wouldn't find it.

The crows were flying above the figure. Two peeled off and landed with difficulty close by. She could just see their red legs and curved red beaks.

'It's the Watcher,' she shouted above the wind.

Kodo encouraged Doon towards the beach. The lizard swam through the breaking waves and waddled onto the sand. Maia slid from Doon's back, her knees buckling as her feet hit the ground and she was grabbed by sinewy hands. The musty smell of spice caught in her throat.

'Sabra? Is it really you?'

The Watcher raised Maia's hands and held them against her wrinkled forehead as she bowed. 'Welcome, Sun Catcher.' Her voice was still as cracked and harsh as a jackdaw's call. 'Greetings, lizard boy.' The silver bangles on her thin arm jangled as the old woman released one of Maia's hands and flicked her fingers in welcome to Kodo. 'And to you, scaly one,' she said, staring into the lizard's unblinking eye. Doon's red crest retracted and she lowered her great head so that the Watcher could pat her. 'Without you the sun-deeps would have gobbled our adventurers and spat them out more dead than alive beyond the saltpans.'

Doon rumbled an acknowledgement as Kodo flicked his fingers in greeting and slid from her back.

The Watcher released Maia. 'Come, Catcher,' she said turning away. 'It will be better if no one knows you are here. Return home, lizard boy,' she called over her shoulder. 'Tell them of the lizard's rescue, but do not speak of the Sun Catcher's return.'

'Wait,' Maia grabbed Kodo's arm and dragged him with her as she struggled after Sabra.

They caught up with her in the lee of the cliff. At least there they were sheltered from the wind and she did not have to scream to make herself heard.

'Why did they attack us?'

'Because they hate the lizards,' muttered Kodo angrily, rubbing his thigh where the stone had struck. 'Because they think Doon will foul and destroy their weed beds even in this storm!' He gestured furiously at the waves. 'When everyone can see that it's the sun-deeps that will damage the weed. They attacked because they will always attack the lizard people.'

The Watcher shook her head. 'They thought you were Sea Thieves. They didn't attack the lizard. They were trying to prevent the boat from coming ashore.'

'I saw them!' protested Kodo. 'They threw stones at Doon to drive her away.'

'It's true,' said Maia.

The Watcher shrugged. 'They were protecting themselves and the weed beds. The Sea Thieves have been seen off the coast. They were afraid when they saw the ship. They would have drowned anyone who tried to come ashore.'

Maia shivered. 'Then we must go quickly and tell them that the men are traders, not thieves. That Trader Bron is a friend and has brought Razek home.'

'I'm not going near the Cliff Dwellers,' said Kodo. He was aware of Maia's gaze. 'They tried to harm Doon. And, anyway, Razek will tell them,' he finished defiantly.

The Watcher nodded. 'Come,' she instructed.

Maia shook her head. 'I must find Nefrar. He was washed overboard. Will Doon take me to search the coves?'

'Nefrar?' repeated the Watcher

'A hunting cat. Our companion,' replied Maia impatiently. 'Will you come with me? And Doon?' she asked Kodo again. 'He might have been washed ashore.'

Kodo looked back at the storm waves. He knew that the chances that the cheetah could survive those were slight.

'If he lives, the storm drift will carry him towards the saltpans,' said the Watcher. 'I will send the birds. They will tell us.'

Maia wondered if the birds had told her about the floundering ship and that was why the Watcher had made her way to the shore. Remembering Sabra's greetings, she also wondered if the Watcher had somehow summoned the lizard. What would Kodo think about his grandfather's lizard being commanded by someone else?

She caught a glimpse of the Watcher's yellow teeth as the woman grinned as she saw her thoughts. 'The stones told me you were coming, Sun Catcher. They told me that you brought the missing Storm Chaser with you. He will find trouble in the weed beds.'

Maia realised that she had thought only of her quest for silk and cocoons and her fear of the far-deeps. She hadn't even considered the hostility Razek must face from the Cliff Dwellers who would never understand why he had deserted the weed beds to follow her to Khandar. Perhaps if she went to them and explained why Razek had followed her and Xania across the Vast to Altara it would make it easier for him.

The Watcher was scanning the cliffs. 'Come,' she said.

'Before the Marsh Lord hears that there is a boat in trouble and comes to collect its men and treasures. He mustn't see you, Sun Catcher. And he will want to know why the storm has washed ashore Ootey's missing grandson.'

Kodo flinched. He didn't want to meet Lord Helmek. The last time he'd seen the Marsh Lord he had been sprawled unconscious at the Gather, having been felled by Xania's juggling discs.

'I'll take Doon to the village,' he said. 'Ootey will be concerned if he finds that she has escaped.' His grandfather cannot have kept the keep-nets repaired if Doon had escaped. He would be furious. He wondered if Ootey would swallow his rage long enough to be pleased to see him.

But the lizard had gone. There was no sign of her. Hoping that she had the sense not to swim too close to the weed beds and encounter another stoning, Kodo climbed up the cliff path after Maia and the Watcher.

Maia huddled into the Watcher's sleeping furs and watched the tendrils of steam rising from the beaker of chay Sabra had given her. Her sodden clothes lay scattered around the fire with Kodo's. They would dry hard and stiff as strips of deer meat unless she rinsed out the salt. She blinked sleepily at the flames. She was too tired to move. Yet she must. She had to find Nefrar. The crows hadn't returned but the Watcher's pigeons burbled contentedly

Maia glanced round the cairn. High above in the gloom a ring of nesting holes circled the curved walls. All of them were occupied by pigeons. The Watcher must keep them for the eggs they laid. And their music. She remembered the wind-flutes that sang as the pigeons flew. The Watcher had given her one of the carved round flutes. She always carried it in her back-sack. It might be beneath the sun-deeps now if Trader hadn't reached the safety of the river running close to the Marsh Lord's holdfast.

She shivered, crossed her thumbs and wished hard that the ship and crew were safe, then stretched her hand out from beneath the fur to feel her tunic. It was still wet. But she had to go out. She must go to the moth-garden. She must collect the silk cocoons and gather the silk that Tareth had tied to the thorn bushes. Tareth needed her. She mustn't fail him. But she had to look for Nefrar. The red-legged crows would return soon with news of Nefrar. She must find him. Yanna would never forgive her if anything happened to the cheetah.

Kodo, shrouded in a woven rug, was feeding a pigeon. He tucked his hand under the bird and scooped out a squab. It sat on his hand, wobbling, its neck too weak to support its head. 'D'you eat them?' he asked.

The Watcher looked at him. 'Are you hungry, boy?'

Kodo flushed and quickly tucked the fledgling back under the pigeon. 'Always.'

The Watcher handed him a dull bronze flesh hook and a pottery bowl with a bird's-foot pattern pressed into the clay beneath the rim. 'I put hot stones into the cook pit just after sun-wake. The meat will have boiled long enough for you to eat. Bring enough for us all.'

Clutching the rug around him, Kodo left the cairn and followed his nose to find the steaming wood-lined pit behind the cairn. The water was still hot. Several stones lay in the embers. Avoiding them, Kodo fished in the water for the hunks of meat, the flesh hook scraping against the cook-stones that the Watcher had tossed into the water to heat it. He hooked out several lumps of meat and quickly returned to the cairn.

The Watcher was singeing flatbread over the fire. Kodo's stomach rumbled. He gobbled the food the Watcher handed him, wiping his torn flatbread around his bowl to scoop up the last of the juices from the meat. He noticed that Maia was making short work of her food too.

The Watcher ate like a bird, stabbing at her dish with her knife as if it was a beak and tossing the small scraps into her mouth. While she ate she talked.

'Much has happened since you left us, Catcher.'

'Yes,' said Maia. 'I've lost a sister. And found a sister who wishes me dead.' She looked at her hands. 'And caught the sun just as the stones knew I must.'

The Watcher paused, a morsel of meat suspended on her knife. 'The Gather juggler?' she asked.

Maia nodded. 'A Wulf Kin blade.' She blinked hard. 'She was my sister, the Story Singer. The blade was poisoned.' She looked across the fire at the Watcher, whose face seemed carved from bronze in the firelight.

The Watcher pushed back her hair until Maia could see the jagged line of scar along her temple. 'I too thought the darkness was my to-come. But the Cliff Dwellers found me and I woke to find that everything had changed.'

Maia put down her empty dish 'Changed?'

'The Marsh Lord has built a new holdfast set deep in the cliffs to protect the Cliff Village from attacks. Its toes sit in the sun-deeps. From there he can watch the sun-deeps and the cliffs. He tells Elder that should the Sea Thieves attack then the children and women can shelter there. The Marsh Lord spends little time on the horse meadows. He rides each sun-wake and before sun-sleep along the cliffs, hunting, watching, seeking.' She glanced at Maia, her bird-bright eyes inquisitive. 'And he searches the beaches below the cliffs. Always alone.' She chewed a lump of meat and picked the strands from her teeth with the point of her knife.

'And the stilt village?' asked Kodo, clenching his fists. 'Does he seek and search there too?' He remembered how he had lied to the Marsh Lord. How he'd told him that the lizards had found the scrap of silk when they were scavenging.

The Watcher shrugged. 'He hunts young lizards still.'

Kodo shuddered. He used to hide when the Marsh Lords and their hounds came to the village and the young unwanted lizards were chased and killed. His mother Jakarta had always tried to comfort him, telling him that the lizards were too swift and too clever to be caught and killed. Only the weakest didn't survive the cull. The others escaped to the wild. They were the strongest and would make good mates for Ootey's lizard when the time came for Doon and Toon to breed. He remembered his promise to his mother and fumbled for the small leather bag of gold hanging round his neck. She had smiled at his dream of bringing her gold earrings to match her stab pin. Soon she would see that he had.

The Watcher was watching Maia. 'So you have returned, Catcher?' It was a question, not a statement.

'I have . . .' Maia glanced at Kodo. He was locked in dreams. Her gaze slid across him so that she seemed to be watching the roosting pigeons behind him. 'Things I must do,' she finished.

Kodo felt a stir of resentment. It knotted his stomach. Maia didn't trust him with her secrets. He had thought they were friends. He wondered if she'd told Razek why she had braved the sun-deeps. He hugged his hurt close. The lizard girl, Caspia, who looked so like Maia, had trusted him with secrets. Why didn't Maia? He knew why she had come. She was going to the moth-garden. She wanted more silk. Caspia had been right. Maia wanted to keep the silk secret and only for herself.

# TWENTY-FOUR

Maia woke. Her head felt heavy, her thoughts befuddled. She stared up at the stones in the curved roof, trying to remember where she was. She could hear pigeons. She could smell feathers and droppings and musty spices and, wafting among them, the scent of hot chay. She sat up, pushing the sleeping furs aside. Her clothes still felt damp and stiff with salt as if she had been bathing fully clothed in the sun-deeps. The leather flap covering the entrance lifted and the sudden bright sunlight dazzled her as the Watcher stooped under the lintel.

'You have slept long, Catcher. The lizard boy left for his village at sun-wake.'

Maia rubbed her eyes. 'Did you make us sleep?'

'He said he will watch for the cheetah,' continued the Watcher, ignoring her.

'Nefrar.' Maia got to her feet. 'I must find him.'

'The birds will find him.' She poured chay into a beaker and handed it to Maia. 'And before you leave here you must hide your hair.'

'What?'

'If you wish to stay hidden you cannot be a flame-head.'

Maia stared at the old woman. Did she need to stay hidden? She had intended to look for Nefrar and find out what had happened to the trader ship. She must visit the Cliff Village to see that Razek was safe. Then she had to go secretly to the moth-garden.

'Hidden?'

The Watcher looked at her. 'The storm brought you again as it did when you were a child. This time you are without the Warrior Weaver and his secrets. Does he still live?'

Maia was tempted to ask why her stones hadn't told her about Tareth.

'Yes,' she said. 'He sent me.'

'And he will not wish his secrets shared.'

'No,' agreed Maia.

'So it will be best if the Marsh Lord doesn't know that you're here. He saw you on the cliff when the wulfen was killed. He will remember you. '

Maia nodded.

'How can I be sure that he won't see me?' she asked.

'We'll dress you like a herder and dye your hair so that you seem like the rest of the Cliff Dwellers, he won't find you.'

Maia noticed that the Watcher's claw-like hands, curving round her beaker of chay, were stained black.

'I'll look just like Laya,' she said, remembering how once

she had wanted the Salt Holder's daughter to be her friend and had thought that Laya had disliked her because of her red hair. It was only on her Naming Day that she had discovered that Laya didn't like her because she thought that Razek did. Laya at least would be pleased that Razek had returned, even if the Cliff Dwellers weren't.

As the Watcher rubbed black dye on to her hair, Maia said as much.

The Watcher's hands stilled. 'The Salt Holder's daughter often walks towards the holdfast now.'

'To the Marsh Lord?'

The Watcher nodded.

Poor Razek, thought Maia. Laya had walked with Razek. Had wanted to leap the handfast fires with him. Even with his silver Weed Master's wristguard he couldn't compete with a Marsh Lord in his bronze helmet with his holdfast, his horse and his hounds.

Razek climbed doggedly up the cliff track. Below and behind him he could see the Marsh Lord's holdfast and, beyond, Trader's boat moored at the edge of the horse meadow. Razek could just make out the heap of goods that he had helped unload so that the hull could be drained and the leaking caulking replaced.

As he watched, Razek saw the gates of the holdfast open and several horsemen ride out. He turned away and continued to climb. Trader had the crew to help him repair the boat and to deal with Helmek. He was glad, as he didn't want to explain his presence on the storm-beached boat. He wanted to find Maia, to see that she was safe. He was almost sure that he had seen the lizard rescue her and swim towards the tiny beach below the cliffs. She might still be there unless she had already sought shelter in the Cliff Village.

He dismissed the thought that she might have drowned. Kodo and the lizard would have saved her. Razek frowned. He should have saved her, but he had been too slow to free himself from the knotted rope that Kodo had lashed about his waist. He squashed the worm of a thought that blamed Kodo for preventing him helping Maia. It didn't matter who had leapt into the sun-deeps so long as she was safe. Kodo might have taken Maia to the lizard village. Razek paused to examine the thought, and then dismissed it too. If she had survived, Maia would have wanted to go home. If she wasn't on the beach, she would have climbed the cliffs to the village.

He glanced across the sun-deeps. The water was green in the sunlight, freckled with tiny, white-topped waves that raced towards the shore. The wind was still strong, threatening to tug him from the cliff path. He wondered how much damage the storm had caused in the weed beds.

Skirting a thicket of gorse, he realised that he was not alone on the cliff-tops. A figure in blue was battling against the blustery wind. Her long dark hair, torn from its pins, danced like a banner. Disappointed that it wasn't Maia, Razek stepped off the narrow sheep track, waiting impatiently for the walker to pass.

'Razek? Is it really you?' Dragging her hair away from her face, the tall girl stared at him in disbelief.

'Laya!' Razek swallowed his surprise and flicked his fingers in greeting.

The girl stepped forward and grasped his arm, turning it so that she could see the silver wristguard he wore.

'It *is* you!' She glanced around and, seeing nothing but the empty cliff and distant shining sun-deeps, continued. 'Did the storm bring you? How are you here? Are you alone?'

The questions tumbled from her. She drew breath.

'Where have you been?' Her eyes searched his face. 'Why did you leave? Leave without a word? I thought you were dead, killed in the attack.'

She took his hand as if to reassure herself. 'How are you here?' she repeated.

Razek, aware of her warm hand clasping his, shook his head. 'A trader ship. Stormbound. We were driven towards the holdfast river.'

'A trader ship,' Laya sounded amazed. 'Is that what you ran off to do? To become a trader?'

'No!' Her disbelief and air of condemnation needled him. He pulled his hand free. 'I followed the Sun Catcher. I have returned with her.'

'Sun Catcher?'

'Maia has become a Sun Catcher,' said Razek.

'Maia?' The changing emotions crossed her face like clouds scudding across the sky.

'I am searching for her. She fell into the sun-deeps.'

'Maia drowned in the deeps?'

'I don't know. I saw her sink. A lizard came,' said Razek.

Laya shuddered. 'Eaten by a lizard.'

Razek frowned at her. Even disliking lizards as the Cliff Dwellers and the Salt Holder's daughter did, no one had ever believed that they ate people.

'I saw it swimming towards the weed beds with Maia on its back. She'll be waiting in the Cliff Village. I'm going there now.'

'Maia!' Laya shook her head. 'I didn't think she'd . . . I thought . . . We heard the beasts baying after she left Elder's cave.' Laya shivered, 'We found a dead beast in the Weaver's Cave. When the Sea Thieves were driven off, Helmek and the Marsh Lords searched the cliffs. There was no sign of Maia or the woman she fetched from the Gather. Just a beast dead close by and the Watcher senseless in her cairn. But when she woke . . .'

'The Watcher! She lives?'

He remembered carrying her into the cairn. He'd thought she was dead. Maia had said she was dead.

If the Watcher lived, Maia could have gone to the cairn. He frowned at Laya, not seeing her. He could see the storm and the lizard. He had seen crows too, tossed like dark spent embers above the flying spray. Yes. Maia would have gone to the Watcher. So he must too.

'Yes, she lives.' Intent on telling her tale, Laya hadn't noticed his preoccupation. 'As old as the cliffs and wind-weathered.' She swallowed and glanced at Razek. 'But, where have you been? Why did you go?' she demanded.

Razek squared his shoulders. 'I thought Maia needed me. I followed her across the Vast.'

'The Vast! You crossed the Vast?' Laya was aghast. '*Maia*

needed you? But the weed beds needed you. You are the Weed Master. You deserted us. You deserted the weed beds. How could you?'

Razek glared at her. He knew what he had done.

'I will have to make my peace with Elder. And hope that the weed beds still need me.'

For the first time, he noticed her appearance. Laya had always been pretty. But in her blue gown with her gold earrings and stab pin and a fine beaten-gold bangle on her slender wrist, she was more than pretty.

'But how are you, Laya? What are you doing here alone? Where are you going, in your gold and your best clothes?'

Laya blushed. 'What is that to you, Razek?' she demanded.

Razek's smile faded. 'Nothing.' He moved to walk past her. 'And I should be elsewhere. The storm will have caused much damage. The weed boys will need my help.'

Laya grabbed his arm to detain him. 'I'm going to Helmek, the Marsh Lord,' she said defiantly. 'Father and I have seen him often since he chased away the Sea Thieves and saved the Cliff Dwellers.'

Again Razek heard the criticism. He hadn't saved the Cliff Dwellers or the weed beds. He had run after Maia.

'Then you'll have to hurry,' he said coldly. 'I saw the Marsh Lord leave his holdfast.'

Laya's face fell. 'Oh.'

Razek had a change of heart. He took her hand from his arm, squeezed it and said, 'I must go to the village and find Maia. The Marsh Lord was riding to the river. The trader ship is there. If you hurry you will find him.'

'If I want him, I know where to find him without your

151

help!' She snatched her hand free. 'Maia's the one you need to help. I hope you find her. If the storm didn't drown her or the lizard eat her.' She whirled past him and hurried along the track.

'Go well, Laya,' muttered Razek under his breath. He was turning away when Laya called.

'Razek! I'm glad you're back.'

Maia lay on her belly in the grass. In the distance, way beyond the reach of a bow shot, she could make out the shadow of the Weaver's Cave. She wondered who occupied it now.

She tugged at the eagle feather in her unfamiliar black hair. She looked like a Cliff Dweller now but it didn't mean this was home. Tareth said her home was in the mountains in Khandar beyond the Vast. But she knew that she belonged wherever Tareth was. She had left him only because she had to find silk for him to weave. He needed to weave. He and the silk were bound to each other. She had crossed the sun-deeps, which she feared, because that need was urgent and the only source of silk was here. She must collect the silk and return quickly. Tareth said Khandar needed silk. And perhaps when she returned with it they could be at peace with each other once more and put aside the disagreements which had driven them apart. She would help him make a new moth-garden. She would fulfil her promise to find a new

Story Singer. She would search high and low for someone able to wear the story-coat if Caspia was not chosen.

Maia nibbled her thumb. Tareth would never accept Caspia. But perhaps the silk would show him what the to-come held. She scanned the cliff above the saltpans then, wriggling closer to the edge of the cliff, gazed at the cove below. Nothing but sand and the green, wind-combed sun-deeps. She rolled onto her back and stared at the sky, searching for the Watcher's birds. She wondered if Nefrar had been washed further down the coast and had made his way inland. She would have to explore the coves beyond the saltpans. Sea-rise always carried storm debris there.

Two red-legged crows flew over the edge of the cliff, towards the saltpans, then swooped out of sight. Her heart missed a beat. Had they found Nefrar? Following the sheep track along the edge of the cliff, Maia found the place she was looking for and started the long descent.

# TWENTY-FIVE

Maia saw the body lying at the edge of the sun-deeps. Small waves washed over its feet and retreated, sighing, across the scatter of shingle and shells. Fingers of foam licked across the sand, reaching for the body, but it was too high up the beach to be sucked into the surf. One of the crows landed on the still form and waddled across its back. The other landed on its head, and leaned forward. Maia shivered. Surely the bird was not going to peck out the eyes of a drowned man. She was reaching for a stone to hurl when a lean, tawny shape sprang snarling from the rocks. The crows took off as the cat leapt across the sand. Calling to each other, they skimmed the cliff-top and disappeared.

'Nefrar!' Dropping the stone, Maia rushed across the beach. Nefrar leapt. Knocked off balance, Maia fell. Pinned beneath the cheetah all she could see were sharp teeth and a gaping mouth and then Nefrar's rough tongue was licking her hard enough to peel the skin from her face. When he had finished, the cat took her chin between his teeth and bit her gently.

Maia wrapped her arms around him and hugged him. 'I thought I'd lost you.'

The cat padded awkwardly across to the figure lying at the edge of the water.

Maia sat up. 'Are you hurt?'

The cheetah was nudging the figure. Grasping its shoulder in his jaws, he braced himself and pulled. The body shifted. Nefrar heaved again and dragged the body clear of the water.

Maia got to her feet and went to help him, hoping that she would not find someone she knew, someone who had sailed with Trader Bron and been washed overboard like her. Together they pulled the figure high above the litter of weed, shells and stones which marked the limits of the storm-driven sea-rise. Maia knelt beside him and pressed her fingers against the clammy skin below a tangle of dark hair. It wasn't a man, as she had first thought, but a boy, with a thin nose, high cheekbones and a straight mouth. His eyelashes were dark crescents against a sun-darkened skin. His clothes glistened with wind-dried salt. Just as she decided that they had pulled a corpse from the water, she felt a tiny flutter against her fingertips. Alive.

A flicker of darkness scurried across the sand. Maia flinched. A black rat ran up the beach.

Slipping her hands beneath the boy's shoulders Maia managed to pull his leather back-sack free. It was lumpy. Maia felt inside and pulled out two flat curving sticks. She could feel bundles of soft cloth. Feeling that she had no right to pick over the stranger's belongings, she laid the strange sticks at his side and tucked the back-sack beneath his head. Then, reluctantly, she pulled back his sodden sleeve and breathed a sigh of relief. There was no fur. This was not a Wulf Kin like the one Tareth had once dragged from the deeps.

She wondered if, like her, he had been washed from his boat. Razek had seen a sail behind them as they'd passed a group of islands. Cupping her hands above her eyes, she gazed across the sun-deeps. Nothing, not even wheeling gulls. The calls she could hear were the gulls crowding on the narrow ledges on the cliff. Hoping that they would not think she was raiding their nests, Maia scrambled up the cliff to summon the Watcher.

The crows were swooping above the cairn. Razek could see the tall dark figure of the Watcher, looking like a gigantic crow herself in her black robes. She lifted her arm and a single crow spiralled from the calling mob and landed on her fist. Razek had never liked the Watcher. She saw too much.

He strode towards her. 'Sun's greetings, Watcher,' he called.

His voice was answered by the derisive laughter of crows.

The Watcher ran her long, bony figure down the feathers of the bird on her fist.

'Storm Chaser,' she said. 'You bring bad weather and ill omens.'

Razek flushed. His intentions to tread warily round the old crone died.

'Is Maia with you?' he demanded.

The Watcher regarded him coldly. 'I saw the storm chase you here.'

'And Maia?' Razek scowled at her. 'Did you see her? Maia, who you named Sun Catcher?'

'What has a Sun Catcher to do with weed beds and Cliff Dwellers, Storm Chaser?' Her eyes mocked him. 'A storm brought her with the Warrior Weaver. A storm will take her,' she announced. 'This is not her home. Her kind do not love the water. They fear it will claim them, will take their gifts.'

'She lived by the sun-deeps until her Naming Day when you gave her a destiny she didn't want,' he replied.

'Give? Give her her destiny?' hissed the Watcher. 'The stones found the Catcher's name, not I. Do you think I named you Storm Chaser?' A bundle of black feathers with blood-red eyes, beak and claw slid from her sleeve.

Razek stared, horrified. He had forgotten the bag of stones made from a filleted bird.

The Watcher held up the bag, shaking it. Razek could hear the runes muttering, chuckling, in the bag. 'The stones found your name, Storm Chaser.' To Razek's relief she tucked the bag back into her sleeve. 'As it chose for the Sun Catcher.'

Razek made one last effort. 'Does she live? Must I search the bays and beaches? Must I send the weed boys to scour the shallows?' He swallowed. 'Must I ask the Lizard Master to send his lizards to hunt through the sea-swell and the drifting storm waste to search for her body?'

'There are some who would wish her dead.'

'Is she alive?' shouted Razek.

'It would be better if no one knew that she has returned. Some seek her still. She has secrets that some desire.'

Razek's knees sagged with relief. 'Then she is alive? You've seen her?'

'She is not what she was,' said the Watcher.

Razek's relief died. 'Not . . . ? She's hurt? Where is she?' He took a step forward as if he was going to charge past her and search her cairn.

The Watcher flung up her hand. 'Listen, weed boy. The Catcher must not be seen, so she won't be seen. As a Flame Head she will be found. As a boy, a weed boy, a herder's boy, an Untouchable with the lizards, she will be like any other. You've been away too long and don't know what has changed. The Marsh Lord has built a new holdfast. He watches the sun-deeps, the lizards, the cliffs. He seeks a secret. He seeks the place where the weaver hid the moths. He mustn't find them. He mustn't know that the Flame Head has returned. Tell no one. The Trader and his crew are close-mouthed. They will keep her hidden. See that you do.'

Her vehemence rocked him. 'I won't tell anyone,' he said. 'Is she in danger?'

The Watcher shrugged. 'She *is* danger. A Sun Catcher is dangerous, weed boy. She is new to her powers. The Weaver is not here to guide her. He has sent her into danger with good reason.'

'Tell Maia that I came to find her. If she needs me . . . Tell her I have returned to the Cliff Village. And that the ship and its crew are safe beneath the Marsh Lord's holdfast at the edge of the horse meadows.'

The Watcher nodded and flicked her fingers in farewell. 'Storm Chaser.'

As he strode away Razek wondered if she would pass his message to Maia. He wouldn't be surprised if the Watcher had her hidden in the cairn where she could hear every word.

His step faltered. Laya. He had told Laya that Maia had returned.

And Laya hated Maia.

# Twenty-Six

Maia tugged the musty fur round her shoulders and tried to wriggle so that her hip was not rammed against the floor. The cairn was crowded with three of them and a large cat. At least from her sleeping place, with the leather door-covering pulled back, she could see the stars. Counting them might send her to sleep. Eventually she found a hollow in the beaten surface and sighed with relief. She could hear Nefrar snoring gently. She wished she could sleep as easily.

The moonlight spilled into the cairn, falling across the face of the sleeping boy. He didn't stir. He hadn't woken when she and the Watcher had carried him there. Only the shallow rise and fall of his sopping tunic had shown that he lived. That and the Watcher's potion, which dribbled from his lips, as he coughed and tried to swallow.

'Was he on the ship?' the Watcher had asked. 'Must we fetch the Trader?'

Maia had shaken her head. 'I feared he was Wulf Kin. We left the city after sun-sleep, because Tareth said no one should know. Elin could have sent them after us. But he's not Wulf Kin. There was a ship in the storm,' she remembered.

The Watcher had frowned and drawn her bag of runes from her sleeve. The tumbled pattern of stones didn't dispel her frown. She had scooped them up and cast again, staring intently at the stones, her forefinger hovering over them, then stirring, rearranging their fall. She had flipped them back into the bag and, pulling her robe over her head, sat muttering until darkness fell.

Maia stared at the moon. The moths would be dancing in the moth-garden. She sensed the silk she wore beneath her tunic listening.

A groan interrupted her thoughts. She crawled across to the stranger. His eyes were open. His hands clutched the edge of his sleeping fur. She could see his knuckles shining white from the force of his grip. She could imagine his night-wake. The terror of drowning beneath the sun-deeps.

'You're safe,' she said.

His head turned towards her voice.

'Caspia,' he said.

When Var woke, fingers of sunlight explored his face and drew bright patterns on the stones that surrounded him. Patterns he couldn't understand. He could hear birds, and smell dusty spice, old fur, smoke and burned grain. He lay and listened to the beat of his heart.

A wrinkled crow's face loomed above him. No, not a bird, human. He tried to reach for his knife but the furs held him and his groping fingers found nothing. The comforting press of his shoulder sheath was gone too. As were his boots with their secret slender blade. He realised he was naked beneath the furs. Without thought, his fingers locked as he pulled his hands free and he stabbed upwards, aiming for the dark eyes and hooked beak nose. Quick though he was, bird face was quicker, swaying out of reach. His hands were swiped aside. A tawny cat, its fangs gleaming, grumbled a warning deep in its chest as it placed a paw on his chest. Var forced himself to relax.

He was surprised by a cracked laugh. 'Stay still and he will not rip out your throat.'

Var lay still. The dappled cat blinked and went to lie across the doorway.

'Perhaps I will not have to kill you after all,' said the bird woman.

She bared her teeth, grinning at his alarm. Var hid a shudder. Her broken yellow teeth looked sharp enough to tear his throat. She held out a pottery beaker.

'Drink.'

Var sniffed. The steaming brew smelled innocuous enough, of spice and leaf-fall when he had walked in forests. Slowly he sat up. His limbs felt as light as a bird's. He noticed the slight tremor in his hand as he reached for the cup and drank. Even that feeble movement made the stone walls swirl.

Suddenly a sickening darkness lapped at the edges of his vision. He fought against it. He could not see. Numbing ice froze his limbs. He could not feel. He was aware of dropping the beaker, hearing it roll away as he crumpled into the furs.

'Who are you? Where are you from?'

'They call me Var.' His voice was not his own. 'The deeps carried me from my ship when the storm broke.'

'Where are you from, boy?'

The flicker of anger brought by her thinking him a mere boy helped him to fend off her question. He had never been a child. Not even before the Finder had found him. He wouldn't babble like one. 'I come from many places.'

He swallowed the bitter taste in his mouth. 'Have you poisoned me?' he croaked.

'You'll live. The stones want you alive.'

He tried to fight off the paralysis of the encroaching darkness. Tried to demand why his fate lay with stones, but the effort was too great. Before he was sucked under he heard a clear voice demanding, 'Will he live?'

And wondered again how Caspia, daughter of the red witch, had followed him here from the mountains and the Tower of Eagles.

# TWENTY-SEVEN

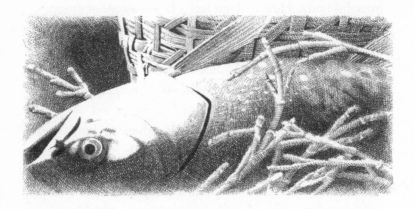

Caspia reined in her black mare. She could see eagles wheeling above the tall stone tower guarding a wide valley surrounded by mountains.

Elin rode alongside.

'See, daughter. The Tower of Eagles. Urteth's stronghold. Now that we have the story-coat and the sun-helmet, the mountain people will follow you. Urteth will have summoned Wulf Kin. He will be training eagles. The Eagle People will fight with them. The usurper Catcher will be overthrown. At leaf-fall when the sun is at its lowest we will return to seize the sun-stone. Then you will learn to become Sun Catcher.'

Three birds broke from the tattered formation and flew towards them. Caspia heard Vultek and Jedhev draw their knives and shout at their wulfen as the birds swooped to attack. Screaming, an eagle passed close overhead, spooking the black mare. She felt the wind from its wings in her hair and ducked from the clawing talons.

Vultek roared, standing in his stirrups, lashing out with his knife as the eagle dived. Jedhev's wulfen launched himself at a second bird. The eagle latched onto its head. Bird and beast fell, rolling in a snarling, screeching tangle of feather and fur.

Caspia fought to control her mare.

'Be still,' Elin screamed. She threw up her hand. 'I command you. The Queen commands. Be still.'

Caspia saw the eagle swooping towards her mother stall and tumble aside as its strike faltered. Saw it climb to rejoin its companion. Watched the earthbound eagle struggle free from the wulfen and fly unsteadily towards the stone tower.

'You dare attack me!' shouted Elin. 'Return to your master. Return to Urteth. He shall hear of this.'

In disbelief, Caspia watched the eagles retreat. Elin cursed, tugging at the reins of her pony as a group of riders raced towards them. Caspia felt for her knife and urged her mare closer to Elin. She could smell Vultek as he kneed his pony close so that it nudged against hers. His curving blade gleamed.

'Protect the Queen,' she cried. He didn't move. 'Vultek. Jedhev. Guard the Queen.'

Elin was laughing. 'Let them protect themselves,' she called and urged her pony towards the oncoming riders.

'Mother!' Caspia struck the flat of her knife blade against the black mare's flank and kicked hard. The mare careered after Elin. A heartbeat behind, the Wulf Kin followed.

'Mother,' shrieked Caspia.

But Elin was too swift. Her pony had reached the horde. It milled around her. Caspia saw her mother launch herself at one of the riders. Then she was among them too and her plunging mare was corralled, her reins seized, her knife knocked from her hand. Someone bellowed. 'Caspia!'

She was swung off her horse, whirled round as if she was a young child and set on her feet.

'Sun's greetings, daughter.'

'Father?' She reached to touch the black wolf pelt bristling on broad shoulders. When the world stopped spinning, she stared at the damaged face. Half she remembered. The other belonged to a stranger. A burn disfigured one side, the skin shrivelled and tight over cheekbone and jaw. One eye was closed, its socket empty.

'Urteth!' Elin lifted the injured man's hand to her cheek.

Caspia hid a shudder. The hand was like a claw. The skin scarred and burned.

Elin was laughing. 'She said you were dead. I knew she lied. I knew I would find you at the Tower of Eagles.'

'Azara is dead,'said Urteth. 'Killed by the Warrior Women.'

'They did this?' Caspia felt hate uncoiling like a serpent. She touched her father's face.

Urteth shook his head. 'I held the stone. She made it flame. It burned. I burned.' He glanced at the old Wulf Kin waiting like a shadow beside him. 'Zartev saved me. Carried me here. Summoned the Wulf Kin.'

'She?' echoed Caspia, even though she knew who the 'she' must be.

'The Sun Catcher,' said Urteth. 'She found the stone. She

taunted and tricked me and I burned.' He glanced at Elin. 'I watched the snows melt and wondered who had caught the sun.'

'She did,' said Elin. 'The last of my sisters. She caught the sun.'

'And will burn for this,' hissed Caspia.

'They will all die when you are the Sun Catcher,' said Elin. 'Maia, the thief Tareth and every Warrior Woman who protects them.'

'Tareth?' demanded Urteth. 'He lives? My brother is in Khandar?'

'A cripple,' said Elin. 'He hides in the Sun Palace. But I have taken the sun-helmet and the story-coat. The stone is in the Sun Palace and will be ours when we return to the Sun City.' Elin shivered as the silk patches on her gown murmured. 'Caspia will be the Sun Catcher,' she insisted.

'And will have my eagles to protect her,' said Urteth.

'Protect! They attacked us,' said Elin.

Urteth shrugged. 'We didn't expect you. They are still young. The Wulf Kin cannot always control them.'

'The Wulf Kin will have eagles and wulfen?' asked Caspia.

Urteth's grin was twisted. 'Many of the Eagle People have refused to join me. Have melted into the mountains. But I have caught many eagles. You will have many fine fighters to take you back to the Sun City, daughter. Until then our home is the Tower of Eagles, our land the mountains, our strength revenge, our people Wulf Kin.'

The Wulf Kin surrounding him drew their long curving knives and shook them above their heads. 'Urteth,' they roared. 'Elin. Caspia.'

The last shout was the loudest. Caspia mounted her black mare and rode at Urteth's side towards the Tower of Eagles.

# Twenty-Eight

Maia scrambled across the scree and wriggled under the gorse and thorn bushes concealing the entrance to the moth-garden. The thorns snagged her hair and clothes and scratched her skin. The undergrowth had grown thicker. At least it meant that no one else had been here since her last visit. She tugged her hair free, licked the bead of blood on her arm and burrowed deeper under the gorse.

The silk was silent. Torn strips hung motionless. The moon-moths, wings folded, slept in the sunlight, the circles on their wings like huge watchful eyes. Maia could just see the white of cocoons tucked among dry curling leaves. The silk looked paler than she remembered. Maia touched a shredded ribbon. It shivered under her fingers. Gently she teased it from the thorn bush and draped it across her wrist. She dreaded what she was about to do. She had to tell the silk what she intended, to listen, to accept its anger. Growing up, she had been warned by Tareth not to touch it, to seal her ears with beeswax when she went to the garden to harvest the cocoons. Now she needed cocoons and eggs.

Taking a deep breath she risked pulling the soft plug of beeswax from her ears, hoping that the moon-moths would sleep and that the silk would listen and not sing and drive her from the garden with its fury.

'I have come to release you,' she whispered. 'Tareth, the Warrior Weaver, has sent me.'

'Tareth, the thief!' The voice was like a shrill bell, a hot ember in her ear.

'Tareth, the Weaver,' she said. 'Who brought you life and stories to sing.'

The silk shivered over her wrist.

'I have stories,' Maia promised. 'From Khandar. Listen.'

She felt the silk's curiosity. A thirst that spread throughout the moth-garden as the silk woke.

She closed her eyes so that the silk's eagerness and greed for stories didn't distract her and summoned a picture of Xania, her face alive with fierce joy, thundering towards her on a stolen pony, the story-coat billowing from her shoulders as she escaped from the Marsh Lord and the Wulf Kin at the Gather. She almost faltered as she remembered that Xania had been killed by a poisoned Wulf Kin blade. She pushed the grief aside.

Then she realised that the silk was whispering, singing Xania's name. She was surrounded by images of her sister. Xania as a child, in the Sun Palace, learning how to wear the story-coat, story-singing by firelight to a spellbound audience with the silk glimmering around her. Xania laughing with Tareth. The silk had loved her sister. Xania had been the true silk-singer. She'd helped Tareth save the silk when the Wulf Kin had set fire to the palace moth-garden. The last of that stolen silk, secretly brought by Tareth to this cliff garden, remembered and honoured her sister.

A hot tear splashed onto the silk on her wrist. She felt the silk shudder and the images of Xania shivered and dissolved.

The silk whispers died.

'I am the Sun Catcher, sister of the silk-singer, daughter of Tareth, the Weaver. I have come to take you home.'

Kodo stretched his feet towards the fire and grinned at his mother's surprise as she unwrapped the strip torn from Zena's scarf. The tiny nugget and flecks of gold gleamed in the firelight.

Eyes wide, his mother looked up at him. 'Is it . . .?'

'Gold,' said Kodo. 'From an ant-bear's burrow.' His smile widened until he felt as if his face would split. 'Gold for the earrings I promised.'

Jakarta touched the gold nugget as if she was afraid it would vanish and gazed at Kodo as if he too was a wonderful mirage. Suddenly practical, she dumped the child sleeping on her lap into Kodo's arms and reached for a woven basket. Pulling out handfuls of samphire and a silver fish, she slit the fish open, deftly pulled out its innards and laid it on the bake-stone.

'You must be hungry.'

'Always!' Kodo glanced down at his sleeping sister. She had grown. He laid her in the small hammock decorated with strings of shells. The shells chimed as he gently swung the hammock. The deep blue cloth lined with saffron that his mother had stitched into a swinging cradle was familiar.

The Weaver's cloth. The price for two hatchlings. Maia had brought it with her story to the stilt village. It had lain in puddles of bright colour at her feet as she had beguiled his grandfather and the villagers. He had seemed a child then. Now he was a trader and had brought gold.

'Where is Grandfather?' he asked.

Jakarta flipped the sizzling fish and tossed the green samphire onto the stone before gesturing at the empty, guano-splattered perch.

'He has taken the birds fishing. '

She pulled the pot warming by the side of the fire towards her and poured chay into a bowl.

'Is he well?'

'He will be pleased to see you. Doon escaped again in the storm. She has been restless. Sea-rise has been higher since leaf-fall. It has scoured the scrape of sand. If she lays her eggs there, they will be eaten by gulls or washed away. Ootey thinks she is looking for a new hatching cove. The keep-nets cannot hold her. ' She shook her head. 'The storms have been bad since you left us. Some of the stilt village has been washed away.'

Kodo nodded. He had noticed gaps in the cluster of dwellings as he had jogged along the cliffs. He wondered if he should tell Jakarta that Doon had escaped to swim through the storm towards the trader ship and had saved Maia. He decided that if the story was ever told it was for Ootey's ears alone. He had never known Doon answer to anyone but his grandfather or her own desires.

'I'll mend the net,' he offered as he gulped down the chay, 'while Trader mends his ship. And follow Doon to see where she lays her eggs.'

'You're leaving?'

Kodo nodded. 'With Trader Bron. And will bring you more gold. '

She tucked the small folded package beneath her belt. 'I don't need gold, Kodo.'

Footsteps stomped along the net platform.

'The lizard is back.' Ootey, fishing tripod in one hand, a pot of eels in the other, ducked under the reed thatch. 'I'll need to mend the keep-net. And the eel trap. Something had bitten through the hazel wands. The birds caught nothing. I hope the chay's hot.' The litany of complaints ceased abruptly as Ootey saw Kodo.

He stood his fishing spears against the wall, crossed to Jakarta and placed the pot of eels by the fire. 'Enough for three,' he said before turning to Kodo. 'So the storm winds have carried you back.'

Kodo felt as if he'd only lived through three wolf-walks beneath his grandfather's glare. 'Yes, Grandfather.'

'Staying?'

'Long enough to mend the keep-net.'

173

'Jakarta been telling tales, has she?' Glowering at her, he took the beaker of chay she offered him.

'About the storms. And the lizard scrape. I can look for the new hatching cove.'

'Humph!' Ootey swallowed his chay in one long gulp. He frowned at Kodo. 'How'd you get here, boy? Has the Marsh Lord seen you? He's always on the prowl. Built a new holdfast in the cliffs.'

'I came with the trader ship. We were running with the storm. The cliff girl, Maia, was washed overboard. We . . . swam ashore. And met the Watcher. She says Trader's ship reached the river. I'll have to go and help Bron. But I'll mend the keep-net first.'

'The trader ship? You found the trader ship. So Doon carried you that far?'

Kodo nodded.

'And Maia, the Weaver's daughter, has returned with you?' Ootey sat by the fire. 'We knew you must be safe when Doon returned without you,' He glanced at Jakarta. 'I told your mother that.'

'And I believed you,' said Jakarta. 'But where did she take you, Kodo?'

'Out to the trader ship, and she rescued the Weaver from the deeps too. He'd fallen from the cliffs.' He grinned at his grandfather. 'Trader was glad to have a lizard boy as crew. I have learned so many things, Grandfather. Seen so many things. Too many to tell. We traded along the coast. I made fishing nets and rope and traded those too.'

'So you remembered what I taught you?' muttered his grandfather.

'Of course. They were good nets. And strong ropes. Then, when we reached Haddra with its tall white tower, higher than the Marsh Lord's holdfast, Wulf Kin were waiting.

'They were looking for the flame-head. For Maia. They'd come from the mountains of Khandar to find her. They almost found Tareth hiding in the boat, but Seth, the oar master, and I tricked them so he was safe. And then he and I left for the Sun City.'

'Sun City?'

'Maia's home. On the edge of the mountains. And Razek, the Weed Master, was there too. He'd followed Maia across the Vast.'

Ootey was shaking his head. 'The Weed Master was killed when the Sea Thieves attacked the Cliff Village. The Weaver too.'

'No, Grandfather. He was there. Now he's back. And the Weaver didn't die. Doon saved him from the deeps. You can ask Maia if you don't believe me. She caught the sun. You should have seen it, Grandfather. Everyone was there. We waited in the Stone Court. They blew golden horns. The sound was like all the lizards roaring together. She is with the Watcher. Oh!'

He swallowed and looked down at his feet.

'I wasn't meant to tell you that. No one must know that Maia has returned. You mustn't tell anyone.'

'Who would I tell?' asked his grandfather irritably. 'And who would believe such a tale? Sun City. Golden horns. Catching the sun.' He rose to his feet. 'I'll not tell your tales. I would be laughed at.'

'Will you laugh if I tell you that Doon escaped the keep-net and swam into the storm to carry Maia and me to the shore?' retorted Kodo. 'We would have drowned. Ask the Cliff Dwellers. See if they laugh. They threw rocks when she tried to swim to the weed beds.'

His grandfather only heard what he wanted to hear.

'Stoned the lizard!' he thundered.

'Is she hurt?' asked Jakarta.

'Since when can the weed boys hit anything with a stone?' said Kodo sulkily.

Ootey strode to the door and grabbed his fishing spear.

'Elder shall answer to me for this. They were glad enough that the lizards helped them to drive off the Sea Thieves. Now they stone Doon when she rescues my grandson and one of their own from the sun-deeps.'

Kodo leapt to his feet. 'No, Grandfather. You cannot tell them that. The Watcher made me promise not to tell.'

# Twenty-Nine

Razek's steps slowed as he approached the track to the Cliff Village. When he had inherited his father's silver wristguard he had promised to care for the weed beds as his father and uncle, both Weed Masters, had done. He had failed them and the Cliff Dwellers.

He turned the silver band on his wrist, his fingers tracing the fish scale patterns. He had forfeited the right to wear it. He stared out across the sun-deeps, squinting against the brightness of the setting sun. The sky flamed red and purple and gold. The colours of fire and warning. Below him he could see the dark outlines of the levees and the indigo smudges of the weed. Smudges that were mottled and broken, not a solid block of dark weed patterning the shallows. Razek frowned. Something was wrong.

Cupping his hand over his eyes he studied the shapes

and shadows of the beds, noticing for the first time that the regular line of the stone walls dividing the weed beds was broken. And he could smell weed. Dropping to his knees he crawled to the edge of the cliff and peered down. Piles of weed lay on the small beach between the weed beds and the cliffs. The storm had torn the kelp free from the rocks and thrown it there. Why hadn't the lizards corralled the floating raft of weed and dragged it away before it reached the weed beds? And if the storm had kept the Lizard Keeper and his lizards in the stilt village, why hadn't the weed boys collected it from the sand? Surely Elder should have been able to tend the weed and mend the breached levees?

As Razek reached the ledge outside the Weaver's Cave a thin woman slipped from the shadows. She looked around furtively and, tucking a hank of saffron-dyed wool into her sleeve, moved swiftly away. Light gleamed on the pearly shell comb she had pinned in the untidy bundle of brindled, grey hair caught at the nape of her neck.

'Mother?'

The woman froze and slowly turned. Razek stared. Gone was Selora, his plump, rosy-cheeked mother with her dark hair. In her place was a greying woman whose disbelieving eyes stared from a hollow face.

'Razek?'

He caught her as she swayed. He hugged her and, scared that she would break, put her down carefully.

'They told me you had fled. They told me you had run from the Sea Raiders,' babbled Selora. 'I told them you were dead. That my son, the Weed Master, would never run like a child from a fight. Yet Elder saw you fleeing.' Her hands were tracing the contours of his face, patting his shoulders, testing his reality. 'The weed boys hunted for you. There was no body. Nothing. Only the Watcher, lying like one dead in her cairn, with a slaughtered beast outside. There was no sign of you. Did the Sea Raiders take you?'

Razek caught her hands in his and held them tight. 'No, Mother.'

Her fingers were as brittle as bird bones. 'What has happened to you?' He glanced around the cave. 'What are you doing here? Have you moved into the Weaver's Cave?'

His mother flushed, pulled her hands free and tucked the wool out of sight. 'Tareth the Weaver is dead. So is Maia, Flame Head. They have no need of cloth or wool. The Weaver would want me to use it.'

She didn't meet his eyes. 'If the Raiders hadn't come, if he hadn't drowned in the deeps, Tareth and I would have been cave mates. He would want me to take his threads, his fleeces. They are no use left here and I can use them'

'But Tareth and Maia live.'

'Live?'

'I've seen him. Spoken to him. He lives. Maia too. They are alive, Mother.' He shook her gently because she was staring at him as if he was a ghost. 'As am I. Maia escaped. I followed her.'

'Followed?' his mother's voice was a hollow echo.

'I had to leave,' he said. 'I went after Maia. To tell her . . . to bring her back'

'Went with Maia?'

'I did what I thought I must. Now I am back. And I see all is not as it should be. Why are the levees broken? What has

Elder been doing? And there are no weed boys to be seen. The beach stinks of rotting weed.'

'Elder!' Selora's disbelief was replaced by alarm. 'He must not see you. They mustn't know. You must go.'

'No.'

'Better dead than shamed,' retorted Selora. 'Go! I will come. Meet you in the Ancient's fort. We can leave. I'm tired of their looks, their scorn, the whispers. They blamed you for the disasters, for the plague of spine-backs who ravaged the weed, for the storms.' Her bark of laughter was bitter as a fish gall. 'As if anyone can chase away the storms. But there have been so many storms and the weed beds were damaged and three weed boys were drowned. And this was all the fault of my son, Razek, who had deserted them. They remembered the Watcher's name for you and blamed you. I told them that my son was the Weed Master, not a Storm Chaser.'

Razek pulled the stolen hank of yarn from her sleeve and dropped it on the floor. 'You have no need to hide and steal from the Weaver's Cave, Mother. I am the Weed Master. Whatever happens, remember that. Wait for me. I will come for you when this is over.'

'They will stone you,' wailed his mother.

# Thirty

M aia remembered that she had once been flesh and blood but now she was just hollow, a collection of bones sucked dry by the silk. She lay where she had fallen, her face pressed into the earth, her hands still clutching the crushed silk strips she had collected from the thorn bushes. It was dark now. Around her the silvered footfall of the moon track had changed the moth-garden into a place of silver and shadows. She closed her eyes against the shining brightness. She thought she could hear the sighing of the sun-deeps. As she opened her hands, scorched flakes of silk fluttered to the ground, fragile as moth wings, and drifted away on the eddies of air. Her story-telling had burned the silk she held.

A touch light as a feather brushed her cheek. Then another and another. Tiny tickles tracked across her hands. She knew she was dreaming when she heard the whispered song. It was an effort to open her eyes. She found she was staring at a moth resting on the back of her hand. Another hung upside down from the thorn bush beside her. The moths were flying. Ash covered her palms but beneath the charred fragments lay bands of silk. Some had crinkled singed edges but they still whispered to the moths. Only the most fragile silk had been destroyed.

Maia sighed and sat up. She could feel the murmur of the silk song trembling through her fingers, running in her blood, flooding her with splintered images, snatches of song, the dance of moths. The temptation to sit cocooned in a cobweb of spun silk, dreaming stories, was overwhelming. Moths fluttering around her head distracted her. There was something else she had to do. She had come here for the silk. She had to do this for Tareth. For his eagle. She looked down at her hands. She had gathered the strands of silk. What else did she have to do? Dreamily, she watched a moth, its abdomen curling, lay a white egg on a leaf. It gleamed like a tiny pearl in the moonlight. Eggs. She had to harvest eggs. And cocoons. Tareth needed silk

The thorns scratched her hands, tore at her clothes, as she robbed the thorn bushes.

Carefully she rolled each tiny leaf with its white seed of an egg and wrapped them in the bands of silk. She dropped cocoons onto another strip of silk and knotted it securely around them.

Finally, when the branches were bare and she had several small bundles, she tucked them inside her tunic, secure against the top of her belt so that she would not lose them as she scrambled down the cliff.

Leaving the moth-garden, she hurried along the cliff path. The way was dark. The moon hidden behind clouds. She stumbled and almost lost her footing.

'Who's there?' demanded a metallic voice above her.

Maia heard the chink of metal on metal. She dropped into a crouch, hiding her face in her sleeve. There was a flare of light on the cliff above her as someone brandished a flaming torch, searching the dark.

'Show yourself.'

The light moved away. The darkness thickened about her. Stealthily Maia felt for a rock. Her scrabbling fingers closed round a stone. She hurled it as hard as she could away from her beyond the flickering light. For a moment she thought she had misjudged her aim, then the rock clattered against the cliff.

She heard a muffled curse. Rising to her feet she threw another stone beyond the first. The light bobbed towards the sound as the pebble struck the rock face.

Silent as an adder, Maia slithered back the way she had come, slid past the overhang that guarded the entrance to the moth-garden and scrambled noiselessly up to the grassy edge of the cliff. She wriggled onto the grass. When she reached the gorse she stopped and listened. All she could hear was the sound of the sun-deeps against the base of the cliff. She searched the darkness. Far to her right she could see a pinprick of light. She would not return to the Watcher's cairn that way.

She wondered who was out in the dark. A man in a helmet. The Marsh Lord. She knew that the Marsh Lord was seeking the silk. She must hide it until she was ready to leave. Maia hesitated for a moment. She searched the darkness. Nothing moved. The light had vanished.

The need to leave tugged at her. She had the silk. She had found Nefrar. She must return to Tareth. She could slip away in the darkness. She nibbled her lip. She had to know that Kodo and Razek were safe. She made her decision and set off towards the bee cave.

# THIRTY-ONE

The bees were angry. Maia was stung several times as she pushed the cocoon bundles far back on a ledge inside the honey cave. She almost wished she had ignored the strange feeling that she ought not to return to the cairn. She trusted the Watcher, but not the boy pulled from the sun-deeps. The boy who called her Caspia. He could be an enemy. And yet Nefrar had rescued him. She wondered why he knew Caspia. He must have been to Khandar and seen the Queen's daughter, the thought-thief. Caspia's gift made her like the silk. It stole thoughts and dreams too. Maia's hands stilled. Perhaps it really was Caspia's destiny to listen to the silk, to the stories the story-coat whispered. She must learn more about Elin's daughter. And discover if Var had been loyal to the Queen and her daughter. If so, he was dangerous.

Maia swiped at the bees attacking her hair, broke off a

small chunk of honeycomb and slid down the rock. She squeezed out the bee barbs, dabbed honey on the worst sting and sat nibbling honeycomb as the light grew brighter.

She had a sudden longing for blueberry flatbread and fish wrapped in weed and baked on stone. Her mouth watered. She was close to the Cliff Village and Razek might be there. She ought not to go there, but Selora made the best flatbreads. Maia gobbled the last of the honeycomb and headed towards the sheep track.

Deep in thought, she didn't see the slender girl sitting on the path, arms clasped about her knees as she stared over the sun-deeps. The girl was dressed in saffron yellow as bright as the gold band on her wrist. It was Laya, the Salt Holder's daughter. Laya, who had always been jealous of her and never tried to be her friend.

The girl turned her head as she heard Maia approach. Maia saw the flicker of alarm widen Laya's eyes as she saw a stranger. She saw Laya's hand slip towards her belt and felt some respect. Laya might be wealthy and spoiled, but she was prepared to stab a stranger who might threaten her.

Maia raised her hand so that it cast a shadow across her face and flicked her fingers in a greeting. Dressed as a boy, her hair dyed, she would walk past her childhood adversary unrecognised.

Laya's hand didn't leave her belt. She stared hard at Maia and rose to her feet, stepping back from the path. Maia lowered her head, lengthened her stride and strode past.

The hairs on the back of her neck prickled, she felt her shoulders tense. For a moment she feared she had been foolish and that Laya would take fright and plunge her knife into her.

Maia spun round and glared. Laya's knife was halfway from its sheath.

'I wouldn't if I were you,' warned Maia.

They glared at each other.

'It *is* you!' Laya pushed her knife back into its sheath. 'Razek said you had returned.' Her gaze travelled over Maia. 'But not that you came back as a boy!'

Maia felt the burn of Laya's derision. Despite herself she responded to the goad.

'It's easier to journey as a boy.'

She looked at Laya's hand, still curled about the hilt of her knife.

'There's no need to jump at shadows. Your yellow skirts have made you fearful, Laya,' she said scornfully. 'And your gold makes you easy pickings.'

Laya's hand covered her bangle.

'No one would dare harm me,' she claimed. 'I have Helmek's protection.'

Maia stared at her. 'The Marsh Lord?'

Laya raised her chin. 'We will be handfast at horned-moon,' she claimed.

Maia digested the news. As ever, the Watcher had seen what was to be. Maia had not really believed her. Laya had plotted and planned to ensnare a Weed Master since she had grown her hair long. She had wanted Razek. The Marsh Lord was old. Why would she want to swap Razek for him?

Laya read her unspoken question. 'I will live in the stone holdfast.' She held out her arm so that the sunlight blazed across the gold on her wrist. 'I will wear gold.'

'You once wanted silver,' Maia reminded her.

'A holdfast is better than a cave,' said Laya.

'Colder,' said Maia, thinking of the shadowed solar in the Sun Palace that even the vast fire didn't warm, even though the palace boys piled the logs high.

Laya laughed. 'And I will wear furs as well as gold.'

Maia shrugged. 'I hope they keep you warm when you leap over the fires.'

'A Marsh Lord doesn't leap over the fires.'

Maia thought that for all her bravado Laya sounded forlorn. Her thoughts must have shown because Laya's eyes hardened.

'So why have you dyed your hair, Flame Head? Who are you trying to hide from?'

'I was trying to look like you,' mocked Maia. 'I always hated red hair.'

Laya glared at her. 'You could never look like me. Now you look like a herder.' Her nose wrinkled. 'You smell like one too.' Her gaze ranged across Maia's clothes, seeing the salt stains and thorn rips. 'You look as if the sun-deeps spat you out.' She fiddled with her gold bangle. 'Razek said you'd come. Why are you here, Flame Head?'

'Since I smell so bad, I'll leave you.' Maia flicked her fingers and turned to go. 'I wish you happy with your Marsh Lord.'

'Wait!' commanded Laya. 'I . . . '

Whatever she had intended to say next was lost in the mournful blast of a conch.

Danger!

The conch sounded again. Two short notes.

A summons.

Maia felt her feet begin to move, to take her towards the

Cliff Village as if she still lived there and was called with the other Cliff Dwellers to answer the conch and work in the weed beds.

The conch wailed. The noise rose and fell like the bellow of angry lizards.

Judgement!

A chill prickled across her skin. She remembered the sound. It had haunted her night- wakes. The Cliff Dwellers had once gathered to pass judgement on Tareth and herself, to decide if they should be accepted or flung back into the sun-deeps which had carried them to the levees. Even though she had only been a tiny child she could remember the noise. It had terrified her. She remembered Tareth bargaining with a muttering crowd. Remembered how Razek had held her tight, had argued that she was a gift from the sun-deeps, that he had saved her and that she should be allowed to live. Razek, who . . .

Maia felt as if she had been punched.

'What is it?' demanded Laya.

'Razek,' whispered Maia. She knew that the conch blared for Razek. The Cliff Dwellers wanted to pass judgement on the Weed Master who had deserted them.

Kodo shouted with laughter as Doon flipped him over her head, tumbling him into the water. He kicked for the surface and a blast of bubbles nudged him sideways as Doon dived beneath him. As Doon surfaced, a wave surged across the sun-deeps, enveloping Ootey, sitting astride his lizard. The rumble of lizard glee trembled against Kodo's legs as he hauled himself onto Doon's neck and watched Toon, his grandfather's lizard, surf the swell. Ootey bellowed as he was half-submerged in the foaming wave, but he was grinning from ear to ear.

It was as if they were all pleased that he'd returned. Perhaps Doon would allow him to follow her to the new lizard scrape where she would lay her eggs. It would save the long treks and games of hide and seek when Doon was ready to lay. As if she had read his thoughts, she was sending him pictures of a cove and an underwater forest of kelp. He was only just quick enough to grab her wide neck collar and suck in a huge breath before she sank. He thought his lungs would burst as she swam through the waving fronds of gigantic weed. They brushed against him as Doon dived deeper until he could have reached out and touched the kelp holdfasts clamped like claws around smooth stones as large as lizard eggs. Just when black spots danced in front of his eyes and he knew he must let go and kick for the surface or drown, Doon carried him back into the air.

Kodo banged his fist against her neck. 'You hide. I'll hunt,' he said.

Doon lowered her nose and blew noisy bubbles across the sun-deeps. Toon warbled at her. Ootey raised his fishing spear in triumph. A long silver fish wriggled on the flint tip. His grandfather knocked it on the head and stuffed it in the bag tied at his waist.

'Home,' he called.

Kodo nodded reluctantly. He didn't want this to end. To swim with the lizards with nothing to do but frolic and fish was rare. To have Ootey in such a good mood, prepared to let the lizards play, was rarer still. He tugged gently at Doon's crest and they turned towards the shore.

The wail of the conch drifted across the water.

Danger.

Anxiously Kodo searched the sun-deeps. He and Ootey were alone.

'What is it?'

Ootey shrugged. 'Cliff Dweller matters. It's the call to settle a disagreement. Three blasts.' He turned Toon homewards. 'Come.'

Doon followed. Kodo tugged at her crest and she turned so that he could scan the shoreline. He could see the dark smudges of the caves with stick-like figures moving down to the shore. He thought he saw a flash of yellow on the cliff-top. He could make out two figures hurrying. He rubbed his eyes and stared again. The one in front was a boy, running down the steep pathway, sure-footed as a goat. The yellow-clad figure followed more slowly, sliding on the loose surface, clinging to the rocks.

'Wait,' he called to his grandfather. 'Something's wrong.'

He watched the figures on the beach. Many were collecting something from the sand; others stood in groups, then started to form a straggling line. Kodo saw a tall figure emerge from a cave and move slowly towards the beach. Sunlight glinted on the silver on his wrist.

'Come,' called Ootey again.

Kodo recognised Maia as she reached the ledges running

between the caves. Then she stopped. Instead of scrambling down to the beach to join the Cliff Dwellers she was running across the ledges, making for the end of the beach where someone was setting fire to a pile of weed. It smoked. Maia disappeared behind the billows and then Kodo saw her standing alone above the shifting gathering, who were moving aside to allow two figures to pass through.

Without knowing he had made a decision, Kodo urged Doon towards the weed beds. Maia might be in danger. Was she being judged by the Cliff Dwellers? He tried to clear his thoughts. Not Maia. She had only just arrived. She had placed herself as a lookout, or maybe a defender. So who was she going to defend?

Kodo urged Doon to swim faster. He knew who Maia had come to protect.

It was Razek.

# THIRTY-TWO

Razek tried not to stumble as he walked across the sand. He could feel the cold bronze tip of Elder's staff pressed hard into his shoulder. The murmuring stopped. He thought he would have to push through the crowd, shoulder them aside as the staff dug into his back, but they parted and closed behind him as he was forced across the heap of stinking storm-weed. He sank up to his knees. Flies buzzed around his head. Why hadn't they cleaned the beach? He felt his anger mount, blotting out his fear as he waded through the weed and staggered onto the sand. He heard Elder grunt and the staff slip to the base of his spine as Elder struggled through the pile of weed. Razek felt no sympathy.

Razek's anger carried him to the sloping, flat rock at the far end of the beach. He made himself look at the crowd. No one met his gaze, not even the gaggle of half-naked weed boys in the front row. His gaze fell to their hands. They were holding rocks. Now he looked he could see that many of the crowd held stones. He could see Selora. He had told her not to come.

He heard Elder strike the rock with the end of his staff. He struck the boulder again. At the signal, the crowds shuffled closer. Beyond them he could see the weed beds and the sun-deeps. Swimming strongly towards the shallows, red crests raised, were two lizards with riders. Lizards were forbidden in the weed beds. Razek swallowed as he recognised the dark head of one of the riders. Kodo.

He didn't blame Kodo for coming to the weed beds. He would have done the same. This was Kodo's turn for revenge. He'd come to witness his shame.

The Cliff Dwellers would be angry that the lizards had come. They would stone them. They would forget him. He had only to lift a stone and hurl it at the lizards and he would be accepted again as one of them. A Cliff Dweller who hated lizards. He had only to shout and point and there would be uproar. Razek clenched his fists and stared hard at the sand. He wouldn't take that way out.

Elder struck the rock until it rang.

'He who was once Weed Master as his father was has come to answer for himself. He was not dead as we were asked to believe.' Razek felt the crowd stir and lifted his head. He saw his mother standing there. She seemed to shrink into her baggy clothes as the Cliff Dwellers turned towards her.

Selora threw back her head. 'My son is a good Weed Master. As was his father,' she cried defiantly. Trembling, head high, she walked through the crowd until she stood beside Razek.

Elder crashed his staff down. 'Silence, woman.' He pointed the rod at her. 'You have not been called here.'

Selora's defiance collapsed. Razek tried to smile at her. 'Go home, Mother.'

She shook her head. A girl in bright saffron yellow pushed through the crowd, using her sharp elbows to carve her way to Selora. She took her hand.

'Come,' dark-haired Laya glanced at Razek and then just as quickly looked away again. 'You shouldn't be here. Come, Selora. He doesn't want you here.'

With an anguished glance at Razek, Selora gripped the comforting hand tightly and allowed herself to be drawn back into the crowd, who parted before Laya's fierce glare before closing ranks again.

'Not dead,' Elder repeated. 'The Weed Master lives. It is the weed that is dying!'

The crowd murmured in agreement.

'Dying because you ran from us.'

Razek cleared his throat. Laya's surprising appearance had banished the ice which had frozen his tongue to the roof of his mouth. He didn't know how the Salt Holder's daughter had known that Selora would need comfort. It was enough that she had. He felt a flicker of warmth and a sudden desire to fight, to defend himself.

'Was it just my leaving that caused the spine-backs to come and eat the weed?' he demanded.

'The Weed Master defends the weed. He doesn't leave it to be attacked by creatures from the far-deeps,' roared Elder.

'Did I breach the levees and let spine-backs into the weed beds?'

'The Weed Master protects the levees,' bellowed Elder. 'It is the duty of the Weed Master to tend and protect the weed. How can he do that if he is not here? You were not here. The storms came. And you were not here. The spine-backs came and you were not here. The levees broke and you were not here to save the weed.'

'The seaweed was not mine alone,' Razek protested. 'The weed boys also look after the beds.' He could feel their hostility seeping like a cold sea-fret towards him. Knuckles whitened as their fists tightened over the stones they held as they saw that he was blaming them. He didn't care what they thought. Since when could weed boys be relied on to think for themselves?

'And the Cliff Dwellers. Can they do nothing when they see the beaches fouled with storm-weed like this and the levees breached?'

He knew he was doing his cause no good, but the ruined weed bed wasn't all his fault.

'He's right.' Razek thought he heard someone say, but the lone voice was quickly drowned in a storm of protest.

Elder had to raise his voice to roar over them. 'Do not seek to blame others. You ran from us. Now you will stay on this stone. If the sun-deeps do not drown you at sun-wake, you will be freed.'

Razek felt the blood drain from his limbs. It was all he could do not to drop to his knees. To be left alone here while the water rose and fell was terrifying. He looked at the sky. Storm clouds were building. If the storm broke and drove the waves across the weed beds he would drown, no matter how low the sea-rise. He tried to remember the phase of the moon but his mind was as blank as the darkness of sun-sleep.

'If the Weed Master needs someone to blame other than idle weed boys or the Cliff Dwellers, then that blame is mine.' A cool, clear voice carried across the beach. 'I will take his punishment.'

Razek spun on his heel. Maia stood on a rock overlooking him.

Elder was glaring at the slight figure towering over him. 'Who are you? Only Cliff Dwellers may speak here, boy.' He gestured to the boys, whose arms were already raised. 'Leave before I set the weed boys on you.'

Maia flicked her fingers.

'Greetings, Elder,' she laughed. 'Don't you recognise me? I am a Cliff Dweller too. You called me Flame Head. You often shared chay in our cave with my father, Tareth. I am Maia, the Warrior Weaver's child, and I speak for Razek, the Weed Master. He chose to leave the weed beds because I was in danger.'

'You lie, stranger. '

'Lies,' chanted the weed boys. 'Lies.' One, bolder than the rest, hurled a stone. It clattered against the rock behind Maia's head. She ducked. Encouraged, another lobbed a stone. A third threw a fistful of sand and pebbles.

Maia rocked back on her heels. She could feel her anger rising like a flame inside her. The weed boys had always tormented her. They would not drive her away. She would save Razek. She raised her hands. Her eyes felt hot. Eddies of wind swirled the flying sand.. The grains hitting her skin were pinpricks of pain, sharp as hot needles. She spread her fingers to ward off the stinging grains. Her fingers tingled. Her eyes blazed.

'Maia!' yelled Razek. 'Stop!'

But Maia had already lowered her hands. Razek wondered if he was the only one who had seen the amber fire in her eyes.

Elder glared at the capering weed boys and they huddled in a sullen group. Razek heard the gentle thuds as their stones were dropped onto the sand. Satisfied that he had regained control, Elder turned back to Maia.

'I will hear you,' he said.

Maia looked down at him. 'You called me Flame Head,' she repeated. 'I hated it, but it was a good name. I have learned the secrets of fire.' She glanced at the weed boys. 'And if they stone me they will feel my fire. But I was – I am – Maia, the Warrior Weaver's daughter, named Sun Catcher by the Watcher. A name I have made my own.'

'And what has a Weaver's daughter to say for the Weed Master?'

Maia took a deep breath. Anger sparked anger. It wouldn't help Razek.

'First I bring greetings from Tareth, the Warrior Weaver, who reminds you that Weed Master Razek and his father rescued him from drowning many star-shifts ago in the weed beds. As I too was saved.'

'I remember. And the Weaver served us well when he chose to remain in the village and dwell with us,' admitted Elder. 'Is he with you?'

'He has returned to the Land of Eagles,' said Maia. 'Where Razek also came.' She waited until the whispers of surprise had died away. 'The way was long and hard, full of danger, of death. Yet one he took to make sure that the Wulf Kin who attacked you when the Sea Raiders came did not kill me before my father could find me.' She looked at Razek. 'He had no choice.'

She scowled at the Cliff Dwellers, willing them to believe her version of the disastrous choice Razek had made. If they believed he had no choice but to leave, surely they would not punish him.

'Razek dragged me from the sun-deeps. He watched over me for many star-shifts before he became Weed Master. He didn't wish to leave you. He knew he must tend the weed beds. It was all that he wished to do. But he also knew that without his help, once the Wulf Kin blade had killed my father's eagle, I too would perish.'

Razek, caught up in her telling of the story, was glad she did not add that it was the Wulf Kin blade he had used that had killed the eagle.

'He knew that I wouldn't be safe here. He thought that my father had been killed in the Sea Raider attack. He saw him fall into the deeps. He saw the Wulf Kin searching for me. I ran away. He followed me across the Vast.'

The Cliff Dwellers moaned softly. No one could survive in the Vast. Razek felt them looking at him.

'We nearly died,' continued Maia. 'He was wounded but still he protected me until I reached the Land of Eagles, while Tareth was rescued by Doon the lizard and came across the far-deeps with the Trader Bron.'

Razek wondered if Maia had seen Kodo astride his lizard, waiting beyond the weed beds.

'A lizard saved the Weaver?' demanded Elder.

Maia nodded. 'As they will help you save the weed beds,' she claimed. 'The lizards are strong. They can move rocks. They will help you repair the levees so that the storms don't tear the weed from the weed beds. So that the spine-backs are kept out. Razek will ask the Lizard Keeper to work with you.'

She thought she had pushed them too far as their muttering swelled. Elder crashed his staff against the rock and they fell silent.

'The lizards fought with us when we were attacked by the Sea Raiders,' Elder reminded them. 'They keep the storm kelp from fouling the weed beds.' He looked at Maia and then at Razek. 'But will they help with the levees?'

Maia nodded again. 'And now that Razek has returned, the weed beds will be in safe hands.' She looked at Razek. 'The Watcher was wise when she found him his name. Razek is the Storm Chaser. He will chase the storms from the weed beds so that the weed can regrow.'

'There have been many storms since his departure,' shouted someone.

'It is his fault that the storms came, then,' called another.

'His fault the spine-backs entered the levees and killed the weed.'

'They made good eating,' called a woman's voice.

There was a scatter of laughter.

'The weed wouldn't have died if he'd remained with us,' muttered a cave wife.

'The weed died. The weed died. The weed died.' Their chant rose and rippled.

'And I would have died and the Weaver lost his only child,' Maia raised her voice. 'The Weaver is a good man. He always helped you even though the fall from the cliffs made him lame.'

Elder nodded. 'The Weed Master failed us,' he decreed. 'He left his mother Selora to suffer. She thought him dead.' He looked around the crowd. Several women could not meet his sharp eyes. 'She carried the shame that others believed he had run from us.'

Razek felt numb. He knew that his and Maia's pleas had failed.

Elder cleared his throat. 'But, he did not fail the storm-found ones. They too had need of him.'

Razek bowed his head. 'Elder is wise,' he said.

A faint glimmer of respect gleamed in Elder's eyes. 'The sun-deeps will decide.'

The Cliff Dwellers turned away. Selora and Laya pushed through them and came to Razek. Selora was in tears. Razek patted her awkwardly on her shoulder and looked at Laya.

'Thank you. Would you stay with her while . . . until sun-wake?' he asked.

Laya nodded.

Maia had scrambled down from her rock and was waiting with Elder.

'Since he came with me across the Vast, I will stay with him now,' she said.

'No!' said Razek.

Maia ignored him.

'Throughout sun-sleep?' asked Elder.

Maia nodded. She knew how the Cliff Dwellers hated the

dark. It was all too easy to fall during darkness. Like the cliff birds, the Cave Dwellers roosted during sun-sleep and did not stir from their caves until the sun rose.

'I'm the Sun Catcher,' she said. 'Why should I fear the dark?'

Elder glanced at the building bank of clouds. 'The wind will drive the sea-rise high towards the cliffs and the beach.' He looked at Razek. 'I will not tie the ropes too tight.'

Razek swallowed. Even with a little slack in the ropes he knew he would not be able to keep his head above the waves. The water would cover the stone before sun-wake.

# THIRTY-THREE

Kodo was angry.

'She had no right to say that,' he complained. 'Why should the lizards work on the walls around the weed beds?'

He had not forgiven the Cliff Dwellers for hurling stones at Doon. He had not believed the Watcher when she had claimed that the Cliff Dwellers had thought they were driving off the Sea Raiders. He knew better. The Cliff Dwellers had never liked the lizards.

But Razek should not drown, thought Kodo. Razek didn't deserve that. The Weed Master had only tried to save Maia. He glanced back at the beach. Shadows stretched across the sand. He could see Maia with Elder. Elder was wrapping himself in a cloak against the fresh wind blowing across the sun-deeps.

'I will stay until sun-wake,' Kodo said.

Ootey nodded. 'Do not endanger the lizard,' he said. He passed Kodo the fish. 'It is better baked,' he added.

Maia waited until Elder fell asleep. Careful not to disturb him, she rolled to her feet and left the fire to slip through the shadows to the water's edge. It was already lapping against the base of the rock.

'Razek?' she whispered.

'You shouldn't be here.' His voice sounded as if he had been a long way off.

'I can free you,' she said. 'Elder is asleep. And the Cliff Dwellers won't leave their caves until sun-wake.'

'They'll know you have done it.'

'I won't be here.'

'And where will I be?'

She was silent.

Razek shivered. The stone was cold. He wondered if he would be too cold to feel the gradual rise of the water. Too cold to panic. He'd heard of herders who had fallen asleep in the cold of wolf-walk as they followed their flocks along the exposed cliff-tops and never woken in the warmth of sun-wake. Perhaps he would sleep. He knew he had been dreaming, slowly falling through darkness, floating like a black crow's feather on a gust of air. Maia's voice had dragged him back.

'I chased the storm that is you across the Vast as far as the mountains,' he said wearily. 'But the weed beds need a Weed Master. I cannot leave again. Perhaps the sun-deeps will let me stay.'

The edge of the water was nibbling at the glistening band of stones and shells that was always covered at high-rise. Soon the stone would be flooded.

'You are a Storm Chaser too. You warned Trader when he should watch for storms. Trader would welcome you as one of his crew,' Maia said. She knew that Razek had loved crossing the sun-deeps. Perhaps the memory would persuade Razek that he did not have to accept the ways of the Cliff Dwellers.

'Trader's ship nearly sank on the rocks beyond the levees. I only watch the sky and the clouds. The Watcher is old and her stones are cracked. Who can chase storms?'

'Who can catch the sun?' demanded Maia.

She glanced at the sky. The darkness did seem less dense, as if some of the storm clouds had disbursed and all she could see now was the black of sun-sleep. The wind was dropping. Perhaps Razek really could hold the storm clouds at bay. She hunted for pinpricks of light. There were none. If there were no stars, the clouds must be hiding them. She stared into the dark, willing the cluster of stars to appear. Seven sister stars. She was one of seven sisters. She needed the comfort of the bright star pattern tonight. She shivered as the breeze from the water tugged at her hair.

The water heaved. A huge shadow loomed. Maia felt her heart thump.

'Is there anything to eat?' High above her head Kodo's whisper was plaintive. 'I had to give the fish to Doon.'

He slid from the lizard.

'You are always hungry, Lizard Boy.' Razek's voice was rough but Maia could tell that he was pleased to see Kodo. So was she.

'If I'd known you were coming, I'd have saved you some honeycomb.'

'Honey. I could eat a whole bee-cleft. And flatbread.' Kodo sighed. He knelt down and felt for the ropes at Razek's wrists. 'So are we going to cut him free?' he asked. 'Doon can carry us all. Trader will be ready to sail soon. The Watcher will hide Razek until then.'

'No,' said Razek.

Doon crouched, her large body making a wall between Maia and the sun-deeps. Could she protect the stone and stop the water reaching Razek? Maia crouched too and felt the sand at the base of the rock. It was wet but there was no water. Doon had stopped the sea-rise.

Maia stood. 'We could stop the water covering the stone. Look, Doon has already started. She's stopped the water. We can get rocks, make the wall longer. Razek will be safe.'

Even as she said it she realised that she was being foolish. She was standing up to her ankles in water now. The slow sea-rise was flowing past Doon's bulk and flooding behind the huge flat stone.

Kodo was shaking his head. 'We'd need too many rocks. Even with Doon we'd never build a wall high enough.'

Maia's shoulders slumped. 'Well, what then?'

'Cut him free,' said Kodo. 'And if he shouts, knock him on the head.'

'No' said Razek.

206

'You'll drown,' said Kodo, 'Can't you feel the wind? It will carry the waves high onto the beach.' His tone said louder than words that he thought Razek was crazy. He looked at Maia. 'Is the stone always under the sun-deeps at sea-high?'

'No,' Razek was goaded into answering. 'Only when the moon is full or when the wind drives the waves over the weed beds. Then the stone is drowned.'

Silence fell as they all looked up at the moonless sky.

'That's it.' said Maia. She knelt down beside Razek. 'The wind. With no wind the sun-deeps will be calm. You can make the deeps calm. Then perhaps the sea-rise will be lower.'

Razek didn't answer.

'The Watcher named you Storm Chaser. What if she didn't mean that you had to leave to chase storms? What if she knew that a Weed Master who could protect the weed beds from storms was what you would become?' She placed her hands on his shoulders and shook him. 'You are a good Weed Master. The weed beds were safe in your care. What if you can chase storms away from the cliffs?'

'No one can.'

'Try,' urged Maia fiercely. 'Try. Become the wind.'

'There will still be sea-rise. The stone will be covered,' Razek squashed the faint thread of hope.

'Believe. Become,' insisted Maia. She closed her eyes and burrowed deep into her memories, seeking the strength to help him. She thought of fire. That was strong. If Razek let the winds take him as sun and fire consumed her perhaps he could chase a storm. She moved behind him so that she too could look over Doon's bulk at the cloud-dark sky. She slid her hands beneath his shoulders. 'Become the wind between the stars. I will help. The star sisters will help. Kodo, help me.'

Razek could feel the heat of her hands. Lines of fire radiated from her fingers in a sunburst across his back, as fiery tentacles seemed to wriggle across his skin and wrap themselves around his ribs. They tightened until he knew he wouldn't be able to breathe. That his skin would be scored with lines of heat and power, branding him forever. The dark was coming for him.

'Maia,' he croaked as he tried to draw breath.

'Become!' she hissed and as the darkness of many wings lifted him he thought he heard her whisper, 'Sisters, help me. Silk sisters, sing for me. Star sisters, come.'

Kodo saw Razek shudder. Saw the veins on his neck bulge. Saw Maia begin to shake. Doon threw back her head, her crest spread wide, and called. The notes ran up and down a scale he had never heard before. The sound was eerie, unreal. Lizards didn't sing.

The sun-deeps sighed.

Kodo trembled. He didn't believe what he was hearing, what he was seeing. He reached out to touch Doon. At least her bulk was solid and real. And her scales gleamed silver with salt. Kodo looked up. Tiny pinpricks of light shone in the dark. He could see stars.

'Kodo! Help me,' cried Maia.

# Thirty-Four

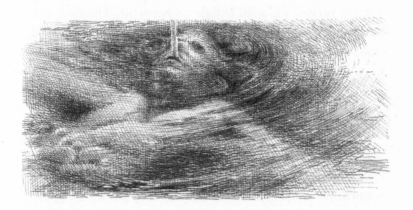

Laya noticed that the setting sun was the colour of her tunic. It was a fine colour. It pleased her. With her dark hair she could wear strong sun colours. Not like Maia with her flame-hair. Laya frowned. She wouldn't think about Maia.

The sun would soon be gone, drowned in the sun-deeps. She loved the purple smudges before sun-sleep. She could ask a dyer to make cloth just that dusky shade. She would like that. So would Helmek. Would he trade for a jewel to match? A ring? A belt with a jewelled clasp. Razek had bartered for a belt for her. She wouldn't think about Razek. She wouldn't think about what she had seen.

She nibbled her thumbnail, realised what she was doing and sat on her hand. She tried to think of words to comfort Selora. Since she had led Razek's mother into the gloom of the cave, Selora had sat rocking, huddled beneath a cloak that she had flung over her head. The cloak was not very clean. Laya noticed that the cloth was old and worn. Selora, once so proud, didn't seem to care any more.

Laya twisted the gold bangle on her wrist. The cave was untidy, the floor not swept. She felt ashamed that such small things should occupy her thoughts when Razek lay waiting for sea-rise. She wasn't used to feeling ashamed. She didn't like it. She wanted to go home. But Razek had asked her to take care of his mother. Laya found herself wishing that she hadn't let curiosity get the better of her when she had decided to follow Maia.

She set the pot of chay closer to the embers. The spicy warm drink would comfort Selora. The chay pot was chipped, its surface blackened with smoke. Selora's cave-keeping skills had left her, just as Razek had. He left me too, Laya thought.

She poured chay. It splashed onto her saffron skirt. It would stain. The cloth was ruined. She would never wear the yellow again. It would only remind her of pain and loss. She nibbled her thumb. Razek would die. They had left him on the stone to drown. They hadn't listened to him. They hadn't listened to Maia.

They would listen to Helmek, the Marsh Lord. In her excitement she broke her nail. She could save Razek.

Doon was silent, her song finished. She crouched as still as stone, watching. The water had reached Razek's shoulders. She lowered her nose and blew. Bubbles skittered across the surface of the water towards the stone, popping as they drifted against him. She blew again and the water swirled around the rock. A tiny wave splashed Razek's face.

Doon turned her head, her crest raised.

Kodo, thigh-deep in water, numb with cold, almost fell over with the force of the images she was sending.

'What?'

Doon ducked her head under the water.

Maia, glaring out across the dark water as if to bend it to her will, knew that they had failed. The wind had dropped. The sun-deeps were flat and calm. But still the water rose. She glanced at Razek. His eyes were closed. He had retreated to a place where she could not follow. She was frightened. She must cut him free before it was too late. He could escape on Doon. Exile was better than this.

'Wait!' Kodo was wading out of the water. 'I know what to do.'

He ran to the pile of rotting kelp and started tearing at the weed, hurling it over his shoulder as he dug deeper. Then he was back, dragging something behind him. He fell to his knees and started hacking at the long stalk of the kelp. 'Here,' He held up a piece longer than his arm. 'It's hollow.' He splashed towards Razek. 'Look.'

Razek opened his eyes.

'When the sun-deeps cover you, you can breathe though this.' He put the tube in his mouth and blew. 'Hollow.' He grinned at Razek. 'You can stay underwater forever.'

The Watcher stirred in her sleep and woke suddenly. Var was bending over her, his shadow hanging like threatening wings above her. The crow crouching on her chest tumbled on to the floor as she sat bolt upright, nearly head-butting the boy. He reared back and almost sat on the hearth-stone. She saw him wince as he put out his hand to steady himself and touched a hot ember.

The Watcher gathered her scattered wits, as the torn fragments of her night-wake dissolved. The sudden waking robbed her of the meaning of the disturbing dream. She sensed that the warning it brought was important. But what warning? She scowled at him.

'Who are you?' she demanded. 'How are you here?'

'I am Var. The storm brought me,' he answered as he had before.

'And before the storm?'

He poked at the fire until the embers blazed. 'A land far from here.'

The Watcher was tired of the game. He was as difficult to pin down as the black rat she had found gnawing a hole in the basket of berries she had foraged. The rat had been too quick for her and had scurried from the cairn. It had dared to scamper over the paws and under the nose of the snoozing cheetah stretched across the doorway. She thought she could see its two small sharp eyes gleaming in the sudden

212

flare of light from the flames. If it had been gorging itself on her store of grain she would hunt it down and hang its carcass from the cairn as a warning to others. If she could catch it. The rat and the boy were the same. Difficult to trap. Even her stones kept his secrets safe.

His eyes gleamed in the firelight like the rat's, as if he knew her thoughts and was amused. If it wasn't for the stones, for the murmurs they made and the thought that this stranger was important to the Sun Catcher, she would turn him out and let him make his own way. She knew that he would be content to go. And that to survive in a strange place would cause him no difficulty.

'Yes, yes,' she said irritably. 'A far land. So why are you so far from your own far land?'

Var looked at her steadily. Despite her gruffness, he liked the old crone. He wondered again if she could be trusted. The girl he had followed trusted her. So did the spotted cat. Var decided he could tell her part of the truth. It might stop her questions, which buzzed like bees around his head whenever he was awake. He yawned and stretched, hearing his shoulders creak. The storm battering had left him feeble. He was stronger now.

'I was sent,' he said.

He heard the soft chink as her hand stoked the bag of stones she always had tucked in her sleeve. He had slipped the bag from her sleeve while she slept, but the stones had told him nothing. He knew that they held magic. Would they betray him? He must be careful what he said.

'I was sent by Azbarak who is also from the far land.' He enjoyed the flash of suppressed anger in her eyes as he made her wait for more. 'Azbarak is Keeper of the Sun Palace. When he learned that the new Sun Catcher intended to leave the Sun City he thought she should not go alone.'

'She had companions with her,' retorted the Watcher.

Var frowned. The Watcher was left in no doubt as to what Var thought of Maia's companions.

'I . . . protect. I was sent to keep the Sun Catcher safe on her journey.'

The Watcher snorted. 'And failed.'

Var flushed slightly. 'She is still safe,' he said quietly. 'She left the Sun City secretly. I reached Haddra too late. She had taken a boat at the port and sailed. I followed.'

'And would have died, if she and the cat hadn't rescued you from the sun-deeps!'

She was just like her crows, thought Var. She even sounded like them.

He nodded.

The Watcher jingled the stones. 'And now?'

'I will protect her when she chooses to return.'

'Return? You think she means to leave? This was her home. She will want to stay.'

Var knew she was testing, trying to goad him.

'She is the Catcher. She will return. I am sent to guide her home.'

The Watcher rose to her feet. 'Then you'd best know this, Var from a far land, who follows the Sun Catcher. There are those here who do not wish her to return. Who will prevent her leaving. She has secrets they want. If they find her they will prevent her return.'

'Then they must not find her,' said Var.

# THIRTY-FIVE

'I've found her!'

Helmek, the Marsh Lord, stretched his long legs towards the blazing logs nudging aside his favourite hunting hound. He quelled the sudden jolt of satisfaction that made him want to leap to his feet and run to his horse. Instead he watched Laya, the Salt Holder's daughter, in her saffron robe, fondling the ears of his hound.

He had not imagined the whisper of silk as he'd ridden through the darkness to the holdfast. It had been faint and he had wondered if it had been the whisper of wind in the gorse bushes. Now he knew that he was not mistaken. The silk had been calling. He had heard it and the girl who kept its secret. He had known that if he kept a close watch on the Cliff Dwellers and the Lizard People he would discover the hidden place where the silk hung. All he needed was the girl.

Laya pushed the hound's head from her knee. It was dribbling on her skirt. 'We must go quickly,' she said. 'Sea-rise will cover the rock.' She got to her feet. 'Elder will listen to you.'

'Why will he listen to me?'

'You are the Marsh Lord,' Laya looked at him with surprise. 'He will listen. He doesn't want to risk Razek's life. He knows he's a good Weed Master. Knows he needs him. He didn't want to put him on the rock. The Cliff Dwellers were angry. He did what they wanted. He always does.'

'It is for Elder to tell the Cliff Dwellers.'

'But you are the Marsh Lord,' she repeated childishly. 'Elder will do as you say. He'll free Razek.'

Helmek's eyes narrowed. 'Why should I save this Razek?'

'He's the Weed Master.' Laya was suddenly aware that perhaps she should have thought through the tale she had carried to Helmek. She had blurted out everything. Had she said too much? She flicked her hair back and was reassured by the waft of perfume the movement released.

'My father says the seaweed is poor, the beds damaged. That spine-backs have eaten lots of the weed. The Cliff Dwellers need the Weed Master's help.'

'Yet they have left him in the sun-deeps.' The Marsh Lord turned the silver thumb ring which covered the brown birth tattoo that his mother had foolishly pricked onto his thumb. The tattoo showed that his mother's people had not been Marsh Lords like his father. 'I cannot interfere with the rule of Elder. What reason can I give?'

'But . . .'

The silver ring flashed as he threw up his hand. Rather than a weakness, his half-blood made him a good Marsh Lord. And when he had the silk he would be the most powerful of them all. The silk had promised him.

'I will not meddle.'

Laya's face fell.

'But I should meet with Elder and speak to the girl and see this Weed Master for myself. I'll ride to the village at sun-wake.'

'It will be too late.'

'Why? Is the girl leaving?'

'What do I care if she does?' Laya's expression was mutinous. She was not used to having her wishes denied. 'Sun-wake will be too late to save Razek.'

'That is in the gift of the sun-deeps.' He clicked his fingers at his hounds. They rose and milled around Laya. She was suddenly aware of how large they were. Their whiskery heads reached her waist. But their tails wagged.

Helmek rose from the carved wood seat he had dragged close to the fire.

'Come. I will take you back to the saltpans.' He picked up a brand lying tossed on the pile of faggots and logs at the side of the fire and thrust it in the flames. 'It is too dark for you to walk alone.'

Laya was about to protest, but his expression as the light from the flaming torch fell on his face silenced her.

He smiled and held out his arm. 'Sun-wake will be soon enough,' he promised as he escorted her, surrounded by his hounds, from his holdfast.

Sun-wake could not come soon enough. Crouching in the water, Maia felt that she had never been so cold. A smooth, rolling wave tried to nudge her off balance. Razek's body shifted. The ropes that held him tightened then slackened. The movement almost tugged the slippery wet tube from her frozen fingers. Instinctively her thumb clamped over the open end which she held above the surface so that the wave did not flood the tube. As the water swelled past and sighed across the sand she lifted her thumb clear of the hole. Even her thumb was numb and stiff with cold. What must it be like for Razek, his body submerged, breathing through the hollow kelp stipe which she held?

Kodo tapped her on the shoulder. 'My turn,' he said. He crouched beside her, carefully taking hold of the tube so that she could stand. The water was above her knees. She turned and stared at the beach behind her. In the grey light she was sure that there was a dark smudge across the sand that the last wave had not reached. It left a trail of white foam as it retreated. The mark was close to the edge of the water.

'Sea-fall,' she whispered.

'And Elder still sleeps like a snoring boar in its den.' Laughter threaded through Kodo's voice.

He looked down at Razek and noticed what Maia had not. The tip of Razek's nose was just breaking the surface of the water. Soon Razek would be able to breathe without the tube. If he lived. He was as still as the dead. Kodo nudged Razek with his knee and saw the whites of Razek's eyes as they opened. He felt Razek's panic and the lift of his rib cage as his teeth gripped the end of the kelp stalk and he tried frantically to suck in air. He muttered an apology under his breath and fed the tube further into Razek's mouth.

Maia padded up the beach to where Elder curled like an ammonite, fast asleep. She twitched the edge of his cloak over his bearded face and knelt by the fire. A few puffs and a handful of dried seaweed, and blue and gold flames were soon licking around the crumbling pyramid of burned gorge twigs and blackened kelp. She sat and fed the fire until it blazed, then keeping high above the sea-rise litter she collected more driftwood and stacked it beside the fire. When he woke Elder would think she had spent the darkness tending the fire.

Maia felt as light and empty as she had after she had caught the sun in the Stone Court. She wondered if Razek's shoulders would show scorch marks where she had held him as he fought to chase the storm and hold back the waves. The clouds hadn't brought wind-streamers scudding across the deeps, driving the waves high across the weed beds and onto the shore, as they had feared

She pulled off her sopping tunic and trousers and wrung as much water as she could from them. The damp clothes felt almost warm against her goose-pimpled skin when she pulled them on again. Forcing her tired limbs to move, she broke into a shambling jog and ran up and down the beach to try and warm herself. When she had done it twice and was gasping for breath a thin finger of gold lined the rim of the horizon. Sun-wake.

The tips of the sun's rays touched the slumbering bulk of Doon, rimming her with gold. The lizard's eyes glowed green then amber as she watched Razek.

'You're safe,' Kodo was saying over and over again to Razek. 'It's sea-fall. Look at the sunrise. You're safe.'

Razek was shuddering.

'Shall we cut him free?' Kodo asked. 'He's freezing.'

'Elder may not believe that Razek survived the test if we do. Let me wake him first so he can see for himself.'

Doon was standing chest-deep in the sun-deeps. She looked over her shoulder at Kodo. Her red crest rose and slowly retracted. She lowered her head into the water and blew a cascade of bubbles towards Kodo. Maia heard a low rumble as the lizard raised her head. Doon was hungry. She grinned. Kodo would soon complain that he was too.

'She's right,' said Maia. 'You shouldn't be found here. Elder might not understand. And the Cliff Dwellers will wake soon.'

'And they hate lizards,' said Kodo. 'Yet you promised the lizards would help them repair the levees.' He remembered his anger. 'You had no right to do that.' Caspia wouldn't have done that. She understood about his lizards.

'No' agreed Maia.

'The lizards belong to Ootey. He's the Lizard Keeper.'

'I know. I was trying to save Razek.'

Kodo splashed over to Doon. She crouched low so that he could mount and started swimming strongly towards the dawn. Maia cupped her hands above her eyes. Kodo and his lizard were edged with light, dark silhouettes against the rose sky.

'You saved Razek.' Maia called after them. 'Without you he would have perished.'

There was no sign that Kodo had heard her. Maia turned

away. Razek, still shivering, was watching her, his eyes wide and dark.

'You're safe,' she echoed Kodo's words. 'You chased the storm and the sun-deeps were calm. You can stay in the weed beds.'

She splashed towards the beach. She must wake Elder. Then she would slip away, return to the Watcher's cairn, sleep and make ready to leave for her long trek. She had already delayed too long. Tareth needed the silk.

# THIRTY-SIX

Maia scrambled up the steep track, welcoming the heat of the sun as it fell on her back. Razek was safe. The Cliff Dwellers would wake soon and marvel that the sun-deeps had spared the Weed Master. There was no sign of Laya in her bright saffron tunic. Was she too afraid to discover Razek's fate?

She reached the cliff-top and hurried towards the bee-cleft to retrieve the hidden bundles of eggs and cocoons she had to take to Tareth. Exhaustion made her careless. She didn't hear the patter of paws, the excited panting of the hounds, until they burst into view. She was surrounded by baying, barking dogs. They circled her, almost forcing her from the narrow track with their eagerness. She tried to push through them. The part of her that could still think was amazed that they didn't attack her. As fast as she shoved one hound aside, another was in its place. It was as if they were corralling her.

Sunlight glinted on metal.

'Stand still or they'll tear you to pieces.'

Maia recognised the man in the gleaming mail cuirass. It was Helmek the Marsh Lord.

She lowered her voice. 'Call them off,' she said gruffly. 'They'll scare the flock.' She gestured behind her. Would he think she was a herder and control his hounds?

He was staring at her head. Then at her clothes. At her face and again her hair.

'Since when does a herder lead and not follow his flock?' he mocked. 'I know you,' he said. 'Where is the silk? It is near. I have heard it whisper.'

Maia turned to run. Helmek whistled. A hound launched himself and she was knocked to her knees. She lurched forward, desperately trying to reach the edge of the path, to hurl herself over and take her chances as she slalomed down the edge. She heard her tunic rip as it was seized in sharp jaws. And before she was buried beneath a pack of snapping dogs she was hauled to her feet. When she tried to kick, he buffeted her head. Her ears rang. She was manhandled past the press of hounds and along the track, her arms twisted painfully behind her back.

Helmek moved so fast she could barely stay upright. She tried digging her feet into the red dusty earth to slow their descent, and he pushed her from the track and sent them sliding down a tiny sheep track towards a tumble of rocks. The rocks concealed a low portal. And then she was in a hollow dark place that echoed with her breathing. A cave. She thought she could hear the song of the sun-deeps as they went deeper into the dark. The ground suddenly vanished beneath her feet and before she could scream and fall into nothingness she realised that she was being shoved down rough wooden steps. Light filtered from an opening. She glimpsed blue sky. The rough stairs twisted deeper, spiralling down. At every turn there was an opening and light splashing onto rough walls and uneven steps. The sound of the sun-deeps was louder. She could hear the call of gulls. She was in a tower built into the cliffs. She was in the Marsh Lord's new holdfast.

She fell off the last step and staggered across the uneven floor as he released her. There was no light. She could hear the slap of water. The rocks were wet. She slipped on weed as she spun to face him, raising her hands ready to spring. She was too slow. He caught her wrists and dragged her to the side of the round room and fastened her hands to a metal ring.

'What d'you want?' she demanded.

'Silk!'

'I'm a herder. Where would I find silk?' she bluffed.

'In a moth-garden.'

Shock nibbled at her bravado. How did he know that? Maia tugged at the ring.

'You will take me there,' Helmek said.

'I'm a herder, not a tender of moths.'

'You are called Flame Head. Your father was a weaver of silk.'

Maia was silent.

'The Sea Raiders killed your father. You disappeared. So did the Weed Master.' Helmek frowned at her. 'I hear he's returned. So have you. I know you even though you are dressed as a boy and have tried to darken your flames.' He smiled. 'You should stay far from water if you wish to conceal your red hair.'

'I am a herder,' Maia repeated even though she knew it was hopeless to make him believe that. As it was to expect him to accept that she was dark-haired like everyone else if the dye had washed from her hair, leaving her like a brindled cat.

'You are the girl from cliffs. The girl the cliff bees protect. The boy with you said his lizards had found the silk he carried. He told me that the silk had been trapped among rocks on the shore. I took the silk and lost it. I want the silk.'

Maia was glad that she hadn't been on her way from the moth-garden when his hounds had found her. The silk was safe in the bee-cleft. If Helmek ever discovered the moth-garden all he would find would be thorn bushes and a few dying moths.

Her silence angered him. 'I want the silk, girl.'

Maia shrugged. 'The silk is not yours.'

'You will tell me where to find it.'

'The lizards found it in the sun-deeps.'

Helmek's eyes narrowed. 'And if I go to the stilt village and search, will I find that the lizards have found more? Will I find the boy who rides the lizard? The old Lizard Keeper said that his grandson had been killed. Did he lie? Has he returned as you and the Weed Master have returned?'

'The silk is not yours,' repeated Maia stubbornly. 'And there was only a torn strand. The lizard boy had it. You said you took that and lost it. There is no more.'

She blanked out the thought of the Marsh Lord rampaging through the stilt village, looking for Kodo, questioning Ootey.

'There's no moth-garden,' she continued. 'I know nothing about silk. I was a Cliff Dweller. I was an outsider . . . they called me Flame Head. Now I am a herder.' She knew she sounded sullen. She hoped she looked sulky, not scared or defiant. 'I didn't want to live with people who called me Flame Head. Even though I dye my hair to look like them they don't like me. I am a herder now.'

He was looking at her thoughtfully. 'That is not what I was told.'

'When my father died I left the Cliff Dwellers,' said Maia. 'And the lizard boy died in the fighting that took my father. '

'And you have been roaming the cliffs, dressed as a boy, since?'

'Yes.'

'I think not. I've never seen you, nor your herds.'

'Why would a Marsh Lord notice me and my sheep?'

'So where are your sheep?'

'Scattered by your hounds. It will take me many sun-wakes to find them once you release me.' She tugged again at the ring. The metal chafed against her wrists. She wondered if she imagined that the ring moved more freely. 'Let me go, before my sheep are lost. And when I find them, I will bring one to you so that you can feast on baked meats.' She felt pangs of hunger at the thought. Helmek did not.

He twisted his silver thumb ring. 'I think I'd wait a long time before you and your sheep came to my holdfast, girl. And I'm not a patient man. You will tell me the way to the moth-garden. I will find the silk. How d'you think I knew where to find you after sun-wake, Flame Head? I was waiting for you because Laya, the Salt Holder's daughter, told me you had returned and what you were doing. When I bring her here you can tell her if the Weed Master survived after all. And then you can take us both to the hidden silk.'

He left her, shutting and barring the door behind him.

# Thirty-Seven

Var lifted his black rat from the basket of hazelnuts and tucked him in his tunic. He collected the empty shells and tossed them on the fire. Nefrar opened one eye as the shells flew past his nose and fell into the embers. Tiny puffs of white ash drifted across his fur. He grunted, got to his feet and padded out of the cairn.

'Any more of your thieving and we'll be thrown out,' said Var. 'If the cat doesn't eat you first!'

He followed Nefrar into the sunshine. The cat was slumped at the feet of the Watcher. She sat pounding seeds in a small stone quern. The cheetah's ear twitched to the beat of the fist-sized stone.

'She's not returned,' the Watcher announced without looking up from her task. 'And if that rat has been eating my store of hazelnuts then you can set him down here and I'll pound his head with this rock!'

Var felt Tiki twitch against his stomach and sent a silent warning for the rat to stay still.

The Watcher glared at him then threw down her pestle and pulled her bag of stones from her sleeve. Var glanced at the red-legged crows. Their feathers gleamed black, shot with iridescent blues and greens, the colours of the sweeping-tailed birds with golden eyes in their tails that he had seen in the lush foothills at the edge of the Hidden.

The rattling stones brought him out of his reverie. The Watcher had cast her runes.

She glared at Var as if it was his fault that they made no sense. 'Darkness. Water.'

It seemed to Var that there must be an easier way to discover the whereabouts of the girl whose eyes glowed amber when she was angry.

'The birds?' he suggested.

'Haven't seen her,' she snapped. 'She is nowhere. The earth has swallowed her.'

'Then she is hiding,' said Var. 'There are many caves.'

'Darkness. Water,' mused the Watcher. 'She may have returned to the Cliff Village. I warned her not to be seen. She may have gone there.' She cast the stones again, muttering to herself.

Var waited until she had stirred the stones and flipped them in disgust back in her bird-bag. 'Did she say where she was going?' he asked

'To the trader ship. But the birds have gone to where the ship rocks below the Marsh Lord's holdfast. He's ready to depart. She wasn't there.'

Var felt relief. Perhaps the girl didn't choose to cross the sun-deeps. If he was to take her to Azbarak after he had discovered the silk Caspia, the red witch's daughter, wanted, he would prefer to travel the overland trading routes. He wouldn't quickly forget the raging waves which had tossed him ashore and then tried to drag him back. The roar of the storm still sounded in his night-wakes.

'So if not the trader ship?'

'She has tasks of her own that she doesn't share with me,' snapped the Watcher.

Var didn't believe her. She was choosing not to tell him where the girl had gone. Yet now she was worried that she hadn't returned. If he wanted her to find her, she would have to tell him where to search. He waited patiently. An assassin learned to wait. He could outwait even this old, wise one.

He didn't have to. The birds rose, cawing harshly, and flew to the stunted thorn tree. The cheetah melted into the undergrowth. A girl ran towards them.

Var stared. She seemed angry, yet anxious and scared too. Her arms and face were scratched. Even so, she was beautiful. He saw the cat slip from the shadows and lope down the track the girl had come along. Var thought about following him in case the girl was being chased. His curiosity stopped him. It would be easier to fight with his back to the cairn, he thought. The Watcher had retrieved her rock and was pounding the grains in the quern. Var felt the muscles in his shoulders relax as the cheetah padded back to her side.

The girl's eyes widened with alarm when she saw the huge cat.

'What's that?' she gasped.

'Nefrar. A guest. He will not harm you.' The Watcher's tone suggested that the same was not true of herself. 'What brings you here, Laya? Do you bring the Marsh Lord?'

Laya shook her head. 'No. He was . . . at the cliff holdfast. He was to have gone to Cliff Village to speak with Elder. You knew the Weed Master Razek had returned?'

'I am the Watcher. I see who comes and goes. I have seen you and the Marsh Lord.'

Var watched the girl flush. 'My father wants us to be handfast,' she said.

'You didn't come to tell me that,' said the Watcher.

'I have seen Maia,' announced Laya.

The Watcher laid aside her pounding stone. 'And?'

'She didn't look like Flame Head. She was dark. Dressed like a boy. Dirty. But I knew her. It was Maia.'

'So she's returned,' murmured the Watcher. 'And you have seen her.'

She rose to her feet. One of her crows flew from the thorn tree and perched on her shoulder. Bird and crone stared at Laya.

'What have you done, Laya?'

'I wanted to save Razek. He would have drowned. Elder tied him on the stone. I told Helmek. I wanted to save Razek!'

The Watcher seemed to grow taller. She towered over Laya.

'What have you done?'

'Helmek has taken her into his cliff holdfast.' Laya noticed Var for the first time. She turned from the Watcher to him. 'I wanted her to go away. I wish she'd never come back. But I never wished to harm her. Razek will never forgive me. Helmek left the holdfast. Maia didn't. She may need help.'

# THIRTY-EIGHT

Kodo urged Doon beyond the stilt village. He ran his hand across her folded crest as the lizard tried to turn towards the shore. He wanted to see Trader, and found him perched on the prow of his ship watching a heron fishing in the river. Bird and man were equally still. Bron bellowed a greeting when he saw Doon and Kodo. The heron took off and flew with heavy wings towards the horse meadows. Doon drifted close to the boat so that Kodo could scramble alongside Bron. She swam up the estuary and dived beneath the water.

Bron studied the spreading circles of water which marked her disappearance.

'Will she return?'

'When she's fed,' Kodo said confidently. 'Will you sail soon?'

'We have replaced the mast. The caulking is done. We're ready to leave. Are you?'

Kodo was silent.

Bron slapped him on the shoulder. 'We'll come again for the Solstice Gather. I will need new crew then for another voyage to Haddra.'

Kodo swallowed and watched the aerobatics of a mob of crows flying along the estuary. They mobbed the stately heron, calling to each other as they circled the anchored ship and holdfast.

'That's good to know.' He'd promised Ootey he would find the new lizard scrape. He could keep his promise and still sail with Bron.

'And I'll have room for passengers too, should the Sun Catcher still be here and wish to return with us.' He glanced at Kodo. 'The Marsh Lord came. He seemed interested in our adventures. He may return, wishing to trade for our furs and timber. He has built a new holdfast.'

Kodo nodded. He'd seen the slender tower wedged in a crevasse in the cliffs. It looked like part of the rocks. Its footings rose from the sun-deeps. He had seen the metal basket of its beacon on the cliff-top.

'Did he ask about Maia?'

'I told him we never carry women. I didn't tell him about the boy who was swept into the deeps and rescued by a lizard. Nor his two companions.'

Kodo grinned at him.

'If you see the Catcher you could return her back-sack.'

'If I see her I could,' agreed Kodo cautiously.

Bron swung onto the deck. 'Then you had best take it and

come and eat. We'll go fishing and wait for your great lizard to return.'

It was going to be a good sun-high, thought Kodo as he followed Bron.

He didn't see Doon surface higher in the estuary and swim towards the sun-deeps.

'I will find this holdfast,' said Var. 'You will show me the way,' he told Laya.

He glanced at the old woman. 'I need my knives.'

The Watcher pulled aside handfuls of black cloth and retrieved a bundle, which she handed to Var. He unrolled it and found his knives. No wonder he had failed to find them when he'd searched the cairn. He should have searched the Watcher. He greeted his knives and slid them into their hidden sheaths, aware of the blue-eyed girl's stare. Her eyes grew wider as the great cat came and stood beside him.

Var fondled the cat's ears. 'I go alone.'

The cat blinked at him. The tip of his tail twitched. The Watcher bared her yellow, broken teeth in a hideous grin. 'Nefrar walks his own path.'

'I will return with the Catcher,' said Var. 'Come. Show me the path and then you are free to go where you will.'

Laya got to her feet. She thought about arguing. Of telling him that she too walked her own path. She glanced at his face and changed her mind.

They heard the sound of a horse approaching. Laya turned pale. 'Helmek. He can't find me here. He—!'

She got no further. Var grabbed her arm and hustled her into the scrub. Nefrar leapt ahead of them. The Watcher threw water on her fire; it bubbled and hissed on the hot bake-stone and steam billowed around the cairn. She knocked over the spit with its roasting laprans. The fire crackled and spat. Var heard her wailing and cursing as he bundled Laya deeper into the wind-stunted trees.

He heard her swear again. 'Control your hounds. Look what they've done.'

He felt the girl's arm quiver in his grasp and wondered if it was with fear or laughter, as he slid quiet as a shadow after the cheetah, dragging her with him.

The Watcher raked charred meat from the fire. She tossed it to the hounds. They fought among themselves, snarling and snapping to get at the food. Helmek's horse whirled and stamped as the dogs rolled under him.

Helmek bellowed and the hounds slunk away to chew scraps of lapran.

The Watcher kicked the scattered fire embers back onto the fire. She threw up her hands, her bangles jangling on her skinny wrists, and whistled. A crow spiralled down to perch on her fist.

'Sun's greetings, Lord Helmek,' she said.

Helmek smoothed the ears and mane of his restless horse. 'Watcher. I hear you've been sheltering strangers.'

He twitched aside the leather hanging and peered inside the cairn before dismounting and stepping inside. The place seemed empty. He circled the room, pulling baskets and jars from the niches in the walls, spilling their contents onto the floor and sweeping his hands across the empty shelves. He tossed the muddle of sleeping furs aside and searched beneath them and kicked over the baskets of stored berries and nuts, hunting through the spilled foodstuffs.

When he was satisfied that what he was looking for was not there he left the cairn. The Watcher still stood by her smoking fire, but now the crow was on her shoulder and her bag of stones murmured and chuckled in her hand as she shook it.

Helmek controlled a quiver of superstitious fear.

'It's not there!' he accused.

'If you tell me what you seek, I will tell you where it is.' She cast her runes across the ground. They scattered around Helmek's feet.

Helmek hesitated. 'The silk,' he said curtly.

The Watcher laughed. 'Silk! What would I do with such a thing? What use is silk to an old woman? I need furs and fire to keep away the cold of wolf-walk.'

'The girl had it. Flame Head. You had the girl. The silk is not here. She's hidden it. Where?'

Stooping, the Watcher appeared to study the stones. She smelled of wood smoke and the musty reek of a pigeon roost. The smell was strong. Helmek stepped back.

'The stones do not say.' She moved closer, following

the fall of stones, her fingers tracing the strange markings scratched on them. The crow flew from her shoulder and strutted among the stones. It picked up a black stone and tossed it aside. Then found the green stone and dropped it into the Watcher's hand. 'You will have to find the girl and ask her.'

He kicked the stones aside.'I will do just that, old woman.'

The Watcher hissed. 'Take care, Marsh Lord. It is not wise to anger the stones. Nor Sabra, the Watcher.'

Helmek swung away and remounted. He glowered at the Watcher. 'Nor is it wise to threaten me, old woman. Ask your stones what happens to those who anger the Marsh Lord.'

He urged his horse through the remains of her fire, scattering it across the ground. A red ember flew onto the hem of the Watcher's black robe.

She stood and watched as he rode off, his hounds behind him. Only when they had disappeared from sight did she rub out the smouldering ember burning her robe. Then she summoned her red-legged crows.

Maia spat on her wrists. The ring was still secured to the wall; tugging had not shifted it. Nor had placing her feet against the wall and jerking backwards using all the force left in her legs to pull the ring from its fixing. She had hoped that the water seeping down the walls would have created fissures around the ring that would open as she tugged. All that had happened was that her shoulders ached and her wrists were being rubbed raw. She spat on them again and tried to slide them from the metal ring.

It took ages. Her mouth was as dry as a lizard scrape and her wrists bruised and badly grazed, but she was free. She licked her sore wrists as she explored the room. There were no openings as there had been on the stairwell but the floor was wet and slippery. She was sure she could still hear the slap of the sun-deeps against rock. She felt the walls. They were damp and some of the rocks were slimed with weed. But the weed slime did not reach any higher than her waist. The chamber must flood that far. She would not drown here when sea-rise started. But she didn't intend to be there at sea-rise to discover if she was right. The door was barred but if the water came in she could get out. The entrance to the holdfast had been a cave. Perhaps the way out was a sea-cave too.

She almost fell into the hole on her second circuit of the chamber when her foot plunged into deep water. Squatting, she felt the edges of the opening. It was big enough for her to slide into. She reached down as far as she could but felt nothing but water. The water moved, slapping against her arm with the rhythm of waves. The way led to the sun-deeps.

Maia sat cross-legged at the edge of the well of water. Dare she risk plunging into the deeps? She took a ragged breath, tried to still the thump of her heart and explored her fear. She had always been afraid of the sun-deeps. She had nearly drowned as a baby. She had been pulled to safety by Razek. She'd been swept from the trader ship when she had tried to reach Nefrar. Kodo had leapt after her and saved her when he had dragged her onto Doon. She'd waited throughout sun-sleep chest-deep in the water, willing the sea-rise not to cover Razek, losing all feeling in her limbs until she had felt as if she was part of the rising water. She shivered. She was still afraid of water, but perhaps not quite as much.

She stretched her arms above her head, rolled forward, curled tight like a hatchling in its egg and plunged into the dark water.

# THIRTY-NINE

Laya had never felt so dishevelled. Or hot. Or cross. Her discomfort was almost greater than her shame. Only the knowledge of what she had done made her put up with it. But she didn't like it. And she didn't like this stranger, even if he was as handsome as Razek. He hadn't spoken to her since he had hustled her away from the Watcher's cairn. And if she was glad that Helmek had not seen her with the Watcher, there was no need for him to ignore her or to expect her to keep up with his breakneck pace across the cliff-tops. Not that he seemed to find it fast. He moved like the terrifying spotted cat that raced ahead of them. They seemed to float over the rough ground. She stumbled, stubbed her toe and twisted her ankle. She screamed and yanked at the hand holding her arm.

'Stop!' she gasped. 'Please. Stop.'

At least he could hear even if he didn't speak. Laya sank into a heap as soon as he let go of her arm. Wincing, she pulled up her skirt, and tugged off her thin leather shoes which were scuffed and ruined. And not made to scamper over rough tracks, she thought angrily.

'I can't run any more,' she said.

The spotted cat returned to Var's side. Laya shifted uncomfortably under the combined stares of the cat and the boy who handled his knives as if they were friends. She shook a small stone from her shoe and pulled it on again.

'I can't,' she said. She pointed along the track ahead of them. 'Follow the top of the cliff.' She got to her feet and hobbled to the edge of the cliff and dropped to her knees so that she could lean out and see the curve of the coastline. She could see the saltpans and suddenly longed to be safe at home with her father. She pointed to the closest headland. 'There. On the other side is the holdfast. It's built into a cleft in the cliff. You'll see a pile of rocks. Leave the track. The ground slopes. It's steep. You'll find a cave. It's the way into the holdfast. Into the tower in the cliff.'

Var nodded. He and the cheetah would go much faster without the girl.

Maia kicked up towards the light filtering through the depths. Her lungs felt as if they were bursting. Bubbles streamed from her nose. She shot gasping into the sunlight, was hit by a wave rolling towards the base of the cliff, and sank again. She heard warbling as she surfaced. She drew her knees into her chest and found she could float, her head just above the water. She rose with a wave and was carried towards the rocks below the cliffs. The wave smacked against them, sending spray shooting into the air. She would be smashed against the base of the cliffs too.

Using her hands like paddles she tried to scull across the swell of water rolling towards the shore. She bobbed like the pods on bladderwrack, turning in a circle but still being swept ashore. At least the sun-deeps were holding her afloat. She crested another wave and could see green sunning lizards on rocks and a small strip of sand. She heard the warbling noise again. It was the lizards. Lots of lizards. Wild ones, not Kodo and Ootey's lizards. She slid down the side of the wave.

Then she was among them. They nudged her, swam under her, surfacing too close, mobbing her. She sank and swallowed water. Panicking, she flailed her arms and legs and grabbed. She was dragged forward. The lizards swam round her, warbling.

She let go and sank again. The lizard dived with her, rolled over, lashed her with its tail. As she sank deeper a second lizard appeared, its body so close she could have touched it. It too flicked its tail. In desperation Maia grabbed at it and was towed deeper and deeper. The lizard swam through tall stands of waving kelp. Maia felt her grip loosening. Darkness flooded through her. The water roared in her ears. A jet of bubbles surrounded her. She was being dragged upwards.

Clinging to the lizard, Maia shot to the surface. A second lizard appeared beside her and flicked her with its tail.

Gasping, she reached out and grabbed it too. Towed behind the two lizards she was tugged towards the cliffs. Ahead she could see the other lizards swimming for the shore and surfing onto the rocks. The wave rolling beside her broke as a huge lizard surfaced. Red crest raised, it bugled. The sound bounced off the cliffs. The noise sent the lizards basking on the rocks tumbling back into the sun-deeps. The two lizards dragging her behind them warbled and swam on towards the shore.

Maia felt sand and stones grate against her. She opened her hands, releasing the lizards, and sank onto her hands and knees. A wave knocked her forward. Gasping for air she crawled out of the water and collapsed onto the sand. Safe. She rolled over and sat up.

Saved by lizards. She coughed and spat out a mouthful of salt water. A bubble of laughter that was half-hysteria, half-gratitude almost choked her. She fell back onto the sand and lay in the sunshine.

A shadow blotted out the sun. A rough tongue rasped her face. She was going to lose all of her skin. Maia opened her eyes. Nefrar bit her chin.

Maia sat up and hugged him. 'Nefrar. How did you know?'

'The Watcher sent us to find you.'

The shadow was not Nefrar. A tall, dark figure stood between her and the sun. Maia squinted up at it.

'Boy from the storm?' she asked.

The shadow moved as he crouched beside her. 'We searched the holdfast. You were not there. We heard the lizard call.'

'It was Doon. Kodo's lizard.' She looked around. 'Is Kodo here?'

'We are alone. The lizard has gone.'

She stared at him and saw a black rat sitting on his shoulder and the hilt of a shoulder knife just showing above the edge of his tunic. The hilt was black too. A memory tugged at her. She reached out and tugged Nefrar's ear while she tried to track the elusive image.

'The Watcher sent you?'

'A horseman with hounds came to the cairn. She thought you were in danger.'

Maia stared at the knife hilt. The rat ran along Var's shoulder, down his arm and onto the sand. Was that another knife snug in a sheath strapped to his wrist? There was another knife in his belt. Maia remembered that the Marsh Lord had taken her belt knife. She flexed her shoulders. She could still feel the wet leather of her shoulder sheath. Good. The Marsh Lord had not known that, like this boy, she also carried a hidden blade.

'I was,' said Maia. She looked at him. 'Am I still?'

'The horseman may return. You shouldn't stay here.'

Maia rubbed her cheek. A flick of her fingers and the knife would be in her hand. The black rat was nibbling the edge of her shoe. Maia watched it for a moment. Black rats. Many knives. A boy from the storm who had called her Caspia. Who was he?

'Are you a friend or my enemy?' she asked.

Var's eyes widened. 'I am Var,' he said. 'The Watcher sent me to find you.' He looked at the cat, sitting beside Maia.

He picked up the black rat and tucked him in his tunic. 'And I wish you'd tell your cat that Tiki is not his next meal.'

He held out his hand. Maia let him pull her to her feet. She felt wobbly. But she had survived the sun-deeps. She realised that she was no longer terrified of the water. And she had swum with lizards. Wait 'til she told Kodo. Putting her hand on Nefrar's shoulder she walked unsteadily beside him as she followed Var and his rat to the precipitous path that zigzagged up the cliff.

# FORTY

Kodo knew he was going to have a long walk. Doon had not returned from feeding. His bad mood settled like a cloud around his shoulders as he thought about Trader Bron sailing without him. He wished he hadn't promised Ootey that he would stay and help him find the new lizard scrape and guard the eggs. If storms hadn't scoured out the coves, washing away sand, making new beaches further along the coast, then Doon's favourite scrape would still be there and she wouldn't keep escaping from the lizard pound to find a new laying site. If Razek hadn't chased Maia all the way to the Sun City maybe fewer storms would have battered the cliffs and the stilt village. If he really was a Storm Chaser he should have stayed in the weed beds and kept the storms at bay.

He continued listing his grievances against the Weed

Master and the lizards until the sound of wind-flutes as a flock of pigeons flew overhead distracted him. One of the birds left the flock and fluttered to the ground close to him. He could see the small red wooden flutes attached to its tail feathers. Kodo fumbled in his belt-bag, tearing the end from the flatbread Bron had given him for the walk home. He shredded it and, kneeling, scattered the crumbs in the grass. The pigeon pecked greedily. Kodo reached out his hand to grab it.

'That's not for eating, lizard boy!'

Startled, Kodo almost fell over as the Watcher appeared. She scooped up the pigeon and cast it into the air. Flutes singing, it flew off to join the flock.

'I wasn't going to eat it,'said Kodo.

'Is Trader ready to depart?' she snapped, ignoring his protest.

Kodo nodded.

'Has the Marsh Lord been here? Or to the stilt village?'

Kodo suppressed a shiver. He didn't want to meet the Marsh Lord. 'No. Why would he go to the stilt village?' he asked anxiously.

'Why does he do anything?' said the Watcher. 'Why did he search and wreck my cairn?'

Kodo felt a frisson of fear. 'Why?'

'You know why, boy. You know what he seeks.'

Kodo shook his head. Somehow he was the focus of her anger. He couldn't think what he had done to upset her. He and Doon had saved Maia. They had also helped Razek. So why was she skewering him with her sharp black glare?

'He's searching for silk, lizard boy. How does he know about the Weaver's silk? He knows because you showed it to him.'

Kodo stared at her. How did she know about the silk? And how did she know that the Marsh Lord had taken a strip of silk from him at the Gather? Only Maia knew that he'd stolen silk from the moth-garden. And Tareth. He had confessed his crime to the weaver.

'But you . . . .. cannot . . . know.'

'I am the Watcher. D'you think anything can happen without me seeing? I saw the Weaver Tareth make his moth-garden. I watched him tend the moths. It was his secret. I told no one. I watched the Sun Catcher learn to climb like a rock squirrel to visit the moth-garden, to collect silk. No one knew where she went. But you, boy, you followed her and you gave the Marsh Lord silk and now he wants more.'

'I didn't,' protested Kodo. 'He took it from me.'

'Silk that you'd stolen!' accused the Watcher.

'And was stolen from him,' insisted Kodo. 'The juggler took it from him. He had no silk. He didn't keep the silk.'

'He kept the dreams the silk promised him,' said the Watcher. 'As you have. And he wants those dreams. He wants the silk. He's been searching ever since. He has built a new holdfast to keep him close to the weed beds. He wants Maia to show him the way to the moth-garden.'

Kodo felt as if fingers had clutched his heart and squeezed. 'Maia. Where's Maia?'

'In his cliff holdfast. Betrayed by one she thought a friend.'

'No! I told no one that she was here!'

'Perhaps you didn't. But Razek did.'

The relief that he had not betrayed Maia was instantly swamped by fury. 'Razek! Razek!'

He would kill the Weed Master. Would send the lizards to tear him apart. How could Razek betray Maia? He loved her! She was his friend.

'And the Marsh Lord has found her,' said the Watcher.

'I must find her!'

He moved to push past her. She threw up her hand and he felt as if he had hit a rock face, even though she did not touch him.

'I have sent another to find her, lizard boy. One who will not fail. He'll take her to safety across the Vast. Take her home to Khandar.' She glanced at the sun. 'They will be on their way already.'

Kodo stared at her. 'What? Who? Where is Maia? I must find her.'

'Another protects her. One who followed from the Sun City.'

'Followed?' Kodo's hand clenched. He knew Maia was in danger. 'We had to leave the Sun City in secret. We left in darkness.' His voice rose. 'Who followed?'

The Watcher shook her head. 'One was sent to follow and protect her,' she said.

'Did Maia tell you that someone tried to kill her after she caught the sun? That someone made their way into the Sun Palace? We left in secret. Nobody followed to protect her. Where is she?'

For a heartbeat the Watcher seemed as shaken as he felt. She reached inside her sleeve. He heard the soft rattle of her stones. The sound seemed to reassure her. 'Safe. He has her safe.'

'I must find her.'

The Watcher shook her head. 'Not yet. You have something still to do here. I will take you into the Vast to meet her, but first . . .'

The Vast! He wasn't going across the Vast. 'I'll find her before she reaches that . . . place,' he said. 'She can leave with Trader. The sun-deeps are safer than the Vast.'

The Watcher shook her head. 'The Marsh Lord must think she has gone with the Trader. I will make sure he does. The Salt Holder's daughter will see Maia leave on his ship and she will tell the Marsh Lord. She will make amends for her betrayal. And Trader will do as I ask. If the Marsh Lord should follow the ship and find them as they trade he will have a tale of storms and drowning to tell.'

Kodo nodded. Bron would do that for Maia. But what could he do? He must find her. He didn't trust the Watcher's stones. Who was the stranger who had followed and now took Maia away?

'I will find her,' he repeated.

'We will . . . together,' said the Watcher. 'The cat is with her. She will be safe. But she needs the silk. She came to get the silk. She must take it with her. You must collect the silk.'

'The silk? But . . .' Kodo knew he had imagined the whisper which sang in his blood. Remembered that Caspia had asked him to find silk.

'She went to the moth-garden. She took the silk.'

'Then where is it?' Kodo felt a lurch of alarm. 'Has the Marsh Lord taken it from her?'

'No. He searches still. The Catcher has hidden the silk.'

Kodo looked bewildered. 'Then how am I to take it?'

'You will know where it is.'

He'd always known that the old woman was mad.

The silk will let you find it, lizard boy. Just as it let you steal it from the moth-garden. The silk has a purpose for you.' Her voice was bleak; her eyes stared past him. Kodo glanced over his shoulder. There was nothing there. Yet still she gazed into the distance. Kodo felt the hairs on the back of his neck prickle. He was glad he couldn't see what she saw.

'You will find the silk and take it to the Catcher. She can't leave without it. I will go to Trader and tell him what he must do.'

Kodo caught himself wishing that he could witness that meeting.

'I will visit the Lizard Keeper and see that he understands why you must leave.'

Kodo was glad he wouldn't be there.

'Jakarta . . .'

'She will miss you. But she'll think you too have gone with the Trader.'

'It will be true. When this is over I'll be a trader again.'

The Watcher nodded. 'It is a good dream,' she agreed.

Kodo was about to tell her that it was more than a dream but she swept his words aside.

'The Salt Holder's daughter will tell her tale to the Marsh Lord . . . and the Weed Master.' She glanced at the sun. 'Go. Find the silk. By sun-wake we must all be gone. When the Marsh Lord discovers that the Catcher has slipped from his net he will be angry.'

She grinned at Kodo.

Even the lizards' teeth were whiter than hers, thought Kodo.

'He'll search,' the Watcher said, 'but he will not find. Nor must he. The silk is not for him. Go, lizard boy. Do not fail. Find the silk. Go!'

# FORTY-ONE

Maia smelled the smoke before she saw it.

She could hear Var scrambling behind her. The tip of Nefrar's tail disappeared. Six breaths later she joined him on the cliff-top and flopped down beside the cat. Then the top of Var's dark head appeared.

She felt as if she was in an eagle's eyrie. She could see right along the coastline. Even the distant smudge of the Marsh Lord's holdfast at the edge of the horse meadows was just visible. She saw the smoke she had smelled. There was a fire on the cliffs.

She was on her feet running before she was even conscious she wanted to move. It wasn't the cliffs that were on fire. It was the moth-garden.

Suddenly Var was alongside her. He pulled her to a halt.

'We must leave here.'

She tugged her arm free. 'The moth-garden.' She started running. 'It's burning. I have to put out the fire. The gorse will catch light. The flames will spread.'

She was jerked to a halt again.

'Others will come. We should leave.'

Maia felt the slow burn of anger. She glared down at the brown fingers biting into her arm. 'Let me go!'

His calm, gold eyes met her angry ones.

'What is there in the garden?' he asked.

Maia had been about to tear herself free.

'Moon-moths,' she said.

Even as she spoke she knew that was no longer true. The moths had flown from the garden as she had collected the old silk and cocoons.

'Thorn bushes. The Marsh Lord must have set fire to them.'

She realised how silly that sounded. What did it matter if the thorn bushes burned? She had stripped the stands of silk from them. The moths would not lay their eggs there now.

'Thorns?' Var sounded puzzled.

Tareth had made the garden. She couldn't let it burn.

'The Watcher said you must leave.'

'I can't. I have to collect . . .' She hesitated. Could she trust him? The Watcher had sent him. She and her stones must trust him. Nefrar liked him. She was not so sure, although the cat had never been wrong. But, Var had called her 'Caspia' as he woke from drowning. He knew Caspia. Did that make him friend or enemy? Was Caspia a threat, just like her mother, Elin? She wished her torn silk would whisper. Tell her who to trust. But the silk was silent.

'There's something I must take with me.'

Var nodded. 'The Watcher said she would have what you need.'

Maia stared at him. 'What did she say I needed?'

Var frowned at his feet as if trying to recall the exact words the Watcher had used.

'She said she would bring what the Weaver had sent you to find. What the Weaver had shown her many star-shifts ago. That she had watched it for him when he went away,' reported Var. 'That she would know how to find what you have hidden,' he finished. 'Now we should go.'

He hoped she wasn't going to argue. He wasn't used to having to explain himself. To talk. Silence was easier.

'Come.'

Nefrar nudged the back of Maia's knees and set off along the track.

Maia glanced again at the smoke. She couldn't see any flames. Perhaps the fire would not spread to the gorse. She heard the conch call. Someone else had seen the smoke.

'Come on, then,' she said and ran after Nefrar, leaving Var staring after her.

Kodo saw the smoke drifting over the gorse. Someone had set fire to the moth-garden. The silk would be burned. He saw two figures running away in the distance. He started to scramble down the cliff. In his haste he slipped and tumbled into a gorse bush. An angry swarm of bees flew from the bush.

Kodo yelled and brushed the stingers from his hair and arms. Buzzing, they flew at him, a dark, angry cloud above his head. He ducked and darted back up the track. Tripped over a root, fell, the breath exploding from his lungs as he steeled himself for the stabbing hurt of bee stings.

Bees crawled from his hair. Others landed on his hands. He shut his eyes as one crawled along his nose. It tickled. It didn't sting. As suddenly as it had erupted from the gorse the swarm, led by a huge queen bee, flew towards a tree clinging to the rock face. The dark mass settled and hung like a monstrous swollen fruit bat in the lowest branch.

Kodo heard the conch call. Someone had seen the smoke. He got to his feet. Far below he could see the Cliff Dwellers running like ants across the beach. He turned to scan the cliffs. Something had disturbed the gulls. He was almost certain he saw a golden shape on the cliff-top. It was a cat. A very large cat. Nefrar. And Maia would be with him.

She must have started the fire in the moth-garden. She had hidden the silk and set fire to the garden so that Helmek the Marsh Lord wouldn't find either the silk or the moon-moths. He was too late to catch her. Even if he followed, he might not find her. And he had to meet the Watcher. And find the hidden silk. The Watcher trusted him. She had said he'd know where Maia would have hidden it before the Marsh Lord had found her. How was he supposed to know?

A bee landed beside him. Kodo watched it explore and feed on the nectar in the yellow gorse flower. It settled on his hand. And he knew where Maia had put the silk.

'Thank you,' he said to the bee and blew it from his hand. Then set off towards the honey cave.

Laya thought that Razek looked pale. Selora looked radiant. And the cave was tidy. A fire burned on the fire-stone and a pile of flatbreads oozing dark sticky blueberry juice was keeping warm on the edge of the stone. Selora flipped one onto a wide leaf and passed it to Laya. She wondered how she was going to bite into it without all that juice spurting over her tunic. Then she didn't care. They smelled too good, and blueberry flatbreads cooked by Selora were her favourite. She broke off a corner, blew on it and tucked it neatly in her mouth. It was as good as she remembered.

'I'm glad to see you, Razek,' she said.

'I'm glad to see you here, Laya,' he replied formally.

He took the beaker of chay his mother handed him and watched her over the rim as he drank.

'Elder is pleased with the judgement of the sun-deeps. So is Father. So am I,' Laya finished in a rush and bit into the flatbread. Juice spurted down her chin. She mopped it up with her hand and licked her stained palm clean.

Razek pushed aside the sleeping furs his mother had insisted on placing over his legs. He stretched his toes towards the flames. 'So am I,' he said.

'No one wanted you to drown,' said Selora brightly.

Silence fell. Laya finished her flatbread and refused another.

'I went to the horse marshes to see if Trader had amber amulets.'

She fingered her blue beads and wondered if Razek remembered bartering for them at another Gather.

'He's a fine trader,' said Selora.

'I saw the trader ship leave. He took others with him,' said Laya quickly. 'A boy and a huge spotted cat.' She glanced at Razek and then away again. 'I've never seen a cat like it. It was the colour of sand.'

Razek's fingers tightened around the beaker of chay. His knuckles gleamed white.

'A boy? Just one boy and a cat?' he asked.

'Two boys,' said Laya.

Razek set the beaker down carefully. His hand trembled. 'And the ship sailed?'

Laya nodded. 'Sea-fall carried it swiftly downriver and into the sun-deeps.'

'I would not like to cross the sun-deeps,' said Selora.

Razek stared into the flames and was silent.

Laya fidgeted, pleating the fabric of her tunic, smoothing out the creases she had just made. She watched Razek from under her lashes. She hoped Razek would never discover her lie. Nor Helmek. Laya suppressed a shudder. It was not such a huge lie. Maia was leaving. The Watcher had promised. And insisted she bamboozle the Marsh Lord and Razek too.

'I must go to the stilt village,' said Razek suddenly. 'We will need the lizards to help repair the levees. I must see the Lizard Keeper.'

He rose to his feet.

Selora started to protest.

Razek ignored her. 'I must see the Watcher too.'

'You aren't strong enough. You should rest,' worried Selora. 'I will fetch the Watcher. She will come if I ask.'

She hurried from the cave.

'The Watcher, coming here?' asked Laya. She didn't want to see the Watcher ever again. She wished she hadn't confessed what she'd done to the old woman and then been told what she had to do to make matters right. Told to say she'd seen two boys and a cat leave on the ship. She hadn't even seen the trader ship leave.

Razek sighed. 'She'll have seen Trader leave. She sees everything. She was watching in the storm when we arrived. She named me Storm Chaser.'

'A good name.'

'I asked her how a Weed Master could chase storms.' He frowned at the flames.

'Storm Chaser,' repeated Laya. It made her see him differently. 'It's a good name. Is that why you left the weed beds? To chase storms?'

'I am the Weed Master. Can I protect the weed beds and be a Storm Chaser?'

# FORTY-TWO

The silk whispered. The silk was angry.

It was angry with what Maia had done. Kodo could see the smouldering ember of scorched silk, the flicker of flame as the cliff breeze blew it to life. Could feel wings brushing across his face. He could dream . . .

Kodo dropped the bundle. The images vanished. He must be careful. But the silk wanted him to dream. It had stories to tell him. Just as Caspia had promised him. He closed his eyes. It was good to dream with the silk, to listen to its song. Caspia had said that the silk would sing to him. But, all he could hear was the buzz of bees, the shriek of a buzzard, the sound of gulls. Caspia and her tiny jewelled lizards would show him its secrets when he found silk for her. Caspia wanted silk. So did Maia. So did he. The buzzard called again. Reluctantly Kodo opened his eyes. He knew he must go. Knew what he must do.

He tugged at the strand of silk he had loosed from the bundle. It came free. He tucked the silk in his belt sheath and carefully eased the knife back into place. He found a large leaf and pulled up stands of tall grass and quickly rewrapped and secured the bundle. He pushed it with the others inside the back-sack the Watcher had thrust into his hands.

Kodo settled the back-sack over his shoulder. The Watcher had told him to find the hidden silk. She would be waiting for him. She would be angry with him if he did not hurry.

Var touched Maia lightly under her ear. She woke.

'Someone comes.'

Var put his finger to his lips and vanished into the darkness. Maia slipped her knife from its shoulder holster. She was clumsy and dropped it. The blade chinked against the stone. She held her breath. Sun-sleep was quiet and still. What had Var heard? Had the Marsh Lord followed her? She felt for her fallen knife and and smelled spice and stone dust and pigeon.

'Greetings, Watcher,' she whispered.

The Watcher laughed softly as she sat. 'Has the lizard boy come? Did he find the silk?'

Kodo? Was he coming across the Vast with them?

'The silk?' Maia asked.

'I sent him to find it.'

Maia was dismayed. How could Kodo find the hidden silk? He would go to the moth-garden, expecting it to be there. He would be found by the Marsh Lord who would be searching the cliffs or returning to the holdfast. She had to find Kodo. She had to find the silk. She rose to her feet.

'He comes,' said Var. 'Sun-wake brings him.'

Maia could see the thin bright band that heralded the rise of the sun. Their journey would begin in the dark but before they had left the sun-deeps behind them it would be light. She slipped her knife into its shoulder sheath and walked away from the others to wait for Kodo.

The Watcher grumbled to herself. Twitching her long black robes around her and filling the dawn with the dusty smell of spice, she turned to Var.

'So it begins,' she said. 'I will take you into the Vast.'

Var nodded. 'We must make for the Hidden. The way is hard but the journey is shorter. The Sun Catcher must go quickly.' Azbarak was waiting. And the red witch's daughter, Caspia. And if the Watcher was right, the boy had the silk.

Kodo slowed to a halt. He was out of breath.

'Did you find it?' Maia greeted him.

'Only stingers could guard it so well,' he replied.

'I could have left it with the lizards.'

Kodo shook his head. 'You hate the sun-deeps.'

She smiled at him. 'Not as much as I did. I have swum through a kelp forest clinging to wild lizards. And stood with a friend in the darkness and felt the flood of sea-rise.'

She held out her hand. 'Did you bring honeycomb?'

Kodo shrugged the bag from his shoulders. 'Just silk.'

Reluctantly he passed her the bag.

Maia slipped her hand inside the back-sack, counting the bundles. Kodo held his breath. His hand dropped to his knife. The hilt felt warm. Was that because it touched the silk he had hidden? He almost confessed but his need was strong.

Maia drew the drawstring tight and smiled at him.

'The others are waiting.'

'Others?'

'Nefrar. Watcher and Var.'

Not Razek. So the Storm Chaser was staying in the weed beds. Good.

'Watcher and . . . Var?' he asked.

Maia nodded. 'He will guide us across the Vast.'

Kodo felt the hairs on the back of his neck prickle as the silk whispered beneath his knife. The silk was uneasy. It didn't trust the stranger. Nor would he.

'Shall we go . . . home?' said Maia.

She tasted the word on her tongue. She had never wanted her home to be the Sun Palace where Tareth waited for her return. She had felt an outsider there, just as she had in the Cliff Village. But home was anywhere that Tareth was. Tareth and his eagle KiKya.

Kodo thought of Bron and the Trader ship making its way to the port of Haddra. He would meet it there. 'Home,' he agreed.

Maia watched him join the others. She faced the golden band of light gilding the edge of the world. If she waited long enough she could watch it cross the sun-deeps to the weed beds to where she knew Razek would greet another sun-wake and be glad that he was home too. He would chase the storms and keep the weed beds safe. If he was wise he would remember what she had said and ask Ootey the Lizard Keeper to help repair the storm-torn levees.

She raised her hand to the spreading light and flicked her fingers towards the Cliff Village, which still slept.

'The sun's greetings, the wind's blessing and the earth's song be yours, Storm Chaser.'

Like the rocks guarding the weed bed, Razek was part of her has-been. Her shadow and protector in the Sun City. She would miss him, she realised with surprise. The Storm Chaser was a good friend.

She wondered what had happened while she had been away from the Sun City. What of Elin and Caspia?

Maia's heart sank as she remembered Elin's threat to destroy Altara. Perhaps the Warrior Women had returned to their holdfast leaving Tareth alone in the palace. She remembered how weary he had looked when she had left. It was as if his strength depended on the silk. He needed her. He needed silk.

She must leave. She pulled her back-sack over her shoulders. She had kept her promise. She was taking silk, cocoons and moth-eggs to Khandar. Tareth could make a new moth-garden. He could weave silk so that new songs could be heard. Could heal his eagle and himself. All would be well. But . . . Maia nibbled her lip. She knew that finding and bringing the silk to the palace was not enough. Just as flying Kikya wouldn't be enough for Tareth.

Blinded by her desire to fly an eagle she had ignored Tareth and harmed Kikya. She had been afraid to listen. Unwilling to discover that catching the sun was not all that she must do.

'I'm sorry,' she whispered. 'I understand now.'

As Sun Catcher she had promised to protect Khandar. Silk

protected too. She must find a Story Singer to sing its stories again. If Elin and Xania's stolen silk coat had reached Urteth then she would go to the Tower of Eagles to challenge her sister again. She knew she had to find the story coat before the next sun-catch.

Maia slipped her hand inside her back-sack and touched the bundle there. The silk would know. If she listened, perhaps it would whisper to her.

The silk was silent. She tightened the drawstrings again. She mustn't lose the last of the precious cocoons and eggs from the moth-garden.

She looked at her friends. Should she ask them to brave the perils of the way across the Vast and the Hidden?

Her thoughts must have shown.

'You can't leave without us, we'd just follow you,' said Kodo.

'The crows and I follow you, Catcher,' said the Watcher. 'We will cross the Vast together.'

Kodo nodded. 'To the mountains and Khandar. Trader Bron will be waiting.'

'To the Hidden and the Sun City,' said Var. To Caspia, the red witch's daughter.

'To Tareth,' added Kodo. 'And Zena.' The silk beneath his knife shivered.

Maia hesitated. 'There may be danger.'

Var shrugged. 'We are ready.' He lifted Tiki from the grass at his feet and tucked the rat inside his tunic.

Nefrar butted Maia's thigh, encouraging her to move.

Maia smiled at them.

'Come then,' she said and set off towards the rising sun.

# BRONZE AGE INFLUENCES

*Sun Catcher* is a magical reality story set in an imagined Bronze Age. It's a fascinating time. A time of change.

The Bronze Age happened at different times in many parts of the world so it's possible to 'borrow' ideas from many cultures: artifacts, ideas, customs, buildings. I've done this in *Sun Catcher*.

Thanks to archaeologists we know quite a lot about this period but wonderful new discoveries are being made all of the time. It's really exciting that the ingenuity and skills of Bronze Age people are continuing to intrigue and surprise us. I think that people who lived thousands of years ago were just like us, curious, innovative, people who were engineers, artists, explorers, astrologers, herbalists, even scientists. They managed without computers and the internet and steam, electric or oil powered engines. But, like us they were busy shaping and changing their world. They told stories, exchanged ideas and passed their knowledge down through the generations.

Since our ancestors were very practical and intelligent and understood the world they lived in, I think that many of the imaginary things from *Sun Catcher* would be feasible in the Bronze Age and perhaps one day we'll even discover that this was so . . .

# NAMES

I often found when I was writing the story that things I thought I had imagined and made up actually had some basis in reality. This was especially true when I was naming things, trying to make them sound as if they were from a distant past. Some historians think that there were no kings and powerful leaders in Bronze Age society, but I wanted a powerful warrior figure who could protect the land from Sea Raiders. I imagined the Marsh Lords and they needed a stronghold. I thought I would have to invent a neat word to describe it. I liked the word hold. I eventually decided that holdfast was a good name as Helmek the Marsh Lord holds tight or fast onto his land and his power. This seemed the perfect made-up name. But holdfast is not actually my invented term. After I'd written the story I discovered it is the name of the root that attaches seaweed to rocks. So I wasn't nearly as clever as I thought I had been. What is amazing is that the word holdfast fits so well because of course seaweed is important to Maia's adopted tribe.

# TRADING

We know that Bronze Age people travelled great distances using both overland and sea routes and when I was writing *Sun Catcher* my daughter was sailing round the world in a race on a yacht not much bigger than a Bronze Age boat. This gave me the idea for Kodo's dreams and adventures. He joins Bron, a sea faring Bronze Age trader. Bron's imagined ship with its painted figure-head is probably more seaworthy and bigger than Bronze Age boats although they did have large ships and they did sail along extensive trading routes. So this is the true bit about Kodo's dream. However, this is not a history book and so Kodo . . .

'. . . *heard the creak of wood on wood. The voices rose and fell. Suddenly his world was full of the crash of oars, the chant of rowers, the cry of their Oar Master. Above him, a dragon with green eyes and gaping jaws emerged from the mist to swallow him . . . Kodo made out figures pulling at ropes, lowering the limp russet brown sail as the boat disappeared, leaving a spreading wake and a falling song.'*

Yes, they did sew the planks together to build boats. Yes, they did have oars, sweep oars for steering and sails. I don't know if they had painted figureheads or if they sang as they rowed or had an Oar Master to keep them rowing in unison. But why not? They did carry cargo and people. We know this because wrecks have been discovered and because many things, pottery, weapons and jewels have been found a long way from the place where they were made. Precious things were traded too. In the Bronze Age the blue beads Laya covets at the Gather would probably have come from Egypt or perhaps the beads were lapis lazuli, a wonderful blue stone which would have been mined in Afghanistan.

People or tribes who lived in areas with rich mineral deposits became wealthy. So if you had access to copper, tin, gold, silver, salt, rare wood, ivory or lapis lazuli gem stones, people would want to trade with you and you could become rich and powerful in the Bronze Age. So in *Sun Catcher*, the Salt Holder is the richest man living near the cliff dwellers.

# TIME

Time is something you have to think about in a story like *Sun Catcher* which doesn't happen in one day or in one place. There were no mechanical clocks in the Bronze Age. Well, none have been found. They would have measured time using what they could see; the sun, phases of the moon, maybe the shift of star constellations, tides, changes in plants and animal and bird migrations. Some civilizations did invent calendars. Seasons, Solstice and equinoxes were important, special times for people in ancient societies. Meeting for festivals and trade at special places at certain times of the year certainly happened. So Maia goes to a Gather close by the holdfast and horse meadows and sees people from many different places.

To have a sun-catching ceremony at Solstice fits with the importance of the sun and the seasons of the year for people dependent on farming. The successful planting and harvesting of crops could mean the difference between life and death. If there really was such a person as a Sun Catcher they would have been very important.

# HOMES

Many people were still nomadic in the Bronze Age, which means that they moved from one place to another, so there are horse herders on Maia's journey, and nomadic shepherds, as well as settled communities. Around this time hunter gatherers were being replaced by settled families in areas where food was plentiful and where farmers had learned to grow grain. Houses were being built, and in some places villages, towns, and even cities, were growing.

If there were habitable caves I think there would still have been cave dwellings as well as bone burial caves. So for the Cliff Dwellers and Maia to live in a kind of cave village on the edge of an ocean seemed an interesting idea. Transitional places, places on the edge, and boundaries were important to people in the past. People often lived near water so the cliff village by the sea, a boundary between one world and another, seemed a good place for a settlement, especially as seaweed is a rich source of food and of course the cliff dwellers would have fished too.

# GAMES AND SPORTS

Games and sport were part of Bronze Age life, and in *Sun Catcher*, Tareth knocks over his gaming board and pieces.

I always assumed that like us Bronze Age people would enjoy playing board games and that they would make their own gaming pieces. We know that the Egyptians played board games. I was fascinated to read a few days ago that 49 small stone gaming pieces, dice and three shell and stone tokens have been found in an archeological dig in Turkey. I wonder just how many of the goods on Bron's boat originally came from that area too . . .

# CLOTHES

Bronze Age people liked adorning themselves, their clothes and their horses. Roaming tribes had gold ornaments on their horse bridles. Many of these were of plants and animals. The horses ridden by the warrior women have these.

*'The icy wind churned through the standing horses, whipping their manes into a frenzy. Gold harness ornaments swung and glinted in the pale sunshine.'*

Huan, the Eagle Hunter, would have decorated his horse's bridle too. Bronze Age jewelry was beautiful. Brooches, or stab pins, were used to close garments as well as to decorate them and to show how wealthy or important the person wearing them was. They are made from bone, gold, precious stones; Maia is given a silver stab pin. Jakarta has a gold pin. Kodo wants to give her gold ear studs too.

People were often buried in their finest clothes with prized objects and jewelry, and so, in *Sun Catcher*, Maia's sister, Xania, has an elaborate burial.

# TATTOOS

Bronze Age people would have known about tattooing. There were many reasons for having a tattoo, not just for making the skin of the wearer look beautiful. Often they had special meanings or purposes. Tattoos could have been magic symbols to help heal rheumatism or an injury or tribal markings or decorations and symbols to mark ceremonial rite of passage.

I wanted my characters to have tattoos too. The Lizard people have tattoos on their thumbs. This is how Kodo realises that at the powerful Marsh Lord must have been one of the Lizard People. Zena has a tattoo on her neck. Xania has a leaping cat tattooed on her wrist. Xania's tattoo has the same design as the special silver stab pin Maia has been given. A pin that belonged to her mother. This helps convince Maia that the stranger is her sister.

# TOOLS, WEAPONS AND ARMOUR

Although bronze was a new technology, people in the Bronze Age still used old tool making skills too. I decided that the community of seaweed farmers would still be using flint for knives and tools. Bronze weapons would be high status and expensive so at first probably only important or rich people would have them.

Razek, as Weed Master, wants a metal knife. This is why he decides to keep the dead Wulf Kin's silver and bronze and eventually trades the stolen silver armband at the Gather with disastrous consequences.

Tareth comes from a different land and lived in the Sun Palace, so he would also have had valuable, state of the art weapons. Luckily he did not lose everything when he was shipwrecked with Maia near the cliff village so he has metal as well as flint knives.

Tareth is the Warrior Weaver. As well as being trained in unarmed combat skills, Tareth also has a bow. So do the warrior women. They hang their silk wrist bracelets on their bows to give the bows special powers. Their bows are used for hunting but of course they are weapons too. I wanted Tareth's bow to be precious and special so it has a name, Blackwood. I think that special weapons would have been given names because their owners believed the weapons had magical powers. If I was a warrior and had a special weapon I think I would name it too.

Whenever I visit the British Museum I go and see the wonderful galleries exhibiting gold and treasures troves and weapons from the Bronze Age and visit the Sutton Hoo treasures. The famous Sutton Hoo helmet is later than Bronze Age but Bronze Age warriors did have shields and helmets, swords and spears so it was easy to imagine the Marsh Lord with his helmet.

Maia's sun catching helmet with its silk eye pieces woven by Tareth to protect her eyes from the glare of the sun would have been much more elaborate and precious than these. I'm hoping one day that somewhere in a drowned or buried treasure trove a beautiful gold helmet will be discovered to remind me that *Sun Catcher* was influenced by the Bronze Age although I don't expect there to be any traces of the mysterious magical whispering silk. But who knows? Perhaps hidden in a dusty cabinet in a dark forgotten corner in a museum or folded in an ancient chest in an attic the moon moth silk is singing.

# Acknowledgements

This is my chance to say thank you.

To Dave who read each page as it fell from the printer, corrected my crazy spelling and kept asking what happens next? I couldn't have done this without you. My family deserves a big hug and thanks too.

*Storm Chaser* has reached this landfall with the dedication and enthusiasm of the wonderful Orion Children's Book team. Thank you all. I hope you loved the adventure. I did. A special thank you to Fiona Kennedy, my brilliant editor, who chased the narrative line and whose suggestions are always superb. Any flaws are mine, not hers. I hope I listened well.

Geoff Taylor's evocative drawings are a delight. I'm so lucky to work with an artist whose illustrations add new realities to Maia's world. A world which would never have been more than dreams without the belief of John McLay my agent extraordinaire and now an author too. Thank you.

And of course, a huge thank you to all my friends and readers who have turned pages, eagerly time travelled into a fantasy and have waited more or less patiently for a year to find out what would become of Maia and her friends after *Sun Catcher*. (I couldn't tell you until the characters told me.) Without you there would be no stories. I hope the wait was worth it. There is more. Enjoy.

Sheila Rance
January 2014